Compassion

THE EXTENDED EDITION

USA TODAY BESTSELLING AUTHOR

XAVIER NEAL

Compassion – The Extended Edition

By Xavier Neal

©Xavier Neal 2022

Cover by Dana Leah, Designs by Dana

All Rights Reserved

Subscribe to my newsletter!

http://bit.ly/XNNLSL21

Dedication:

To the Universe...Thank you for always showing me compassion.

Playlist Selects

Here are ten songs from the "Compassion" playlist!

Feel free to follow the playlist on Spotify to find more songs I felt related to the book.

1. Religious – Ne-Yo (R&B)

2. Phenomenal – Eminem (Rap/HipHop)

3. Too Much – Spice Girls (Pop)

4. Irish – Goo Goo Dolls (Alternative Rock)

5. Thank God – Kane Brown, Katelyn Brown (Country)

6. You Saved Me – Gary Clark Jr. (Soul/Blues)

7. Eleven: 11 – Pell (Rap/Hiphop)

8. Take Me Home Tonight – Eddie Money (Pop Rock)

9. Dream – Queen Naija ft Lucky Daye (R&B)

10. Low Life – X Ambassadors, Jamie N Commons (Pop Rock)

More songs: https://spoti.fi/3Nssn7b

Chapter 1

Jaye

Moms don't really **always** *know best, but let's keep that between me and you, okay? Oh! Oh no! If you're a mom, I really didn't mean to offend you. I'm sorry! I am so, so sorry! I probably should've been more specific and said* **my** *mother doesn't always know best. Words and sentence structure matter. I know this. I literally get paid to know* **and** *teach this to an extent.*

"Don't slouch, Jaye," my mother, Margaret Jenkins, not-so-gently reminds me at the same time she places a plate of gourmet eggplant parmesan in front of me. "It's unbecoming, *and* it's terrible for your back. Keep that up, and next thing you know, you'll be going to see Dr. Smiley for a visit." She twists the plate to a more picture-perfect position prior to flicking her thick, wavy, caramel locks away from her honey, tawny skinned face. "And while smile may be in his name, you can rest assured, going to see an orthopedic physician will leave you with *nothing* to smile about."

"I don't know," Charles Jenkins, my father, nonchalantly argues while leaning back in his stool seat, dark hickory hands folding together in his lap. "He *does* have the best candy jar in the game, Mags." His dark brown stare shoots me a small wink. "Freshest Whoppers in all of Highland. He leaves me with no choice but to confiscate at least a handful on behalf of the good people in this city."

And this is what makes my dad so damn magical. An entire city full of people to serve and protect yet he always, always starts at home with me.

"Neither you *nor Jaye* need any more Whoppers in your life," she scolds as she puts his plate down in front of him.

"Candy or burgers?" Dad playfully pokes.

"*Both.*" Her snip is given to him on an unhappy glare before she relocates the disapproval my direction. "And speaking of things you should be avoiding, you need to be careful about adding extra cheese to your dish tonight." The expression of discontent deepens. "Not only could eating too much *increase* your risk of high cholesterol and high blood pressure therefore increasing your risk of a heart attack – something to always have in the back of your mind even at twenty-nine – but also your pants are beginning to look a little…*snug.*"

You know it's bad when your doctor says shit like this to you during a yearly physical, yet when your mom says it, your mom who is **also** *a doctor – a thoracic surgeon to be more exact – the low blow pain is much,* **much** *harsher. It's pretty much a kidney shot. It hurts so bad that you wanna scream bloody murder but can't. I also wanna tell her that I could've bought these pants this way! That maybe they aren't fitting tighter because I've had one too many snowmen shaped cookies from the children at school who gave me some as a holiday treat! Whatever the case may be – fashion or frosting – extra cheese would be just fine on this Gordon Ramsey inspired meal. I'm not going to explode, although if I keep bottling up all my feelings like this I may* **implode.** *See. Words matter.*

"Now," Mom begins during her stroll back into the main portion of the kitchen where her plate is waiting to be relocated, "what was I saying before all this?"

That you think your daughter is going to turn into The
Hunchback of Notre-Dame if she doesn't straighten her spine.
Oh...maybe that should be a book we read for book club! The
adults the version by Victor Hugo – great writer – and the children
the Disney adaptation. I'm sure it exists. Disney basically has a
book for **everything** *they make animated.*

"Something about the Phillipsons," Dad loudly reminds yet quietly adds, "who are also probably to thank for whatever this shit is." His confused expression meets mine on a barely above a whisper snap, "What the fuck is this?"

After cutting a quick glance to where my mother is snapping a social media shot of the dish that she created, I answer at the same volume, "Eggplant parmesan."

His thick eyebrows pull together. "Did the grocery store stop selling pasta?"

"Not that I know of."

A low unhappy grumble begins. "Is there at least *meat* hidden in this leaning tower of veggie?"

I slowly shake my head which causes the low mumbles to get louder.

"What's that?" Mom asks in tandem with finally picking her plate up. "Did you say something?"

"*Bread?*" Dad swiftly investigates, in desperate need of something high in calories. "Is there garlic bread to go with this, Mags?"

"Of course," his wife warmly coos while reaching for an additional dish. "What kind of monster serves Italian without garlic bread?"

Should we really call this shit Italian? Wouldn't they riot in disgust at whatever this cooking channel class project is?

"Not one I would ever marry," Dad lovingly teases upon her arrival.

She beams brightly, places the bread near him, and slides onto the stool that's at his side.

I swear she isn't always the big, bad, waistline wolf. She isn't always dead set on huffing and puffing and blowing away all my self-esteem.

"I wish *we* were having grandchildren like Lucy," she sighs as her grip leaves her plate to grab her glass of white wine. "Unwrapping a box with the sonogram inside would've been so," her hand clutches her dark blouse covered chest, "*special.*"

Yeah, she's just that way...most of the time. You know like during months that have at least thirty days in them.

"I always just assumed I would be a grandmother by now. At least to my *first* grandchild."

The pause she takes may in actuality be brief yet feels like eons.

Literal.

Fucking.

Eons.

"*Definitely* before Lucy," my mother sneers on a snip of wine. "I mean, don't get me wrong, Bernard is a nice enough young man-"

"He hoards cats," Dad casually inserts into conversation before having a bite of bread.

"However, I never thought he'd get *married* let alone start a family."

*I'll openly admit to you that going to all his cat themed wedding events last year really knocked me down a few pegs. Primarily because my mom spent each one whispering shit like this to me but also because if the creepy cat dude can find love, why can't I? He's ten years older and ten times weirder and **still***

12

managed to find someone who wanted to live in holy catrimony with him. What's so wrong with me? And I'm asking you, not the woman who has a list that she checks twice like she's fucking Santa Claus for criticisms.

"This is actually Brenda's recipe," Mom announces after swallowing a bit more wine. "She gave Lucy *this* while Lucy gave her a few healthy alternatives to some of the nastier pregnancy cravings." Her pale blue eyes that she inherited from her biological father swing my direction. "You know I have a list, too...Just in case it ever happens in our family."

I offer her a forced sympathetic grin and ingest the smallest nibble I can stomach.

Look, it's not that I hate children. I totally love children. I love them so much that I have literally worked with them my whole life. Babysitting. Tutoring. Lifeguarding. Birthday party hosting. Nannying. Tumbling guide. I absolutely want children of my own someday. And it's not like I didn't want them then when the possibility was there. It's not like that shit wasn't in the plans despite his privately spoken indifference. However, sometimes – through no fault of our own – plans change. **Life** *changes. And the change isn't always a predictable one.*

"Can this dish never happen to us again?" Dad slyly shifts the subject with a point to his meal. "At least not without more cheese."

"*Charles!*" my mother fusses his direction causing him and I to immediately snicker.

See why I love him.

"So, how's the book coming along, sugar?" Dad reaches for the small tub of parmesan that's in the middle of the table. "You refused to talk about it on Christmas – I assume to not steal the spotlight from the baby news – but that doesn't make it not important or even *less* important than what they announced."

"Come on, Charles, it's not nearly as important as bringing *life* into this world."

"Maybe it is to *our daughter*." My father swiftly argues while dumping a spoonful of cheese on my food for me. "And maybe this book is her bringing life into this world in a different way. Have you ever considered that?"

Writing and illustrating a children's book is something I've been trying to do since my freshman year at Clover Rose University. Keyword to take away from that is trying. See, back then, it was just one of those things I doodled and daydreamed about while ignoring my Writing and Culture's professor who – by the way – never included women nor people of color in his teachings. I loved the idea of my own children holding something that I created. Something that they could pass down to their own children. I wanted them to be proud and able to say to others 'look at what my mother accomplished.'. Regardless of how overly critical of my existence my own mom is, I love that she's accomplished so much in her life. She's one of the best surgeons in her field and one of the top ones at her hospital. She's got accolades hung in expensive frames all around her office as well as a growing collection of medical periodicals she's contributed to. And Dad? I'm very proud of him as well. He's a blue blood. A lieutenant now with more responsibilities than his paycheck could ever cover. It's not an easy gig, even at his mainly administrative level. There are always cases and crimes and people who are quick to point out your every minor mistake while just disregarding every life you've ever saved. It's a thankless job, especially when you're on the cleaner side of things, yet he does it and keeps doing it because he believes that human life, human rights matter. He often tells people blue bloods are boots on the ground while those that sit in congress or the senate try to figure their shit out. He knows the world isn't black and white or even fair but does his best to do what's right *in spite of the bullshit. The admiration I have for them both…is admiration I want my own little ones to have for me. During my college days and even the first few months out, I kept working on the book, but once Chris Garrity, my now deceased fiancé of three years, entered my life, I completely stopped. And the only reason I started again is because all the experts my mother more or less forced me to speak to said focusing on a project would help the healing process. They claimed it would give me control over my life again. Give me a new purpose outside of work. A new vision. Allow myself to plan for the future I wanted. Truth? The only thing working on this book has done is give me an excuse to buy more wine, which I didn't need. My mother is reason enough.*

"Still not in the mood to talk about it?" Dad cautiously questions prior to cutting into his dinner.

A small headshake is presented on a forkful bite of the now cheese-covered dish.

"What about work?" Mom adjusts her wine glass at the same time she changes topics to something that may actually interest her. "How is it? Have you been promoted yet?"

15

"Mom, there is *no* promoting, remember? I'm as high up as I'm gonna go."

Being a librarian at an elite preschool is honestly my dream job! Doesn't sound like it would be – and for most people it isn't – but it's everything I love all rolled into one very nerdy, very book-filled career. The place isn't at all like your average daycare. It's more like a child college for lack of a better term. It's a private academy that's geared towards those with lots of money to throw at their child's education. It's a learning organization that offers your precious ones art classes designed and written by those with degrees in the field, musical classes by the future composers of our time or past award-winning ones looking for a different pace in life, as well as gourmet meals that borderline on haute cuisine yet kid friendly enough to still be devoured like they're a run of the mill basic PB&J. I'm lucky enough to work at one of the most unique and innovative institutions for early child development in the entire country. You're probably wondering what do I do exactly, right? Well, I'll tell you, and hopefully it sticks better for you than it does my mother. You see, it's my responsibility to pick the books we keep on the shelves, coordinate with the owner/director, Presley Morrison, about the ever-changing curriculum, and travel from classroom to classroom reading stories to help drive a literary passion. The older afterschool kids, I occasionally help with additional homework if their teacher, Sienna O'Hara, sends them to me, which she typically does. She doesn't like doing the homework portion of her job. She prefers the fun science experiments, the cooking projects, and crafting things with them from her own Ojibwa – or Anishinaabe – heritage. While I don't love *her pawning them off on me, I do love getting her feedback on Native books to include in the book fairs that are also my responsibility. On top of those things – as if those aren't enough – I also run the book drives – collecting books to donate to single parents in lower financial brackets – and our twice a month book club. One is for the children to attend with their parents, which is basically just a book they're given each month to read weekly with their kids before coming to me at the end of the month*

where I'll read to them the same book while they enjoy
refreshments. It's meant to be a bonding exercise as well as to
build healthy reading and studying behaviors between adult and
child – or in too many cases **nanny** *and child. The other book club*
is for adults only that are looking for ways to socialize with other
parents – or again nannies – without the crutch of their children.
Basically, the English degree everyone swore would never be
useful – mother included – got me a life that revolves almost non-
stop around books. Combine that love with the other – kids – and
yeah. Doing what I do is nothing short of a dream come true.

"You could always look into switching to an *actual* private academy or even a boarding school." Mom's head tilts in a judging fashion. "You would probably make more money *and* be able to work your way into administration where you belong."

"I *belong* right where I am," I promptly argue, fork being gently placed down. "And I know it drives you crazy that I'm not a supervisor or in any type of management position, but I'm *happy,* Mom. And I love what I do. Hearing kids like Sylvie, this sweet, mousy, four-year-old with coke bottle glasses read books like *Green Eggs and Ham* all on her own brings to me more joy than any amount of zeroes on a paycheck ever could."

To my surprise, she flashes me a small smile. "That was the first book you learned to read."

"Dr. Seuss was basically a drug dealer in this house," Dad teasingly adds. "She always needed another hit of *One Fish, Two Fish, Red Fish, Blue Fish* and *Fox in Socks.*"

"*Hop on Pop,*" Mom promptly contributes.

17

"There's a Wocket in My Pocket."

"Don't forget *Oh, the Places You'll Go!*"

Warm giggles are given on a minor blush. "I read that one to my graduating pre-k kids every year."

"You were *addicted* to Dr. Seuss," she happily coos.

"Addicted to reading in general," my father says between bites of his dinner, mirth heavy in his tone. "I didn't hate it, though. Afterall, there were worse things for a three-year-old to be obsessed with."

"That's not at all how you felt when she pulled out a box of condoms from the grocery bag and started reading the back of it like a box of cereal."

Dad's uncomfortable cringe causes the three of us to chuckle in unison.

See. She's not always so bad.

"So, sugar," he begins again once the laughter has died down, "nothing new to report at all?"

18

"I'm thinking of doing *The Very Hungry Caterpillar* for the kid's book club this coming month and serving a tray of snacks to match the ones touched on in the book." I reach for my water glass while rambling off another idea. "And since Eric Carle is such a staple in the art of picture books for children, I'm thinking of maybe mirroring that message with picking a graphic novel for the adult book club. Possibly *Maus* by Art Spiegelman, which I'll have you both know was the first graphic novel to win a Pulitzer Prize."

"And now that you bring up *prizes…*" Mom giddily segues with a mischievous grin.

"Something tells me that you're not talking about the same *type*," my father mumbles on an exasperated eye roll.

"There's this *prize* of a young doctor at the hospital who is *single* and according to the rumor mill *very ready* to mingle."

"Mags, no one uses that phrase anymore."

"You hush," she swiftly scolds his direction and resumes her gushing towards me. "He's about thirty-five, no more than thirty-seven. About 5'9, 5'10. Thick, dark hair. Not quite shaggy but long enough you can help brush it away from his crystal blue yes."

"Did Patrick Dempsey leave *Grey's Anatomy* to work at Highland North Medical Center?" Dad good naturedly jabs exactly what I'm thinking.

"Donates to children's charities. Does volunteer work with animals. Likes to spend his free time down in South Haven where he has a *beach house* with an incredible view."

"Why do you know so much about this young man?" my father's joking continues. "Did you have someone run a background check on him as a solid to the lieutenant's favorite wife?"

"*Only wife,*" she offhandedly corrects yet doesn't skip a beat in her verbal pushing. "I think you two would make a *perfect* pair."

Yeah, she said the same shit about the bottlecap collecting Frost Luxury Hotel tax accountant. And the male thong obsessed lawyer from Dornan Law Firm. And the LARPing marketing director that works at Bennett Enterprises. And the toothbrush obsessed dentist. The dentist who – I'll have you know – was by far the worst. It's beyond words weird having someone stare at your mouth not because they wanna kiss you but because they wanna clean your teeth while listening to slow jazz.

The only response she's given is me picking my fork backup.

"Jaye," her voice attempts to take a softer, more sympathetic tone, "you really should be out there dating."

My retort is barely above a whisper, "I date."

Not enough to call it actively dating, but whose side are you on?

Her attempt at a compliment occurs as my fork cuts into my food. "You're a great catch."

"The first greatest after your mother," Dad states on a sweet wink.

"And you shouldn't just be wasting your life away. You shouldn't be spending your Friday and Saturday nights baking cookies and re-reading classics like *Pride and Prejudice-*"

"I liked the one with zombies more," I quietly inform around the newest nibble in my mouth.

"You should be out there with your colleagues – if you can call them that – grabbing cocktails and accepting drinks from doctors or lawyers or directors of sales at one of those upscale wine bars downtown. You should-"

"Mags," Dad cleverly cuts off, "is there more sauce for this? Because I gotta admit, the sauce...well, the sauce is the best part of the whole damn thing."

Mom – *thankfully* – falls for the distraction technique. "Can you believe there's no meat in it?"

"I believe I could use a little more sauce on mine." His circumventing the truth tactic is one I may have inherited. "Any chance you could grab me some since you're about to reheat your plate?"

She looks down at her untouched meal prior to tossing him an adoring smile. "How do you know me this well?"

"Years and years and years of marriage, Mags." This wink gets her giggling, planting a kiss on his cheek, and abandoning her glass of wine to grab both of their plates. "Appreciate you."

My mother beams brighter and saunters away to deal with their dishes.

The instant she's out of earshot, I faintly coo, *"Thank you."*

"You're welcome, Sugar," he responds in the same muted volume.

I offer him the warmest smile possible and force myself to have another bite of the food I have no genuine interest in eating anymore.

Okay. Here's what you need to know. Contrary to the unbecoming way my mother makes me sound, I really am working on moving past Chris. I've been on a few dates in the last three years, although most are – admittedly – the ones my mother keeps stuffing down my esophagus like this gross excuse for dinner. The few that weren't were ones that I let myself get roped into by drunk, meddlesome coworkers in between their rounds of 'Kill, Bang, or 2nd Wife' using the dads from the school as their subjects for the game. All the dates failed – including those with the stamp of approval from my mom – for the same reason. I'm too quiet. And I know it. I mean I've heard the same shit for pretty much most of my life. The thing is when there's something I wanna talk about, I talk about it. And I keep talking about it. And I can't stop talking about until someone basically says shhh. Chris – may he continue to rest in peace – was the same way, which is one reason he never said that to me. And one reason we were probably a good fit. Not **perfect** *but good enough to have a future together.*

Post the last leg of the painful meal – in both taste and conversation – I make the short drive home to the somewhat soothing sounds of The Fray, a band both Chris and I enjoyed separately as well as together.

What? No. I'm not missing him. Really. I'm just craving that time in my life where I had less lectures about who I should be dating and more about proper care for these curly fries I'm blessed to call my hair.

The second I've crossed the threshold into my luxury two-story home that's much too big for just me, I drop my workbag near the stairs and head straight for the kitchen in desperate need of alcohol reprieve.

Don't worry. I'm not going to drink a whole bottle of wine in spite of the fact my mother makes me want to. Or…need to if we're being more candid. I'm just gonna have a glass. Maybe three. Perhaps six. Is that the really whole thing, or are you just trying to stop me from drinking my problems away because I'll have you know…I plan to eat them away, too.

I grab a bottle of red from the wine fridge prior to opening the one that contains the food in search of carb reinforcements.

You saw what she served. I can't drink ¾ of a bottle on an empty stomach. No one likes that feeling the next morning.

Seeing the two-day-old delivery pizza that I know I'm not going to eat has me abruptly stopping the hunt, putting the wine on the nearby island, and removing the box for immediate disposal.

I swear to you I'm really not that anal retentive. When Chris was alive, he had a strict – and I mean strict – 'no more than two days' policy for cooked food. Didn't matter if it was takeout or something I had made. Two days and it had to go. I'm not sure if it was the smell or the possible bacteria build up or the fact that he hated clutter of any kind that inspired the rule but nonetheless, it was one. The first one he had when we moved into this place, and I use the term we rather loosely. He preferred the penthouse downtown; however, we both knew it wouldn't be ideal for raising a family, so he bought this place. This mini mansion in a gated community next door to what it would look like if Maleficent married Jafar's long lost American cousin. You laugh now but wait until you meet the wicked pain in the asses of Elm Ridge for yourself.

It doesn't take long to walk back the way I came with the leftovers in tow, yet when I open my front door, I instantly become frozen in place. Near the edge of my curved driveway where my trashcan and recycle bin are cleverly hidden in a white fenced in enclosure is a tall, bearded man with tattered clothing, a beanie, and an old backpack digging in one of the containers.

Aw, that poor guy. I wonder if he's looking for bottles or cans to recycle for a few coins that he can use to help get him whatever it is he needs. If he is, then he definitely picked the right neighborhood because practically everyone has a shit ton of those in their recycle bins.

Not wanting to scare him off, I continue to silently watch him rummage around until I realize he's not after what he can recover for financial gain but what he can salvage for a nutritional one when he pulls out the end of a loaf of bread in victory. His head falls slightly back in relief as he squeezes the bag containing a few stale pieces in absolute joy. Like he's receiving a Christmas miracle that's a little late yet one he wasn't certain he'd ever actually get. He enthusiastically starts nodding. Mumbling to himself. Stuffing the bread in his backpack so that his hands are free to go diving again. This time, his foraging is faster. More anxious. Determined. Now invested in his discovery, his success, I lean in little closer, ignoring the winter wind that's hellbent on convincing me to go back inside where it's warm.

And safe.

An apple I don't remember chucking along with an orange I do remember ditching make it into his possession, yet the second, he lifts a wedge of old cheese to smell, I can't stop myself from squeaking, "Don't eat that!"

The man whips his head my direction, his tan face full of sharp features and hard lines.

Seeing the flash of instinct to run away is what prompts me into croaking, "I don't want you to get sick."

Confusion causes his thick eyebrows to dart down.

Yeah, I see yours crinkling, too. And I don't know! I don't know why I said that out loud, but I meant it. I don't want him to get ill, especially not when it could've been prevented. This man's…human, ya know? He doesn't deserve to be sick…nor sick with no way to get better. Nowhere to go. No one to take care of him.

"I mean it's cold out, but not like *refrigerator* cold out, so the chances of you getting an upset stomach from old, not properly stored cheese or something much worse like an allergic reaction or even hospitalization if you have a compromised immune system are still pretty high."

His face instantly twitches in horror.

"*Sorry*," my sheepish apology is given on an embarrassed cringe, "I swear, I wasn't trying to like food shock you into fearing cheddar. It's just my mom's a doctor, and sometimes I unconsciously find myself word vomiting what she has word vomited at me to unsuspecting strangers who didn't want the word vomit any more than I did, and as I keep saying the actual *word* vomit I realize that's disgusting and should probably stop before I make one of us physically vomit."

The faintest flicker of a smirk unexpectedly occurs.

Ohmygod, did he just smile at me?! Did I just make someone besides a bunch of preschoolers smile?!

"Want some pizza instead?"

The male carefully lowers the lid to my trashcan with his other hand, eyes never leaving mine.

"It's um…pepperoni, sausage and mushroom."

He smoothly slides the recovered fruits into his backpack while continuing to keep his gaze locked on me.

"Thin crust because it's less bread but between you and me, I really like it because I feel it holds the pizza sauce better versus making it too soggy. Like who in their right mind wants to eat tomato soup bread?"

Another small smile is sparked as he attempts to warm up his hands by cupping them over his mouth and blowing big breaths of hot air.

"It's from that little place on the corner," I thoughtlessly keep talking, body unconsciously gravitating closer to him. "The one that's at the next light up by the entrance to the Rose Patch subdivision." Treating this like it's an everyday conversation with a run of the mill random new neighbor effortlessly continues. "You know where I'm talking about? They have that godawful sign that looks like it was designed by a homecoming committee that couldn't pick a direction."

This time I receive a snicker.

It's light.

Airy.

Almost missed around the howling wind, but it's heard.

And it's adored.

And it's making my heart race faster than it ever has before.

What on earth is going on with me?! Did I do tequila shots with my dad and totally forget about it?! Why am I not even remotely afraid of this man? Oh, and why can't I stop talking like someone put fresh batteries in me?!

"The pizza's only a couple days old." My movements come to an eventual stop with me closer to him than I anticipated. "And it was in the fridge the whole time. Okay, not the *whole* time because I did eat it when it was hot, and then had to let it properly cool before *Tetris*ing it into my fridge, but other than that," the grin on my face I didn't realize I had gets wider, "it was appropriately stored." Extending the box his direction, I playfully add, "On top of an unopened container of liquid egg whites and bag of fresh spinach I'm totally gonna eat."

He quirks a challenging eyebrow at the same time he lowers his empty hands.

"*Probably* gonna eat," I correct in a giggled fluster.

The look remains.

"*Possibly*?" More sniggers of frustration escape prior to me shaking my head. "Ugh. Fine. I don't really *like* spinach, but I force myself to eat it. My mother on the other hand, likes the shit so much, she probably would've named me *Popeye* had I been born a boy instead of a bubbly, babbling, baby girl."

He unleashes a chuckle that's attached to a full-fledged grin that causes my knees to wobble.

Gah…

What a sound.

What a beautiful, beautiful sound.

His face tips a little forward during the laugh allowing the moonlight to illuminate green eyes so gorgeous that I momentarily forget how to breathe.

The whole *purpose* of breathing.

Is it so that I can stay conscious just to stare into them because then that makes total sense to me. Hm? Am I really sounding that crazy again? Well, be a good person, and shout out red flags you see. From him, not me. I've got me covered. I'm very aware of why Detective Inspector G. Lestrade would be knocking on my door first thing in the morning with a shit ton of questions.

"Go on," I sweetly insist, item shoved his direction further. "Take it."

His gaze sweeps the box for what I imagine to be clues of tampering or possibly poisoning. If it weren't for the fact that I can physically see his hunger increasing with every blink, I might be worried that this was a mistake.

That I should've kept my distance.

Let him continue to scramble to find something decent to eat out of my trashcan.

But I *know* this was the right call.

Is the right call.

He's starving, and there's no reason I have to let him.

"You know you want to…" I tease on a crooked smile, expression warm to indicate I'm being playful not mocking. "I mean *I* would want to. It's gotta be better than the shit my mom was trying to pass off as eggplant parmesan."

The male lightly laughs again, shrugs in an almost disbelief nature, and relocates the object into his possession after showing me his open, unarmed, palms.

I knew he didn't wanna hurt me. Not once did he reach for a weapon or display an aggressive behavior. Add in that I haven't seen him twitching – like he's on something or coming down from it – and being kind without fear is a no brainer. Besides, it feels right in my gut, and I was taught to always follow that. Dad's not wrong about people, and honestly? Neither am I.

The trash spelunker grips the box now in his hands tightly, even tighter than the loaf of bread. A multitude of emotions cycle through his face, yet it's the tiny tear in the corner of his eye that causes an ache in my chest. Rather than acknowledge it or remove his hands from the object he's holding, he simply meets my stare.

Delivers a curt nod.

Grins to the best of his ability as the frigid wind reminds us both to get out of its way.

"Stay warm," I quietly command at the same time I begin backing up towards my house. "And just knock if you need help making that happen."

31

He doesn't nod a second time.

Hell, the only reason I even know I didn't give him a heart-attack from my totally absentminded offer is due to the slow blinking that occurs while he watches me disappear back inside.

Once I'm there, I lock all three locks like normal and rush to the nearby dining room to sneak one final peak at the unexpected visitor.

The homeless man continues to linger for a moment staring at my front door as if concerned for my safety rather than his own. He suspiciously glances around the cul-de-sac in search of any possible intruders before placing the box down on top of my trashcan. With a simple flick of the wrist, the top flies backwards, exposing him to a sight that irradiates his entire expression. His bright beam kindles my own and the gratulation of his first bite is so palpable, I can practically feel myself shaking in excitement with him.

Wanna know what's really crazy? Talking to him…hearing him laugh…giving him that pizza…all of those things have felt better than any date I've had since Chris's death. That's the real red flag here. What does that shit say about me and the pathetic excuse I've come to refer to as my so-called life? Don't worry. There's no need to phone 221 B Baker Street for the answers. I, sadly, already have them.

Chapter 2

Archer

Pizza. Fuck, I love pizza. I've always loved pizza. Since the first time I had it in foster care, it became the one food I've always searched for whenever traveling somewhere new. And the worst part about the shit isn't even found with the food itself! It's the way people forget to treasure the treat. We're talkin', every little portion of it. They undervalue the bread whether it's flat and thin or thick for a deep dish. They underappreciate the sauce regardless of if it's traditional red or untraditional pesto. They overlook the true experience of various cheese flavors and types. Fail to notice when it's fresh rather than frozen. How they melt slightly different. Oh, and don't even me started on the blatant disregard of the veggies and meats that they're so fortunate to have. The sheer combination of all those components, hot or cold is the equivalence of sex for your taste buds. It's something that when people are getting it on a regular or have easy access to it, they can't fucking be bothered to truly cherish the masterpiece that it is. They just take the shit for fucking granted and assume they'll get it again at some point in their lives. Well, let me be the first to fucking say to you – in particular – to stop doing that shit. You don't fucking know when it could be your last chance, or when you'll be left wondering if you'll get a chance again. Hm? What do you mean if I'm talking about sex or pizza? Pizza…but now that you bring the shit up? Both.

Still in slight disbelief, I give the door guarding the gorgeous woman who gifted this to me another glance.

Did you see her? I mean…really see her. She was fucking beautiful. The most beautiful woman I've ever seen, and I've seen quite a few in my time – side perk they don't tell you about being in

33

the military. I've been fortunate to admire and have some of the most stunning females in various shapes, sizes, colors – ladies love a man in uniform – but Pizza Woman? Well…she takes that shit to a whole other level. That creamy coffee shaded skin makes me a type of thirsty I haven't been in a long, long time. And that curly bouncy hair? Man…I can just picture spinning a single curl around one of my fingers just to hear that breathtaking sound she calls a laugh. Oh, and those eyes…Fuck me. Did you see those toffee-colored eyes? Yeah, they were a stop-in-your-tracks shade but more importantly they were filled with warmth. Kindness. Compassion. There wasn't a fucking ounce of disgust in them. It's rather surreal if I'm gonna be up front with you. Believe it or not, those aren't the sentiments most people offer me.

The decision to devour or savor is a difficult one.

Logic and starvation push for the former. I should shove as much as I can in my mouth, ditch the box, and be on my way before someone *less* kind and *less* understanding catches me where I obviously don't belong; however, hope has me anxious to appreciate the flavors.

The unexpected freshness.

The eyebrow raising amount left in this box that makes me wonder if Pizza Woman ate more than two pieces.

Another gust of wind shoots a chill up my spine prompting me to split the difference of the two options. I continue moaning in content over the slice dangling from my lips while securing the remaining portions in my backpack. After ditching the box in the recycle bin, I hastily stroll away towards the manicured walking trail that's just on the other side of Pizza Woman's back fence. More bone-chilling air brutally whips around me, and the noticeable drop in temperature provokes a sharp sting to rip through my right leg causing my slightly noticeable limp to be painfully more apparent.

Honestly, most of the time I completely forget it's even there. The shit only seems to bother me when it gets too cold out or when the memories make a surprise appearance to strangle me alive. Hurts like a motherfucker then. Makes me wish I could just remove the whole damn thing. Remove...me. The world would be better off if I did.

Dragging my shivering frame along faster is done at the same time I slip my hands back into the pockets of the army green trench coat someone tossed out right after Christmas.

I assume his wife got him a new one. This was left in the box, but it didn't match the picture. Grabbed the box, too. Made for an alright place to store food. Well, it did until someone in Rose Patch ratted my ass out to the cops, and I was forced to move without my belongings that weren't on me. It wasn't the first time something like that had happened, and I know it won't be the last considering where I choose to collect supplies from. Knowing how people operate, especially in these types of areas, is the primary reason I keep everything I absolutely need in my backpack. I'm always prepared. To move. To flee. To start over. You know it's funny, people think the only battlefield worth talking about in this world is the one we fight with assault rifles over bullshit politics, false ideologies, and greed. Trust me. The one you face when every person you encounter is just as desperate to live another day as you, you see the real war we should be fighting. The real soldiers. The battles being ignored day in and day out. Just because I make the active choice to stay out of the trenches by living off the grid near nicer neighborhoods doesn't mean I'm not still in the struggle. It simply means I'm willing to use alternative tactics to

35

stay alive. To hopefully survive and someday be invited back into society.

Despite the burden I call my leg, I slyly hustle my way through the wooded area surrounding the path, dodging windows, streetlights, and security system cameras to the best of my ability. Eventually, I veer further away, taking my own created trail that leads me to the backside of the neighborhood club pool. Climbing the fence is easy. Avoiding the poorly angled security camera isn't as easy but isn't exactly infiltrating a sleeper cell difficult. Once I'm securely out of sight, I take a brief moment to dip my hands in the currently heated pool water and scrub away the crumbs that may have gotten into my beard.

I'll bathe in **non-chlorine** *water in the morning. It's okay. You don't have to worry about me. No one else does. I'm not worth it.*

I shake my hands dry into the cold night air on my way over to the back corner storage shed that the teenagers who run this place always forget to check at closing.

As long as everything is generally in the area it's 'supposed to be' and nothing is obviously missing, no one seems to give a shit. Hey, their lack of giving a fuck about their job works highly in my benefit. It gives me a warm space to sleep when the temperatures get this low.

Inside the small structure primarily used for storing buckets and other loose pool tools, I rearrange some of the former and crawl around to rest behind them.

If anyone comes in before I have a chance to sneak out, I won't be the first thing they see. It's strategic. Which is probably my personal key to surviving nowadays.

I carefully dig out the fleece toddler blanket from underneath the food in my backpack accidently causing my dog tags to clink against something inside.

The subtle sound feels anything but.

It seemingly echoes around the dark room.

Taunts.

Mocks.

Do you know how much easier it would be to just end all this shit? How one precise slit of the wrist would stop the memories from replaying in my mind, emotionally pounding me in the balls, mentally bleeding me fucking dry? How one well tied rope swung over the right tree would stop these voices in my head from whispering that no one would even fucking notice if I was gone. And they wouldn't. Fuck…Do you know how fucking depressing that is? To know I could disappear right now, and no one would even mourn me? Do you have any fucking clue how hard that makes it to open my goddamn eyes every morning?

The unexpected overwhelming amount of bleakness is one that indicates I'm long overdue for some rest. Knowing that's the only time those thoughts manage to seep through the cracks of my fractured mind pushes me to speed up the sleeping process. I arrange my backpack to double as a pillow, curl my body into a tight ball, and spread the blanket out to its fullest capabilities.

Gotta count the wins, right? That's another key role in survival. Let's see...I have a warm place to sleep tonight. I have breakfast of real sustenance for tomorrow. Probably even lunch and dinner if I really make it stretch. And I know how to do that like a pro. I've been having to make that shit really last lately. People haven't been throwing out their holiday leftovers yet, so pickings have been a bit scarce.

On a loud yawn, my eyes shut and a vision of the kind, smiling, brown-eyed female clutching the pizza box immediately greets me.

Meeting her was a win, too. The biggest win of the day. The type that almost makes life worth living for. Not quite but definitely almost.

Chapter 3

Jaye

Thoughts of the striking, homeless man I gave cold pizza to are still lingering on my mind.

The initial ones when he walked away from my house were understandable.

And then the ones I had when I went to actually eat something for myself that night were still in the category of understandable, definitely not crazy.

And then the ones I had on my way to sleep were fine – because reflecting over your day is totally normal – but when thoughts about him *three times in one day* became thoughts about him *nonstop for three days* – basically all my non-work time – that now successfully qualifies me to be placed in the insane section of life's library.

Everything about our interaction has just been on one giant re-read. I mean the entire thing. From the first time I looked at him to the point where I backed away slowly with our eyes still glued on one another. Those green eyes that were so beguiling yet so broken. His light laugh that sounded like it hadn't been heard in decades. The look of pure, unbridled pleasure on his face the instant that pizza touched his tongue…Okay, so that expression totally sent my mind whirling in the absolute last direction it had any business going but…it definitely went there, if you know what

I mean. And it stayed there probably a little longer than it should've. Add those things to the way he kept a guarded watch over my front door – we're talking prepared to take down any possible threat that challenged my safety – while he ate and maybe you can see why I'm a total goner. Or maybe you can't. Maybe something is fundamentally fucking wrong with me. After all, most people wouldn't have done what I did if they saw some random dude dumpster diving in front of their house. They'd probably would've called the cops or chased him away with a broom or mace or maybe even a gun. They damn sure wouldn't have walked **defenselessly** *over to him with their leftovers like they had no choice because that's the way it was written in their poorly scripted teleplay. Yup. I heard it. Something has gotta be wrong with me. However, let me just say this for the record. I* **wasn't** *completely defenseless. Don't forget my dad belongs to the red and blue club, so I learned self-defense tactics at a very,* very *young age. I also read some of the scariest statistics about sex much too young, but I'm pretty sure that was part of his 'keep my daughter innocent for as long as I can' strategy.*

"*Jaye*," an unexpected voice calls over my shoulder. "You good?"

I casually turn to face Merrick McCoy, the preschool's personal painter, leaning on the navy-blue doorframe to the library.

Oh, down ladies. Yes, I'll admit it. He's extremely dreamy with those bright blue eyes, mouthwatering muscles, and intricate tattoos, but he's also extremely *taken. His girlfriend – though he sometimes uses the term fiancée – is an absolute doll. Met her when she brought him dinner one night a few weeks ago. I don't think I've ever come across a couple – outside of books – that is more meant to be than them.*

Swinging my workbag over my tan trench coat covered shoulder, I present him with a forced smile. "Yeah, I'm fine."

"You sure?" He cautiously asks again. "You look like someone's on your mind."

"You mean something?"

"*Nope.*" His cocky grin is accompanied by the folding of his arms across his chest. "My oldest brother is a professional brooder. I know the difference in the two better than I know the difference between plum and mulberry."

Bewilderment bursts onto my face. "Those are different colors?"

"That's like asking me if there's a difference between comic books and graphic novels."

The gasp that escapes is thoughtless.

"*Exactly.*" McCoy lightly chuckles and kicks his chin my direction. "You wanna talk about him?"

"There is no him."

You. Shh.

41

"Her?"

"There's no her, either."

"*Them?*" His eyebrows lift in curiosity. "I won't judge. My boy Vinnie back home has a relationship like that. To each their own and all that shit."

Them?! I could barely make it work with one other person. I cannot imagine juggling two.

"I'm good, McCoy, but thank you for the offer." After presenting him with a warm grin, I cradle my bag closer to my frame and change the subject. "You know I haven't really seen you since the holidays. Did you enjoy your break?"

"Mostly."

"Do anything special?"

"Went home with Jo and visited family, both hers and mine. Hadn't heard from or seen my brothers in a few months so you could say that was special."

Moving closer is done at the same time I innocently question, "You guys not close?"

"We're really fucking close," his reply comes with a crooked smile. "Just…had a small communication hiccup that's over now."

Huh. Wonder what kind of communication hiccup would make you stop talking to your family for months? Someone refuse to pay the cell bill, maybe?

My mouth opens to ask for more details, when he cuts me off, "What about you, lovely library lady? You enjoy your break?"

Spending Christmas dinner for the third year in a row with my dead fiancé's parents who also happen to be my parent's best friends is how every twenty-nine-year-old woman wants to spend her time off from work. It's not too hard to find the holiday spirit when you're staring into the eyes that gave birth to the person you had planned to spend the rest of your life with yet somehow can't seem to move past fast enough despite your own mother's demands that you do so. Oh? Too much sarcasm? Should I tone that shit down before speaking to this poor unsuspecting colleague?

"It was nice," I blatantly lie. "Thanks for asking."

He skeptically nods prior to pulling his paint cart inside the massive room.

"Need anything before I go?"

McCoy shoots me a teasing smirk. "Not to kill me if paint drops on your books? The leaves on the reading tree mural are always such a bitch to touch up."

"Oh…," a sweet, humor-filled coo comes from me, "playful painter boy, while I understand your problem, we both know if you harm my books that's a murderous offense." My body turns to maintain eye contact during my exit. "And we also both know I'll be examining every last spine I know you were near *first* thing in the morning. Punishment will be served accordingly."

"I've been threatened more for less," he loudly chuckles as he turns his black baseball cap around. "Have a good night, Jaye."

"You too, McCoy."

On the drive home, the mundane routine of being stuck in rush hour traffic gives my mind more time to aimlessly drift the direction it can't seem to refrain itself from going.

Are you wondering the same things I am like how did he become homeless? Is he a drug addict? And if so, what kind of drugs? Is he another victim of the opioid crisis? Maybe some sort of drug mule who has an easier time moving product by 'blending in' with the homeless? Hm? Yeah. You got me. That was the plot to an organized crime novel I started yesterday after I finished my favorite author's – Sloan Mathers – latest book. While I know it's probably not the latter, he honestly didn't seem like the former, either. I didn't see or sense any of the signs of drug use or withdrawal symptoms, which I am pretty good about identifying given what both of my parents do in their respective careers. The real question is why I do care so much? It's not like he's the first homeless person I've ever come across and sadly, I know he won't be the last. It's just…they don't usually show up on my doorstep, ya know? That was definitely a first. And me actually speaking to him was too. That was the first I've ever given an actual second thought about someone in his position. Is it because he was literally so close to home? Or because he was attractive? A combination of both? Guilt over bitching about my mother's cooking when there are plenty of people who have no food at all? Fuck, am I seriously that emotionally callous? Self-absorbed? Insensitive?

The horn behind me blares spurring my foot to slam on the accelerator, anxious to bridge the large gap between me and the SUV far ahead. Desperate to get the unknown male off my mind, I prepare to turn up The Lumineers song just seconds before the Bluetooth in my car alerts me to an incoming call from my mother.

Does it make me a bad daughter for wanting to hear them rather than her?

All it takes is a single push of a button for my mother's voice to flood my vehicle in full surround sound. *"Tell me he called."*

Taken completely off guard by her demand, I quietly croak, "Who?!"

"Dmitri."

"Who?"

"Dr. Dmitri Chappell, the very *single,* very *looking for love,* pediatric doctor I told you about at dinner the other night. Remember?"

Ah. Prince Charming with a stethoscope.

"Surely, you remember, Jaye. You're not having cognitive processing issues already, are you? You're too young for that. Have you been having enough broccoli? Salmon?"

Swallowing my annoyance is barely done. "Why would this *stranger* I don't know magically call me on a Tuesday night after work?"

"Because I gave him your number."

"*Mom.*"

"*Jaye,*" she begins in such a familiar way I can practically recite what's coming next as I change lanes, "I showed him your picture at work-"

"That's not weird-"

"-and he thought you were attractive. Actually, he thought you were stunning. Yes, I'm quoting him. The direct quote is 'Your daughter is quite stunning, Maggie. How is she still single?'."

Perhaps because I lack a personality people want to spend time with?

"I told him, you won't be for long, so he better hop on it while you still are."

"Wow," is quietly whispered under my breath.

"Bit of an oversale-"

"Ouch."

"-but people love the idea of getting something before everyone else does."

What am I? The latest trending sweater?!

"I simply offered him your number afterwards and was just curious if he had used it yet."

Meet the original version of all dating aps. Mothers.

"And he *will* use it. I know people, Jaye."

Just not her daughter.

"There's no reason to be worried about him not having called at this point."

"I'm not worried."

Not even sure I care, honestly.

"And there's no reason to be upset about me taking the initiative to facilitate this connection for you."

Upset isn't the right word. More like…annoyed. Look, I get it. She…means…well. I know this. I know this like I know every line of If You Give a Mouse a Cookie, but it doesn't change the fact it irritates me. Severely.

"I'm not upset."

"You sound upset."

"I don't."

"You do. You sound like you're trying to pretend you're not because you really are and don't want to get into it with me about it."

Oh, that she picks up on? Not the whole…uninterested in being matchmade again?

"Nonetheless, it's fine. You'll get over it, especially once you *finally* have someone to come home to again."

48

Yeah, coming home to Chris didn't occur nearly as often as she's picturing. Curse of having a significant other who traveled a lot for work.

"You need this, Jaye. You need someone in your life to take care of you. To build a family with. A *life* with. You need to move on."

Instead of outwardly screaming that I am well aware that life continues on after the death of a loved one, I quietly lie, "Hey Mom, I gotta go. The other line is ringing, and it's work. I probably forgot to lock up something in the library, and my boss is just calling to ask me did I know. I'll talk to you again soon."

"Wait, are you *sure* you're getting enough brain foods in your diet? What about blueberries? Have you been having blueberries in your yogurt like I told you?"

"I swear my brain is fine-" – just tired of dealing with you – "-but I need go."

"I love you."

Reluctantly, I echo the sentiment, "I love you, too."

Hitting the end button allows me to finally breathe again.

I know *she's the reason my wine intake has increased over the past year, just like I know my ordering of Chinese takeout tonight isn't going to help my tight pants dilemma. But you know what? Sometimes, we just do what we gotta do to survive another day. Between you and me? I look forward to a point in my life when I'm no longer just trying to make it and actually enjoy living again.*

Chapter 4

Archer

I turn off the hose after my two plastic water bottles are filled.

You know what most people don't realize? Just **how** *fucking routine based they truly are. The average person does the same little shit day in and day out. Humor me. Take a minute and really give some thought to your own basic habits both inside and outside your home. Alright, now those little thoughtless moments when you're on autopilot are what make it easy for me to slip by and live off of you when I need to. For example, when you leave for your morning thirty-minute jog or to go grab that coffee you just had to have from your favorite shop up the road, it gives me the opportunity to pick up the peaches or pears or pecans from your tree that fell overnight. The ones you won't notice until the ants or other rodents come for the taking or your lawn crew is tasked with their disposal. Yeah, I said* other *rodents because that's what you think I am, right? A giant rodent. A pest on society. Useless. Pathetic. Well, fuck you for that and let that be the reason I pee on those petunias you only wanted because your snotty neighbor's yard was beginning to look better than yours. Oh, don't worry. I piss on theirs, too.*

The sound of a car approaching pushes my back flush against the side of the brickhouse so that the manicured bushes can block me from view. Staying completely still, I actively listen to the overpowering male voice yelling at whoever is on the other end of the phone. His volume booms as he calls them incompetent and slams the car door. Disorganized is the next insult that precedes the honking of the horn which lets the world know his vehicle is locked.

Unacceptable becomes the last thing I clearly hear prompting me to count to a hundred before coming out from my spot.

This shit happens like clockwork. Mr. Yelling comes home relatively around the same time every evening either shouting at someone who works for him or screaming at someone to make his latest 'indiscretion' disappear; however, he usually ends that particular call before stomping into the house where his wife – who has a habit of watching girl on girl porn before cooking dinner – is waiting to greet him. And before you ask me how I know so much about these people, I already told you. The average person is more routine based than they realize and learning their habits is a crucial method to my daily survival strategy. First, I study the terrain. Which homes have what angles and locations closest to the things like neighborhood security or roads with heavy traffic. Once those have been eliminated, it's about separating them into two categories, those who have security cameras and those who doesn't. Those that don't are then surveyed a little harder for what value I may be able to extract from them such as this one. Due to the barrier bushes and her distraction with getting herself off in the living room with a big, black, vibrating club I'm left with a good window to brush my teeth, bathe, and get clean drinking water all before she runs away to hide her toy, and he storms his ass inside. I guess you could say my tactical military training still plays a productive role in my life.

Wandering away from the Yell House is casually done as to not draw attention to myself.

The trick to keeping suspicions down – besides the obvious action of sticking to the shadows whenever possible – is to avoid eye contact while walking like you know exactly *where you're going. People tend not to think twice if you look like you're headed somewhere in particular versus just aimlessly roaming. That little rule applies regardless of if you're slinking around the 'burbs or*

52

prowling the streets downtown. It prevents you from looking like a hostile to be watched and presents you more like noncombative to be ignored.

Another night of frigid wind ruthlessly makes itself known. Despite the well-insulated coat and several layers that I'm bearing, cold creeps its way through every crevice it can find, forcing me to acknowledge the unbearable ache it creates in my bum leg.

Should've known this below freezing bullshit was here to stay. Then again, it's hard to be sure of what the weather's gonna do when the best version of a daily forecast you have is whatever you overhear people bitching about during their morning walk. Please note that 'totally Ugg boot weather' doesn't equate to an actual number on a thermometer. Just sayin'.

"You're a cheating bastard, Franklin!" The woman on the other side of the sidewalk shouts at the top of lungs at the same time she hauls a vase of roses at him. "You think fucking flowers make up for you fucking our nanny?! Our nanny?!"

"Babe, I-"

"Fuck you! I never wanna see you again!"

His pleas to take the fight inside grow louder in volume as I decide to veer the opposite direction of their confrontation.

Most people don't realize just how good they have it in relationships until they've already trespassed into an area that they have no business being in. Until they've already violated the simple treaty of trust. Yeah. I said simple. Because it is simple. Say the shit you mean. Do the shit you say you'll do. Be honest. If you say you're going to be fucking faithful then fucking be faithful. Don't negotiate the terms of a relationship, shit on them, then act surprised when your ally turns on you.

Seeing Pizza Woman's house in the near distance naturally causes my body to gravitate towards it.

Yeah. The nickname stuck. At least it has in my head. That's how I've been referencing her whenever she's crossed my mind. And to be brutally honest, she's done that a lot. More than any person has in years. Before our pizza incident she was simply the 'Two Day House'. For whatever reason the food in her trash was rarely more than a couple days old whenever I would check. It's wasteful shit, but I won't complain. It's provided me with a steady supply of non-rancid food. I appreciate that, even if I don't agree with what she's calling trash.

The clearer sight of her home has the smile I didn't realize I had grown growing bigger.

Wider.

What! Putting aside the fact she's...drop dead beautiful... she spoke to me. She actually spoke to me. Do you understand what I'm saying? She didn't yell. She didn't scream. She didn't insult me or threaten to call the cops. She talked to me like she viewed me as a person rather than a pest. And yeah, the conversation was a little one sided – given that I didn't say shit – but it didn't deter her from continuing to try. And you know what?

54

I haven't been able to shake that small high of humanity since. The need for another hit has been pushing me to go back every day. To see if I can have another or if it was just a fluke. A flub. A one-off. That…irresistible feeling of being treated like an actual human being has me curious to see if maybe I just caught her in an unusually kind mood or perhaps in a charitable mindset. Part of me is anxious to know if she sees me as an actual living, breathing, individual worthy of kindness or love or if she's just like everyone else who labels me as a parasite of society.

As much as I wish I could just walk up to her door and knock, I know the invitation extended was just *politeness.*

She wasn't actually offering me a chance to go inside.

To get to know her.

To *talk* like a date versus a stranger you're just shooting the shit with.

Fuck, a date? Did I really just…even…think that shit? What the fuck is wrong with me? Am I suffering from lack of nutrition again? You'd think my body would be used to this shit by now.

I cautiously approach the area her trashcan and recycle bin are stored, eyes continuously sweeping the scene, knowing two of her neighbors are not only nosey, but meddling. Last week one of them – I'm pretty sure the one that lives directly next door – left a note on top of Pizza Woman's trashcan labeling me a bum and threatening to call the cops if she saw me digging around again.

55

Which makes coming back here even riskier than it was when I showed up on Pizza Day. But...I...can't seem to help myself. I wanna see her again. And hear her again. And get another dose of kindness that I haven't had in fucking years. Plus, her trash is still some of the freshest around and a guy's gotta eat.

Just as I prepare to open the door to the white fenced enclosure where the supply treasure chests are stored, the sound of her front door opening halts all my movements.

My breathing.

I don't even consider fucking blinking.

"Hey, you," Pizza Woman warmly calls out causing my heart to beat a little harder against my ribcage. "How about Chinese tonight?"

Fuck. Me.

She's still using the same *tone.*

Offering the same...*compassion.*

Sucking in a deep breath, I run my hands along the front of my jacket to iron out any wrinkles I possibly can, anxious to look more presentable.

56

Not that it fucking matters. This isn't date number two or number four when she invites me in for a drink that's clearly going to lead to sex. This is just...Well, it's just...Look, I honestly don't know what it is other than an unexpected meal I didn't have to pick off maggots from. Or cook maggots with to have a better source of protein for the day.

By the time I finally turn around, not only is she casually cradling the container of food ready to hand it over like its Tupperware and we're neighbors, but she's standing closer.

Much closer.

Almost *too* fucking close.

I wouldn't hurt her. I would never hurt a woman. It's just her being so close to someone like me...is the last thing I would ever expect. It's crazy enough she's this...welcoming. I can hardly fathom the idea she's not repulsed by the look of me or the smell. Yeah, I mean I took a shower a little bit ago and do my best to keep myself somewhat groomed – that whole blend in with your surroundings shit – but she knows what I am. She has to. She knows and still doesn't mind being in my presence. How is this shit possible?

"It's from Phȯcking Duck, this Asian Cuisine restaurant that's in the same shopping complex as Loca Mocha Casabloca." She gives a small bite to her lightly glossed bottom lip. "Have you ever been?" A small cringe unexpectedly occurs on her face, which I assume is from worry that she offended me. "To the Chinese place, not the coffee one."

57

Huh.

Not the clarification I was expecting.

"*Or* to the coffee place? Have you been there?" Anxiousness to know more information has her beautiful eyes widening. "Have you tried both?"

My mouth drops open to respond yet nothing comes out.

The first time we met I swore the reason I didn't say anything was because I didn't want to scare her off. I mean I don't have like a horror movie voice or something that sends people running for the hills, it's just in my experience, I've learned talking makes the situation – my situation – too real for some people. And I didn't want her to go through that. Especially when she was just so…open, ya know? So…sweet. However, now I'm beginning to wonder if maybe I just **can't** *talk around her. Like maybe my mind has morphed into believing that if I speak it'll ruin everything. Because that's what I fucking do. I fucking ruin everything. Ruin shit and get others killed. That's my fucking M.O.*

"I ask too many questions," Pizza Woman brushes off when she doesn't receive a response. "I'm sorry. Would you believe me if I told you that that's totally *not* usually how I am? That most of the time people have to like *yank* me into a conversation?" She has another bashful bite of her bottom lip prompting my eyes to steal a hungry glance of the damn thing. "Holy shit, I just asked two more questions right after declaring I ask too many questions!"

It's impossible not to smirk.

Quietly chuckle.

"God, I hope you're laughing *with me* and not at me."

Still unable to form words, I hastily nod.

"Good," she warmly coos, empty hand curling around the edge of her long, tight-fitted, black sleeve shirt. "So, I just ordered this about an hour ago." Pizza Woman casually continues, our eyes locked once more. "It's not hot, but it's far from cold. Definitely warmer than anything you *might* find over there." Her head makes a small motion towards the bins. "And I hate leftover Chinese food above all others."

My head tilts to the side in a wordless questioning nature.

"First there's the way the rice hardens and then you can't reheat it because gets gross and mushy and who wants that shit in their mouth? And then there's the way the bread on the chicken gets too soggy or stale. I mean even if you reheat it in the oven there's really no bringing that shit back to life or restoring it to its natural glory. But you wanna know what I hate most of all? The way its smell just commandeers the whole fucking house when you simply open the fridge! Seriously, are there really people out in the world who would rather wake up to the smell of sweet and sour pork versus *Folgers*? Not that I drink Folgers – I have one of those fancy single serve machines that comes with the pods – and not that this is sweet and sour pork. It's Sesame Chicken. I wish it were General Tso's because I love the little kick that peppers give when it's done right but unless I'm sharing it with my dad, I tend to order this because…well…because it's what I'm expected to."

Her choice of phrasing furrows my eyebrows.

"*Was* expected to."

The correction deepens the concern.

What the fuck does that mean? Was she…tortured into eating a certain type of fucking chicken?

"*Ohmygod, I'm rambling,*" Pizza Woman mumbles in obvious shame, curly ponytail whipping back and forth as she shakes her head. "I'm sorry about that. I don't mean to. You're just…I guess…really um…," her eyes cut a glance down to her shuffling feet, "easy to talk to."

First free food.

Then judgement free conversation.

And now a fucking *compliment*?

Am I hallucinating or is this really happening to me?

"And I hope someday we are talking *to* each other instead of just me talking *at* you." She offers the container a little higher for me to finally take. "I promise I'm a pretty good listener even if I'm terrible talker."

I take the unexpected prize into my possession at the same time I prepare to playfully argue as well as express my gratitude; however, my jaw has barely finished lowering when the sudden repeated flashing of headlights occurs interrupting my intentions.

Instinctively, my entire frame wavers.

Changes mechanisms.

Makes me unsteady on my tactical boot covered feet yet pushes the rest of my body to fumble onward.

Get the fuck out of dodge.

Avoid the bullets whirling by.

It's the middle of a fucking warzone! Of course, I gotta stay low to avoid being hit.

High pitched screams and barbaric last cries have me unsure of which way I should go for my next move.

Is it left to run towards my team? Right? And where are those women we saw earlier? Were they in on this? Were they innocent victims killed by a stray bullet?!

Gripping my gear tighter, I clumsily hustle around the lifeless soldiers, determined to get to Hiltz and St. Clair. Adamant about doing whatever it takes to get them out of this shit. *All of us left* out of this fucking ambush.

Smoke suddenly blurs my vision preventing me from seeing where they should be.

Where they were.

The thick white puffs begin to be sucked in by the mouthful, strangling my ability to breath.

Think.

I maneuver myself until I reach the safety of the nearest brick wall and slam my body against it. The impact sends the container I'm holding flying out of my hands revealing contents that don't make any fucking sense.

Is that…Sesame Chicken? In the middle of the combat? Who delivers that shit to-

Confusion and consternation clamor quickly around my mind commandeering my thoughts and convincing me that I'm in two places at once.

But I can't *be* in two places at once.

It's not possible.

Chinese food in the middle of a mission *isn't* possible.

Another glance at the box seems to push away the smoke.

Reveal the frost on grass.

Or is that blood?

My eyes grab a glimpse over my shoulder to see a tree rather than the white wall I rushed to only seconds ago.

Bark instead of brick.

Missing wood as opposed to bullet holes.

More panic seeps into my system forcing me to shut my eyes and cover my ears. Thoughtlessly, I begin to rock. Slow. Intentional. Command that my body connects to the ground beneath me.

63

Demand that my mind acknowledges where we physically are this moment. Under my breath, I quietly recite the trained phrase I taught myself to use in these situations, "*That was then…*," my frame continues to sway, "*this is now.*" The rhythm syncs to that of my statements. "*Hiltz was then.*" Pushing harder on my ears blocks out any unwanted noise. "*Sesame Chicken is now.*" Pressure unhurriedly begins to remove itself from my chest. My arms. "*That was then…this is now.*"

The repetition relentlessly continues at a low volume until I'm successfully yanked out of the hole that is my horrific past and plopped remorselessly back into the present. At that moment, that exact moment when I know without a doubt *where* I am as much as *who* I currently am, I let out a deep breath, slam the back of my head against the tree trunk, and drag the open container over to me with the tip of my finger.

You know being without a steady place to live, a job, or people who give a fuck about you is hard enough. Having a trigger that can spiral you back in time with no way of escaping is like having cancer in remission. You're never sure when it'll wake back up or if it will at all. You can only **suspect***. You can pray to whoever it is you pray to that it* **won't***. But the truth? The full, ugly, no punches pulled to the balls truth is that it doesn't fucking matter. You still have a ticking time bomb waiting to blow up inside of you. You are a walking disaster. A tragedy on two feet. No one should have to suffer through that* **or** *this. No one. Fucking. No. One.*

Chapter 5

Jaye

Shit, I'm late! So late! So, so late! Um…alright maybe not exactly late. At least not yet. But I will be if I don't put a little Panic! in my Disco. You know…like the band? Anyway, this is exactly why I do everything I can to avoid falling asleep on the couch. On one page, it's the closest thing I ever *get to peaceful sleep. Whether that's two in the afternoon or two in the morning, this couch, this comfy purple clashes with everything else in the room couch, provides me with just enough guilt free mind space to sleep like I imagine the masses do. It's one of the* only *things in this house that I bought* after *Chris's death. We had a couch when he was alive, of course. It was white. We're talking,* painfully *white. Unfortunately – or fortunately for my purple couch – during one of my postmortem sob fests about him, I managed to get red wine on it. And by on it, I mean all the fuck over it. Cushions. Pillows. Legs. I felt like a such a monster that I rush ordered a new one through the tears that night only to have the wrong furniture delivered to me, yet when this plum piece of crazy came, I loved it. For some reason, it called to a little piece of my soul. I didn't wanna send it back, so I didn't. Now, on the other page of this cautionary Princess and The Pea like tale, sleeping on this thing is dangerous because I* always *sleep through everything when I do! Phone calls. Texts. Alarms. Which is what happened this morning and why I need you to excuse me now to quickly go get ready for work.*

In impressive timing, I shower, change into black pants, a black camisole, and purple blazer I hardly *ever* wear, and manage to get on just enough makeup that will prevent my mother from bitching about my appearance if I happen to swing by after book club tonight.

Not promising I will. I typically pretend it runs too late. Thankfully that's bullshit she always buys.

Downstairs, I quickly wiggle on my flats while silently reassuring myself that my curls are tamed enough for work. While I prefer having the extra fifteen minutes to stop them from looking like I stuck my finger in an electrical socket, shit happens, which is why I made sure early on in my career to perfect the sleek high ponytail for these emergency situations.

The grabbing of my coat as well as my workbag – that doubles as a purse during the week – is swift yet instead of charging out to my car that I auto started when I only had one shoe on, I'm blocked by a piece of ripped brown paper being held down by one of the rocks from my garden alongside a gorgeous, red rose.

There's no stopping the bright smile that jumps onto my face from the unexpected sight. I carefully lean down to pick up the morning surprise, grin growing even wider from the words left behind.

Thank you.

Two words.

Just two very simple, very common words, yet the way butterflies are fluttering around my stomach, they feel like ones he scoured the entire world searching for.

Chomping down on my bottom lip is done to prevent from swooning.

*What? Of course, I know it was Mr. Green Eyes who left this. Who else could it have possibly been?! The woman across the street? Why would she leave me a thank you note and a flower? For returning her cat? She didn't even realize the damn thing was missing. Come on. We **both** know who left this. Hm? Oh, don't be silly! He was clearly just trying to express his gratitude, nothing more. This was just him being...thoughtful. Returning the kindness that was extended to him. It's sweet. Super sweet. And from my experiences in life, if I've learned anything it's that sweet without an agenda is **rare** in this world.*

I happily add the objects to the others I'm holding and pull of an award worthy juggling act to lock my front door. On my way to my car, I brush the edge of the rose right underneath my nose, and inhale deeply, letting myself get lost in the sweet scent versus distracted by the shouting match from next door.

What! A crush?! You think I have a crush on the guy who eats my garbage? First off, that's...that's such a weird sentence to say, and second of all...I...don't have time to have this conversation with you. I'm late for work, remember?

The morning pushes forward in its typical fashion. Some people are too indulged in their morning coffee or fixing their mascara to focus on the green lights while others who are clearly running late cut people off or abuse their horns to express their frustrations.

Personally?

I'm too distracted by the thoughtful gesture to care.

Outside of Teacher Appreciation week and Employee Appreciation weeks, the last time I got flowers was the Valentine's Day the year before Chris died. He hated buying flowers. Called them a waste. Told me it would just be easier to put the cash directly in the trash. There was always a big hub bub about why they were worthless, yet every Valentine's Day, he bit the bullet and bought a dozen. Er...correction. Had his secretary buy me a dozen and pick out a card, although he did sign the card himself. That...counts for something, right?

By the time I'm headed through the employee only entrance, my mind has managed to venture past the initial excitement of receiving such a sweet sentiment to the dangerous, obnoxious why zone.

Why'd he flip out last night? And I mean you saw him. He freaked. The. Fuck. Out. One minute he was about to speak – or at least I hope he was about to speak – and the next he was grumbling and rumbling and then fumbling away. Is he that afraid of the cops? Would it have brought him comfort or more horror if he knew I was a cop's daughter? Was it something else? Could it possibly be anything else?

"Morning, Miss Jenkins!" A little girl cheerfully greets, putting herself directly in my path to the library.

"Morning, Sandy!" I warmly acknowledge in return. "Oh! What a beautiful bright purple bow you have on today!"

Reaching out to fix it is done at the same time she announces. "It's da same color your jacket!"

Rather than reprimand her for the missing words – like too many parents do – I straighten out her accessory while verbally rewarding the accurate comparison. "It *is* the same color! You are so smart." Once the oversized object is where it rightfully belongs in her blonde hair, I meet her glowing blue gaze again. "Do you remember how to say purple in Spanish or French?"

"*Violette!*"

"*Ohmygod*, look at you! Learning your French vocab words!"

"I am! I am!"

"Maybe we should read *Purplicious* during your library time today."

"Yeah!"

"No, Justin, I'd rather take the effing Greyhound than effing fly coach," her mother scoffs, Bluetooth conversation still in progress in spite of the fact she should be focused on getting her daughter to her classroom. "Ugh! Come on, Sandy! You're making Mommy even more late!"

"Bye, Miss Jenkins!" She giggles seconds before her mother yanks her away by the hand, worried more about her phone call than the small human in her care.

Unfortunately, that shit right there is pretty common. You get used to it. Even if you wish you couldn't.

Resuming my trek for my office space, I allow myself another brief inhaling of the sweet scent from the object I can't believe I'm still clutching.

Where should I put this? On my desk in my back office so I have a little piece of him here at school or on the kitchen table at home so it feels like he's finally taking me up on my offer to come inside? Am I maybe…a little…too into this stranger? Especially considering the fact he hasn't said a single word to me. And why hasn't he? Why leave me a thank you note – which more people really should do in general – when he could've just said it? Writing me a note is way more effort than saying those two words. Think about it. He had to find a pen. Okay. Maybe he didn't. Maybe he already had a pen. That's fair, but he had to find paper. Or maybe…maybe he had that too. But what about the flower? The chances he had that just sitting around in his backpack are slimmer than a romance novel winning a Pulitzer Prize. That means at some point post his flip out, he had to go find this flower, walk all the way back to my house, and leave it there for me. During that entire process he could've stopped. Threw away the idea of wanting to do something nice for me and just hightailed it to someplace warm, which would've been the smarter idea considering how cold it was last night. Hell, the couple minutes I was out there with him, I felt like that moment when Little Penguin, the star of the finger puppet books I read to the baby class, gets chilly and needs to snuggle. See what I'm getting at? Instead of safely sheltering himself from the dropping temperatures, he marched through the cold, got this flower,

70

marched back to my home, and left it. Why? Why do all of that
instead of just saying *thank you? Is it because the action says*
more? Means more? Did he want it to say or mean more? Did he
need it to? Uh…feel free to chime in at any point here. I'm all
ears.

"That's a pretty huge smile," Presley Morrison, my boss, the
owner of the school, and by far one of the most gorgeous women in
the entire building, casually comments.

Startled by her voice, I completely lose my footing and land
on the hard hallway floor, contents of my workbag spilling out.

"*Ohsheesh*," Presley immediately rushes to assist in
collecting my lost objects, starting with my book club planner. "You
okay? I really didn't mean to scare the living 'ish out of you."

I prepare to insist that she didn't, that that's why I shouldn't
walk while distracted yet stop to briefly observe the way so many
people walk past me without even a second look. How so many
individuals don't even acknowledge the fact there's a fucking human
being on the floor potentially in need of help. They don't know why
I've fallen. They don't know if I can get up on my own or need
medical assistance. And from the focused looks on their faces to the
way they simply swing wide or step over my scattered items, it's
clear they don't care either way.

Is this what Mr. Green Eyes feels like? Does the world ever
stop to try to lend him a hand? Maybe I was the first one. Maybe
that's why he went out of his way to say thank you. Hm. No. No
way. That can't be it. People have tried to help him before, right?
Maybe? At least once? Probably at least *once.*

71

My boss's voice cautiously calls out to me at the same time she offers me the notebook, "*Jaye?*"

"Yeah!" Shoving the item back into the bag is followed by two more objects being treated the same. "I'm totally fine. If *Pete the Cat* doesn't cry about stepping in stuff, no need for me to be upset about tripping over stuff even if stuff is technically me." The smallest giggle escapes as I rise to my feet. "Thanks for the help, though. It's…nice to be reminded kindness isn't an extinct thing like the Mosasaurus."

"Is that a dinosaur of some kind?"

"Not exactly. They were marine reptiles that ruled the water in the same Cretaceous period *as* the dinosaurs."

Her eyebrows lift in surprise at the random fact.

The realization she didn't ask for a history lesson has me cringing and profusely apologizing. "*Sorry.* Lawrence needed help with his fact versus fiction school report on dinosaurs last week, so naturally he came by the library for help, and some of the weird stuff about them we learned just sort of stuck in the brain." My shoulder shrug is innocent. "And may or may not have convinced me to add a couple more *How Do Dinosaur* books to our small collection. I really thought we had more than we do."

Presley folds her light chocolate arms across her black button up shirt and teasingly grins. "Now, I don't know if you're smiling about whatever made you smile before or over the new books you bought."

Warmth undeniably coats my cheeks. "Both?"

"I like both."

I do, too.

"Wanna tell me about the *non-book* thing making you smile?"

Telling my boss that the homeless man who likes to eat out of my garbage left me a rose on my porch for giving him fresher food doesn't seem like a wise idea. It probably doesn't paint me in the sanest light, and the last thing I need is the person who signs my paycheck rethinking that decision.

"I might have made a new…friend?"

"Oooo," she girlishly giggles on a silly shoulder shimmy. "Friend or *friend*?"

"Friend."

Maybe the other type of friend someday. Wait. No. That definitely sounds crazy even if I'm more attracted to him than all the men I've been out with in my entire life. Yeah. Chris included.

73

"Well, I hope your new friend keeps giving you reasons to smile."

Hold your judgments.

"Unfortunately, I'm about to give you a reason to frown."

"Oh?"

"Yeah, I can't make book club tonight."

Thankful it's not something more devastating, I let out a small sigh of relief. "It happens. No need to stress."

"Is it that obvious that I am?"

"Kind of." Adjusting the strap on my shoulder is done as I ask, "Is everything okay?"

"It's fine." She pauses, internal debate scrunching her soft, brown skinned face. "I um…I just have a prior engagement."

"Gotcha."

"If it's alright with you, I'll just grab the new month's read on my lunch break tomorrow."

Before I have a chance to reply, Clemmy, the main school assistant, nabs her attention from the end of the hall. "Boss, you've got a call on line one!"

She presents me with a polite smile. "Remember to CC me the book fair decorations order, please."

"Will do."

Presley's the best boss. She really is. Intimidating model worthy looks aside, she seems like a beautiful person. Genuine. She puts everything she has into this school and in turn allows us – the employees – to put everything we have into our roles. We're given the best training, the best opportunities for growth, and some of the best bonuses for simply doing what we love to do – educate kids. On a more personal level, we have similar tastes in books and T.V. shows – at least that's what I've gathered from the non-child related small talk we've shared – which makes me believe we would be good outside of work friends if we tried. And honestly, I don't try too hard to connect to anyone past the surface level anymore. Chris's death became my scarlet letter of sorts. In general, people either avoid me completely – unsure of how to approach a widow adjacent woman – or avoid me for more than a quick hello, goodbye – to theoretically prevent them from saying something that could trigger me into a blubbering mess, which for the record I haven't been for last couple of years. There are few exceptions to those groups, but those people really view me more as a pet project they want to reward themselves for when they 'help me find love again'. Yeah. That shit is more obnoxious than just having people stay away from me, yet the never-ending nagging from my mother to 'be more social' pushes me to endure such irritations over the occasional cocktail with coworkers.

After a long workday filled with making book orders for the library, orders for the classrooms, orders for the book fair, participating in reading to kids as well as helping some of them read out loud to me, and managing the adult's only book club meeting, I'm finally able to head home with just enough time to miss the predicted sleet storm.

I fucking hate them. Mainly because Chris died on an icy road trying to get out of one.

Pulling around the corner, the sight of a police car parked near my house with its lights on sends me back in time in all the worst ways.

My heart instantly lurches into my throat.

My fingers swiftly become slick.

Tense.

Dread drags itself the length of my spine and down my leg until my foot is no longer on the accelerator.

I got off late from work that night, too, although it wasn't because of book club, but because I was working on last minute scheduling changes to the winter wonderland book fair, something

76

I could've easily done from my laptop at home had that been allowed. See, Chris could bring work home, but he didn't like for me to. If I was home, he wanted me home. Present. Focused on him. Or us. Or whatever family portrait bullshit moment we were pretending to have. He wanted a housewife – so to speak – and in some ways I wanted to give him that.

Several slow deep breaths are executed at the same time I gently remind myself that that scenario repeating itself isn't possible.

I don't have a fiancé anymore.

Or boyfriend for that matter.

Fuck, I haven't even had a recent enough date to be the person they contact as the individual who last saw him alive.

Yeah, I hear how pathetic my dating life is. Let's wait to discuss that subject until we're safely inside the house and out of the pending sleet, okay?

I park in my driveway and do my best to casually give the commotion next door a once over.

What! We can't just brazenly stare. That's rude!

Waiting in my car to see who "Perfect Mrs. Prescott" is having arrested crosses my mind yet getting out seems like the more natural option. The one that says I'm not at all interested in which

77

little neighborhood piggie has caught the attention of the big, bad, bitchy wolf.

And she is a bitch. I don't call her that label loosely. She once called HOA because she believed the leaves in my yard had been there too long. Never mind the fact, we hadn't been home for a week because we were on our engagementmoon, which was why we hadn't done anything about them. Her needless whining cost us a hefty fine and an increase in lawn maintenance fees. I swear the woman lives to nitpick her neighbors. Last week, I watched her nastily point out to the woman in the house on the other side of her, where the carwash had missed spots during its cleaning prior to proclaiming she needed to get that taken care of to keep up the prestigiousness of the community. Yeah...That's the type of person she is. Pain in the ass would be a compliment at this point.

The officer turns the individual they've cuffed towards their vehicle revealing to me a face that sends my heart back into my throat.

No! No. No. No.

"Excuse me!" I exclaim and grab my workbag from the passenger seat. "Wait!" Slamming my car door, I hastily hustle down my driveway towards the men in uniform. "Please wait!"

The arresting officer ceases his movements and meets my brown gaze with his. "Well, well, well, if it isn't Little Jaye Jenkins."

78

Yes, yes, I know, but when I was five, my dad always introduced me that way. It stuck. Pretty much the entire force – including rookies who are younger than me – refer to me this way.

"Evening, Officer Brallon!" Hiding my anxiety is difficult but done. "I didn't know you were back on patrol already. I thought you had a couple more weeks."

His stubble covered, warm ivory face lights up on a small laugh. "Anymore desk duty, and I would've considered eating my own brass."

"True story," his red headed partner pipes in, joining the conversation. "Evening, Little Jaye Jenkins."

"Good evening, Officer McAdams. How's life with a newborn?"

"*Loud*," he lightly laughs as he arrives at his partner's side. "That girl has a set of lungs on her that is unmatched."

"Could you please stop being so *chummy* with my neighbor and resume arresting that vagrant?" Gwenith huffs from the sidewalk space she's occupying in her satin and lace sleep robe.

First of all, kudos to her for using a top shelf word. Second of all, why did she raid a Kardashian's closet for something to

79

wear while she had this poor man arrested? That was just unnecessary.

Officer Brallon rolls his eyes wordlessly informing that he doesn't want to be making this arrest either.

Which is good.

Because if I have anything to do with it, he *won't*.

"He's not a vagrant, Mrs. Prescott, he's my friend."

The unexpected declaration slowly lifts Mr. Green Eyes's head up until our stares can lock. Confusion and gratitude battle for the right to be seen, yet he gives no other indication that what I said is untrue.

Maybe because it's not?

Maybe because we both *want* it to be true therefore in a weird way it already is?

Please keep comments and concerns to yourself until after we've successfully saved him from wrongful incarceration.

My smile softens while my tone remains kind. "Can you two please tell me why he's being arrested?"

"Friend?" Brallon's confusedly questions. "This man is your *friend?*"

"He's not her *friend,*" Mrs. Prescott sneers and seethes in an impressive tandem. "He's a pathetic piece of garbage that goes around digging through other people's personal belongings. Most likely looking for heroin or women's undergarments to do unspeakable things with." She tugs her black robe tighter together. "Come to think of it, he's probably a serial rapist. In fact, I'm sure of it."

"He's not a rapist!" I loudly squawk.

"*Ma'am,*" McAdams firmly states, stare swinging her direction. "Please, be aware of the weight of such allegations, especially without proof."

"How do you know I don't have proof?"

Her question causes new pangs of anxiety to swell through my chest and my mouth to defensively hiss. "*You don't have any proof.*"

She pulls her painfully thin lips to one side on a quiet snip. "*Not yet.*"

"Not ever, Gwenith, because he's not a rapist!"

"Little Jaye Jenkins, please, lower your voice," Brallon insists in such a manner I have no choice but to back down.

"Sorry, Officer Brallon."

He gives me a kind nod of acknowledgement prior to investigating the accusation further. "Is this individual your friend?"

There's no hesitation in my answer. "Yes."

"Are you aware that he doesn't have any form of valid identification on him?"

"He must've misplaced it again," I casually lie.

Or hope.

Perhaps hope is the better term here.

Hope doesn't leave me feeling shitty for lying to the law.

"You know how that goes for wanderlust lovers like him."

"Got a cousin like that," McAdams says on a heavy sigh, shaking his head. "Swear to him every time he visits another country that he's just begging to be a target of identity theft."

Small chuckles leave the three of us prompting Gwenith to viciously snaps, "What's his name?"

Yup.

Should've seen that coming.

How did I *not* see that coming?

"Pizza Dude," my mouth retorts without my consent.

Officer Brallon's face bunches up in disbelief. "Pizza Dude?"

"Okay, so, you caught me." The tiniest blush creeps into my cheeks. "I don't...know his...*actual* name but tell me you've never had a friend who had a weird nickname that you always used to the point you couldn't even remember their real name anymore." My rushed response seems to be well received given the way that their shoulders slightly relax. "God, there was this guy I graduated high school with we all called Shaggy because he looked *exactly* like the dude from *Scooby-Doo*. To this very day, I still don't know his name. I think it was Michael? Maybe Chad? Er...Brad?"

"Yeah, I know what you mean," McAdams states on an understanding nod. "There's a guy I graduated with from the academy we call Snowy. He's so fucking pale, he practically glows in the dark. No clue what his real name is."

"Speaking of snow," the segue to change the subject is swiftly stolen, "did you get to try those coconut snowball cookies I made for the precinct, or did dad eat them all before you could?"

Brallon warmly chuckles during the process of uncuffing the homeless man who looks almost as stunned as my neighbor that he's being set free. "I had one." His head rapidly shakes. "*One.* That's all that monster was willing to share."

The giggles that escape are genuine. "Yeah, that sounds like Dad."

"*Excuse me,*" Gwenith loudly tries to interrupt pushing me to quickly speak over her.

"You know what? Why don't I make another batch this weekend and drop them off for all of you without telling him first? That way you can help yourselves! And if Dad tries to give you crap about it, you can just tell him, a cookie angel dropped them off. You had *no clue* where they came from."

"You are a cookie angel," McAdams gleefully chortles. "Only woman I know who bakes cookies and wants nothing in return."

Okay maybe not nothing this time. Forgetting this whole little incident happened is the hope.

"Well, before I become a sleet angel," I casually motion up to the sky where it's beginning to fall, "do you mind if me and Pizza

84

Dude go inside? You both probably know I'm still not really a fan of this weather."

Sympathy I hate to see fills both their stares but for the first time in a long time, I'm more than okay playing that card.

"Of course, Little Jaye Jenkins," Brallon quickly nods and kicks his chin towards my garage. "Get inside and then perhaps talk to your guest about some things like boundaries. Private property. Keeping his *ID* on him. And perhaps *answering* questions we ask rather than remaining silent." His eyes briefly cut to the homeless man whose face is expressionless. "You look less guilty that way."

"We'll talk about all those things and more over hot cocoa inside."

"God, you probably make a mean hot cocoa, too, don't you?" McAdam's practically drools.

"One of the best in the city."

He tosses his partner a playful glare. "Why didn't I marry a woman who could at the very *least* make me good hot cocoa? Babs can barely turn on the coffee pot without setting off the smoke alarm."

"That's worrisome," Brallon good-naturedly jabs back.

"Excuse me!" Gwenith squeaks as the homeless man retrieves his bag from the ground. "This isn't the first time I've seen him skulking around in her trashcan!" Her boot covered foot aggressively stomps the ground. "He's not her friend! He's some homeless junkie looking for drugs or needles or-"

"*Ma'am*," McAdams instantly chastises. "That's enough."

"More than enough, Gwenith." My protective nature increases exponentially. "You have no right to say that. You don't know
 anything about him or his life."

"*Neither. Do. You*," she bitterly bites.

Don't agree with her! I damn sure know more about him than she does!

"*Ladies*," Officer Brallon firmly states at the same time he holds his hands out at both of us, "let's just agree from this point going forward to be *better neighbors* and *communicate* when we believe we have a problem. Understood?"

"Definitely," I softly sigh seconds before more sleet starts to come between us. "Gonna go ahead and go." Motioning my head towards the garage occurs next. "Pizza Dude, I've got a couple empty boxes in the garage. Do you mind tossing them in the recycle for me while I go to the bathroom? I *really* have to pee. Traffic was a nightmare."

Only a small lie. I'm not actually going to go to the bathroom. I'm just trying to get him inside without getting him inside, ya know?

Mr. Green Eyes wordlessly nods and follows me to my two-car garage door where I type in a code to open it.

"Enjoy your night, Little Jaye Jenkins!" Officer Brallon insists on a warm wave yet turns a scolding finger point toward Gwenith.

I manage to hear the beginning of a lecture that includes phrases like "unnecessary calls" and "waste of valuable police time" on my way to the door that leads inside. Rather than going all the way in, I step out of view and casually point to the two empty delivery boxes I was planning to use for a library project, silently insisting he throws those away to make my story more believable.

And yes, we're going to call it a story, because lie makes me feel really shitty about doing the right thing, which is **not** *how doing the right thing is supposed to feel!*

Pizza Dude tosses the boxes, casually waves to the officers, and presents me with a single nod to lower it the instant he's crossed the threshold like I just reappeared rather than had been lingering around the entire time.

Once we're officially alone, our gazes meet again.

His stare glows so brightly that I have to fold my hands together in front of me to prevent myself from reaching out to touch it.

Him.

How on earth is it possible to feel so many things just staring into someone's eyes? How can you feel lost in such a way that you never wanna be found but found in a way that makes you feel like you'll never be lost again? How can they give you breath yet take it away? Promise security and showcase insecurity?

It takes longer than I expect to find my voice, "So, they're probably gonna circle the neighborhood for the next couple hours, especially with the way the sleet is picking up. Part of that is to make sure I'm not full of shit about who you are, and the other part is simply routine patrol during inclement bad weather. They get an odd amount of 'emergency' calls during storms like this. It'll probably be better for us both if you wait here for a bit, but after that, I can take you wherever you like. I mean I don't *love* driving in the sleet...," my head gently sways back and forth as I feel inclined to be more honest, "I actually really loathe driving in the sleet, but I totally will for you."

His dark brows lift in surprise.

"I just wanna know you're somewhere safe...and warm..." The confession has me nervously biting my bottom prior to prodding. "Do you um...Do you *have* somewhere like that to sleep tonight?"

Mr. Green eyes keeps his distance.

His wordless nature.

Slowly shakes his head.

"Well, you do now."

The declaration pulls his brow together in perplexity.

"You can stay here in the garage. I have a blowup air mattress you can use, plus the whole thing is insulated *and* has a helluva space heater to help keep it warm. My fiancé," there's no stopping my head from whipping back in forth, "er...*ex-fiancé*," another frantic headshaking is presented, "*deceased fiancé*, which is definitely the worst of those three phrases," I helplessly cringe and try to continue onward less awkwardly, "he used to build model cities out here." Pointing to the covered, untouched structures nonchalantly occurs next. "It was the only hobby he ever had. And now that I think about it, that was probably for the best. That shit was expensive. And he had expensive tastes on top of that. Any other hobbies, and I'm afraid to think what our bank accounts might've looked like. Or our sex life for that matter considering how often he ended up touching those rather than me."

The homeless man's eyebrows twitch in question over the unexpected truth bomb.

Okay, where were you?! Why didn't you stop me from letting that out?! He didn't need to know that!

89

"Anyway, my point was, the space heater out here actually makes this entire place feel pretty hot. Just as hot as inside the house. Definitely much warmer than...*out there*. So...um...what do you think? Wanna crash here?"

Yeah, yeah, what I'm doing is a little insane, but I can't just throw him back out there. Fuck that. I won't *just throw him back on the street with no place to go. No way to stay warm. Nothing to protect him from the fucking sleeting out there. Look, the last thing I want is for him to catch pneumonia or hypothermia or frost bite or one of the other million weather related illnesses my mother has been lecturing me to wear my coat to shield me from since I was four. He needs somewhere* real *to sleep tonight. He could die if I sent him back out there. And I don't want that. I don't want that at all.*

For the first time since we've met, the homeless man finally speaks, proving that he is indeed *capable* of it. *"Why are you so nice to me?"*

Fuck me, even his voice is sexy?!

Deep.

Firm.

Gruff.

Ugh, how is that fair?!

Hm. No. No, I didn't just say sexy. I said…Okay, well I meant…you know what. That's enough out of you for right now.

The retort I offer back is done with a soft grin. "Why not?"

His head immediately cocks to one side as if the question broke his brain.

Maybe it did.

And if it did, perhaps *that's* the bigger issue than my willingness to help out someone who desperately needs it.

And yes, before you ask, if he were a woman, down on hard times, in need of food or shelter or momentary shielding from the Little Twat That Could next door, I would do the same thing. The fact that he's attractive – you have eyes! – is just a weird, unexpected bonus.

Mr. Green Eyes does his best to relax in the moment.

To not fidget with the straps of his tattered backpack.

To not shift his weight.

91

Shuffle his feet.

When he finally speaks again, his voice is still littered in shock. "You're really not afraid of me."

The fact that he says it as a statement instead of a question causes me to smile wider. "Nope. There's no reason to be."

Mr. Green Eyes's expression shifts to one of scolding.

"Pizza Dude, my dad's a police lieutenant – if you couldn't tell by my interaction with the two officers out front – and my mom's a thoracic surgeon, which means I have the capability of stunning you, cuffing you, and then carving out your organs to donate them to science because *Operation* in my house wasn't a game so much as a monthly study session on the human body and how to create a foolproof alibi."

The smirk that slides onto his face sends the dormant butterflies in my stomach into a full tizzy.

"*Truth bomb* incoming."

Intrigue rips through his stare.

Has his body lean forward, anxious for more information.

More knowledge about me.

"I've taken several self-defense classes – enough to basically teach one myself – am always packing some sort of protection on my person – knife, pepper spray, dog whistle – and sleep with a fully loaded Beretta at my bedside." Folding my arms across my chest is done on a teasing beam. "Maybe it's *you* who should be afraid of *me*."

His chuckles are so warm they damn near cause me to break out in a sweat. "*Maybe.*"

You know he's the first person outside of my family and book club since Chris's death that I've wanted to be around for longer than five minutes? That means something, doesn't it? Even if it shouldn't. Even if it's bizarre. Even if it's unideal or illogical, it doesn't erase the fact that it does. Or that it's true.

I casually change topics to one that's just as important as his shelter situation. "Have you eaten?"

"I had lunch."

"Which was?"

He hesitates to answer; however, he eventually does. "Some crackers."

"Crackers aren't lunch, Pizza Dude. Crackers are a *snack*. And not a very healthy one according to the two page email my

93

mother sent me about avoiding things that are so high in sodium due to their ability to cause bloating, heart attacks, and strokes." The eye roll given is absentmindedly done. "The irony is that *she* is probably going to be what gives me the latter."

Another small, amused smirk is shot my direction.

"You like lasagna?" Keeping hope out of my tone is impossible. "It's not made from scratch or anything, but it's still pretty good. Wouldn't kick it out of bed for eating the aforementioned taboo crackers."

My joke successfully receives another light laugh.

"How about I put that in the oven while you get settled?" A new wave of questions rushes over me. "Have you had a hot shower lately? Or just...access to hot water period?"

The joy on his face falls prior to a headshake.

"Okay, then *you* hop in the shower and get warmed up while I put the food in and get the space heater working. After you're all done, we can get the mattress setup and pick out some sheets and blankets and pillows. I wanna say I have some non-floral print stuff for guests, but it's hard to remember. I haven't had one in...um...*ever*...and my mom has a hard on for gifting flower décor items, insisting 'visitors find it welcoming'. Not sure that that's true; however, we may be putting that theory to the test tonight."

More laughter leaks from his parted lips wrapping around me the way I guiltily wish his arms would.

"I'm Jaye Jenkins, by the way." An awkward unnecessary wave is given to him. "Just in case you missed the officers calling me that."

"Oh no, I heard them. Loud and clear." The amused expression lingers. *Little Jaye Jenkins.*"

"Don't make me get the dog whistle, Pizza Dude."

"*Archer.*" His warm correction is followed by him bridging the gap between us, extending his open palm, and properly introducing himself for the first time, "*Archer Cox.*"

Chapter 6

Archer

Jaye. Pizza Woman's first name is Jaye. Fuck…just when I thought she couldn't get any more perfect, she says her name to me. Did you hear what I said? To. Me. Not around me. Not near me for my overhearing benefit. To. Me. She fucking introduced herself. Called me…a friend. Part of me knows it was just to get the cops off my ass – fuck her nosey neighbor for that – but the other part me…the part I call instinct…the part that kept me alive in combat as much as when I'm roaming the streets is insisting that she meant that term. That that's how she really sees me. And double fuck because that shit feels good. Really good. Too fucking good considering I know all this is just temporary.

The burning hot water firmly massages my shoulders, which pulls another pleased groan out of me.

Forfuckssake, what the hell am I doing? I don't belong here. I don't belong in this fancy ass walk-in shower, with this fancy ass seven setting showerhead, with this fancy ass fucking soap that smells like I'm bathing myself with a slice of vanilla birthday cake. No. I belong scrubbing my face with that slightly heated pool water and washing crumbs out of my scruff with a garden hose.

Both of my palms press harshly against the tile wall while my head falls completely forward, helplessly lost in the heavenly sensations.

96

I honestly can't remember the last time I had an actual hot shower. I think it was a few months ago near a holiday weekend. Sometimes if you linger around the cheap motels right off the highway, the maids will take pity on you. They'll go for an 'overdue break'. Sometimes they'll pretend they forgot something in the main office. Leave the door unlocked or cracked open. Let you rinse off right before their cleaning duties are to begin inside. Look the other way if they happen to come up a towel short – after all guests take things all the time, it's why some of that shit is pre-factored into their bill. Maria Claire used to be my go-to. Unfortunately for both of us, her kindness is what got her fired. I should've just gone a couple times and moved on to prevent any damage being done to her or her career. I shouldn't have risked her security for my own selfish momentary satisfaction. I swear to God, I ruin everything around me. It's the only shit I'm actually good it. It's why I need to leave first thing in the morning. What happened to Maria Claire weighed heavily on my heart for weeks; however, just the idea *of causing Jaye any type of turmoil weighs heavily on my fucking* soul. *I have to go. I refuse to hurt her. At* all. **Ever.**

After rinsing off the last of the suds from my shoulders, I turn off the water, open the glass door, and reach for the large, fluffy white towel waiting for me on the nearby toilet seat. There's no stopping the small grumble of continued pleasure that instantly breaks free.

Fuckin' hell, man, even the towel is comfortable?! Feel this shit. Soft, right? God, have you ever had a towel like this in your entire life? Even in my pre-nomad life, I never had anything at this quality. I was more of a buy whatever's cheapest type of guy. I gotta ask – you not her – is this what staying at The Frost Luxury Hotel is like? You know the five-star place I'm talking about, don't you? They've got fancy chains and resorts all around the world. Yeah! That one! Is this comparable? Well, even if it isn't, this shit

beats the fuck out of rinsing off with a hose and using tattered rags
I grabbed out of the garbage to dry off.

Rather than rush to get back into my dirty clothes, I stretch out the once in a lifetime experience.

Slowly run the material along the length of my arms.

Across the tattoo of silhouette soldiers that form a feather right above the phrase "Lest we forget" on my left arm and the Spartan warrior helmet on my right shoulder.

Patting the cushiony cloth against burn marks, bruises, bullet wounds, and scars fills me with both sense of pride and gut-wrenching disgust.

My skin is a reflection of the battles I've fought both as a
grunt and as a civilian. I wish that the blemishes were only from
the former. I wish that the outside world had been fucking kinder
to me than the enemy combatants. God, do I wish I received a
hero's welcome rather than being shunned for returning home a
lot more broken than I left.

The full-size towel has just been secured around my waist when there's a sudden knock at the door.

Jaye, to my surprise, doesn't wait for an invitation to enter. She simply turns the knob and thrusts herself into the steamy room. "Hey, I-"

Whatever the end of the sentence is fails to form.

Her light brown eyes shamelessly sweep my frame from head to toes, soaking in every little inch of exposed skin it can see.

Look, I know it's wrong to even **think** *about how easy it would be to just drop my towel, slip my tongue past her parted lips, and pin her against the doorframe while she moans for mercy we both know by the look on her face right now she doesn't really want, but just because it's morally wrong doesn't mean my dick got the memo not to twitch in excitement over the mere idea. Can you blame it?* **Me?** *Every fucking thing about this woman is fucking amazing. She's not airbrushed. Her true face doesn't start an inch underneath her makeup. She's not prim and proper and overly polished. The tiny tear on the lace portion of her top is easy to spot. She's got strands of hair springing out of the place they're supposed to be. Her chipped nail polish on her big toe is beyond faded from the bright purple color I imagine it once was. Jaye is far from perfect and that distance from such an overrated ideal is exactly what makes her perfect to me. She rambles with full lips moving at such a rapid speed it's fucking hypnotizing. And the craziest thing about that shit is I never want her to stop talking. I love the sound. The jokes. The questions. I love when she cringes because she's crossed a boundary yet lingers for a moment to investigate if it really was one or if it was just a small stone in her way. And if we move away from her bubbly personality back to just her physical portion, holy fuck, did you see the way her hips swayed going up the stairs? How her gorgeous, toned legs stretched up each one, mercilessly hinting at how they would stretch around me while she clung on for dear life as she got ready to come? Fuck, would I do whatever it took to make her come. To make her scream my name. Add scratch marks to my already battered body. Huh. It's uh…It's been a* long time *since I've had these kinds of thoughts running through my mind. A* really *long* *time. They didn't even appear for Maria Claire – who was quite attractive albeit a bit young – when she offered to let me crash at her place for the cost of a single dick ride. I need to reel this shit in and definitely get the fuck out of this house first thing in the morning. Like…sun hasn't even had its fucking coffee yet first thing.*

"Uh…" This time Jaye's voice trails off while her eyes continuously help themselves to a second serving of my surprisingly well-kept figure. "Um…"

Truth? If she asked to come on my cock in exchange for a warm place to say I wouldn't think twice about saying yes.

Her lips purse together on a whimper, summoning my shaft to swell harder under the towel.

Casually, I drop my hands to block my dick at the same time I airily chortle, "*Jaye?*"

The carnal trance she stumbled into seems to remain. "*You have abs.*"

Unsure of where the topic is going yet unafraid to succumb to a little curiosity prompts me to retort. "I do."

"And…*abs.*"

100

"Yeah...I uh...," clearing my throat grows difficult, "have abs."

"And these muscles," her hand brazenly waves back and forth in front of the tatted words "This We'll Defend" on my upper chest.

"Pecks?"

"Yeah, those and arm muscles," her head tilts to one side as she drinks in the Spartan tattoo, "and shoulder muscles and...neck muscles..." The feverish lick of her lips she steals threatens to become my undoing. "How do you have so many fucking muscles?"

"I do the best I can to care for myself in spite of my circumstances."

"I'll say..."

Her teeth hungrily nip at her bottom lip pushing me to get her out of the room before I'm the one doing the biting. "Did you need something?"

Jaye lazily drags her stare back to mine causing my face to slightly heat in embarrassment.

Fuck, I haven't been stared at this hard and this needy since I was on active duty.

She sweetly hums her question, "Hm?"

Realizing she didn't hear what I said has me cockily smirking at the same time I repeat, "Did you need something, sweetheart?"

"*Sweetheart*," she quietly swoons, "I like that." Her grin grows ground shakingly powerful. "I like that way more than Little Jaye Jenkins." The declaration receives a nod of acknowledgement prompting her to return to our reality versus whatever reverie she was just in. "Why am I here?" She doesn't wait for answer from me. "Right!" A rapid headshake seems to plant her back on mentally firm ground. "*Clothes.*"

"The thing I'm not currently wearing."

"Yes." Her smile softens, and there's no stopping my heart from following. "And I got to thinking that maybe since *you* were in need of a shower – not that I thought you smelled or anything – that *your clothes* might be in need of one too – they definitely smell – and so I went ahead and took the liberty of sneaking them out of here to toss them into the wash."

"So, you came to tell me I'm having dinner in a towel?"

Or naked? Maybe she wants me to be naked while she eats? Is that weird? I haven't been this…close or cordial to another person in months. Pretty sure that would be a strange, run for the hills, request, right?

102

"No, no, no," she rushes to deny, face reddening in a way I find myself enjoying, "I brought you pajamas! Well, sort of. It's a jersey cotton robe and matching pants – both never worn. I wasn't sure if you wanted to sleep topless-"

"Topless?"

"*Er*," Jaye flashes me her infamous cringe, "*shirtless. I* wasn't sure if you wanted to sleep *shirtless* or not, so I didn't bring one, but I can go back and grab you one if you need me to." She pushes the folded pile of clothing towards me. "And I also brought you a toothbrush. For tonight before bed or in the morning when you wake up or both. Brushing your teeth is super important at least once a day according to the dentist I avoid because I swear he looks down my top and the *Just Going to the Dentist* kid's book by Mercer Mayer I just picked for dental awareness month which is coming up soonish." Her string of sentences I'm not sure she took a breath between are suddenly followed by a heavy sigh. "*Sorry*. I don't know why I do that. I don't know why I just talk and talk and talk and don't seem to be able to shut up around you."

All previous feelings of flattery pale in comparison to these new ones.

So…it's…just me she does this for? That makes me…special, doesn't it?

My mouth mumbles unapproved words before my brain can conjure proper ones. "I don't want you to shut up around me."

Relief and excitement simultaneously pierce her stare.

103

Alright. Maybe those words weren't so bad.

Transferring the objects into my possession is done at the same time I inquire, "Not to sound ungrateful, but where'd these 'never worn before clothes' come from?"

"They were Chris's."

"The dead fiancé?"

My callousness doesn't seem to deter her from answering. "Yeah. He um…he really only liked silk pajamas when he *wore* pajamas to bed with me – and that's not a because he liked to sleep naked thing, that's a we rarely slept in the same bed thing – but I stupidly thought that maybe if we got a matching pair that he might try them. You know…*humor me?*" She shakes her head in a sad nature. "He didn't. He didn't even pretend to appreciate the thought of the gift I was so excited to give that Christmas."

Prick.

"I wear mine all the time – they're so fucking comfy – but um his…" her hands slip into the back pockets of black dress pants, "his have just been sitting in the back of the closet, waiting for me to grow the courage to give them away to someone who might actually appreciate them."

"I *do* appreciate them."

104

The hint of a smile appears.

"You."

It slowly stretches from ear to ear.

"I just hope you know that I *can't* and *won't* be him."

"I don't want that shit, either."

Her response catches me completely off guard, yet her prompt exit afterward doesn't.

Would you stop calling me a dick already? No, I wouldn't prefer asshole. I just…thought that shit needed to be said instead of simply inferred. The last thing I need is her trying to slyly puppet me into being his replacement. I'm not looking to play pretend I'm the dead dude you're probably not over. To be brutally fucking honest, I'm not looking for anything. Friendship included. I don't think I could live with myself if I lost another one.

I swiftly slip into the charcoal gray pieces – fuck she wasn't exaggerating about comfort – and give my teeth a good, long overdue, hard brushing. Post feeling minty fresh, I immediately haul ass downstairs to apologize – or deliver something awkward that sounds adjacent to one – yet am stopped abruptly in my tracks by the sight of my hostess struggling to reach something off the top shelf of the closet.

Against my better judgment – like staying here for the night – I allow myself a minor moment to appreciate her wiggling, perky ass that would be a perfect fit for my palms.

I mean a perfect fucking fit.

"Why did I put you up here?!" She loudly gripes to something inside. "Why would I put you somewhere I can't even fucking reach!? How stupid am I?!"

"Do not call yourself stupid."

The instruction falters her movements causing her to bump her elbow into the door frame.

"And please be careful, sweetheart." I cautiously approach. "I may know how to bandage a wound or two but that doesn't mean I wanna do it on you."

Joy jumps around in her wide gaze as though pain never existed in her arm. "You called me sweetheart again."

Hiding my crooked, bashful grin is difficult. "You said you liked it."

"I do!"

"Good. I would rather do things you like than ones you don't."

The stunned stare I'm shot fills me with unease.

Why does that statement feel like it's a fucking foreign concept to her?

"Do you need some help get something down?"

She brushes away whatever thoughts are tumbling around her mind with a warm nod. "Yes, please. I'm little vertically challenged."

"You look like the perfect height to me."

Jaye blushes, brushes a random curl away from her face, and does her best to nonchalantly point upward. "The um…The pump's up there."

I wait for her to step out of the space before invading it to retrieve the object.

My reaching is done in tandem with her talking starting again, "I've already got the mattress itself out and in the garage. Genius me thought that it would be a good idea to keep *that* on the ground but not the pump. Where the logic is in that I'll never know." She's cut a scolding glance for her second round of self-chastising.

"I also grabbed the guest sheets. They're fucking hideous but soft. Soft is what matters most, right?"

Inching the box forward into my grip occurs between small chuckles.

"I wasn't sure how many pillows you wanted, so I just took all the ones from every guest bed."

The item is gingerly lowered as I ask for clarification. "How many guests beds are there?"

"Three."

"And how many pillows are on each?"

"Three."

Amusement speedily bulldozes itself on my face. "What the fuck am I gonna do with *nine* pillows, Jaye?"

"I don't know!" She girlishly squeaks prior to giggling. "I just…I didn't think one was enough and then one became two and two became two bedrooms and before I knew I had collected them all like fucking Pokémon." Her hands briefly cover her reddening face which only makes me laugh more. "Ugh." When they fall to her hips, she verbally runs to explain her actions. "I honestly don't know how other people sleep, okay? Personally, I sleep with two. One for my head and one for legs. I would prefer sporking-"

"What the fuck is sporking?"

"It's like spooning except our legs are wrapped around each other."

Fuck me...I would go into **any** *enemy territory right now to do that for even a moment with her.*

"Not *our*," her hand frantically motions in the small gap between us, "legs, but like another person's legs. Like whoever is sleeping with me legs. Legs that belong to the person in bed that isn't me. Legs-"

"Picture painted, sweetheart."

The term of endearment not only stops the panicked spewing but redirects us back to the subject. "All the bedding and pillows are on the couch. I had momentarily put them down to check on dinner."

"You wanna check on it again while I get started on this?"

She enthusiastically nods and saunters off the direction of the kitchen, leaving me alone to relocate myself to the garage.

It doesn't take much thought or effort to latch the pump to the mattress or get it going. The loud noise alongside the inflating action indicates I can take a moment to lean against the wall. Drink in my surroundings. Forget about the charming SOB she's somehow resurrected out of me.

Seriously. I haven't been this…social since Hiltz's funeral. I thought having to hug his pregnant wife and apologize for being the one who made it out alive broke that capability inside. I hate to admit that Jaye's proving otherwise. So…I won't.

Warmth from the turned-on space heater continues to flood the three-car garage in an impressive manner while my eyes survey the area on the opposite side of the room, the one near the door we didn't enter through. Several long tables occupy the territory, each one completely covered by thick, dusty gray sheets.

Cities. She said he liked to build model cities. That it was his hobby. That it was expensive. And when you combine that with this house, his preference for silk pajamas, and the extra set of Porsche keys I passed by on my way in here, it's safe to conclude the guy had money. And once you add that to the way he disregarded his woman's feelings, her needs, her…fucking…efforts to give a shit about him, the manifesto is clear. He wanted a trophy wife instead of a wife that was a trophy. Yeah, I know, the shit's really none of my business, especially because we're not really…friends. Or dating. Or fucking. But…shit. Never mind. Forget I even brought it. Distance is key here. I need to keep a distance. Stop letting me forget that.

About ten minutes later, I'm looking at the first chance to sleep in an actual bed I've had in the last three years.

Doesn't fucking matter if it's not a 'real' bed. It's a real fucking bed to me. And beats the fuck out of the ones I used to have to fight for at the shelters when I still scavenged downtown.

"Sheets," Jaye unexpectedly announces in a singsong voice that reminds me of a schoolteacher. "And two pillows." She steps inside the garage prompting me to scurry to my feet to assist her. "They're kind of big so I can only carry two at a time."

Transferring the gear into my grasp happens prior to me suggesting, "Why don't I start with these two and grab more after dinner if I need them."

She happily nods in agreement and informs, "The lasagna's cooling, so it'll be just a few more minutes before we eat. Do you want bread to go with it? I sort of just assumed you wanted garlic bread and put a loaf in the oven, too. I actually just assume everyone eats bread with their pasta dishes but now that I think about it, I don't remember there being any in the *On Top of Spaghetti* book the PreK kids love so much."

Aha. I knew she was a teacher. Good to see my observation skills are still sharp outside of scrounging for supplies.

"You um," her shoulders innocently bounce during her return to the conversation at hand, "you obviously don't have to eat it if you don't want to. I'm not gonna force feed you carbs."

"Bread sounds great, Jaye."

111

"Good. Good. Good," she nervously repeats, hands fidgeting around her frame for somewhere to put them. "Did you want a glass of wine to go with your meal? I've got red. And white. And sparkling. And maybe a bottle of Rosé. Oh! I have grape juice if you're not into that. And cran-grape. And bottled water. I always have bottled water. No soda, though. My mother periodically comes over to do a soda sweep, so I just learned *not* to keep it on hand. Cuts down the lectures, too, and heaven knows that woman doesn't need more things to lecture me about." Her bottom lip briefly slips behind her top teeth. "Oh! Oh! I could probably make you iced tea. It'd probably take a bit, but I could give it a shot if you like?"

God, it's like she can't help herself no matter how hard she tries. Her mouth just starts running away and to be blunt about the shit, all it does is make mine want land on top of it to help slow it down. Fuck. Me. It's been a really, really long time since I've been bombarded with this many goddamn hard-ons. I think my dick has done more pushups tonight than I did in basic training.

"Whatever you wanna pour me is fine." Lowering the material to block my swollen cock since the pajama pants do nothing in that department is followed by a small throat clearing. "I'm good with whatever you decide."

"But what is it *you* want, Archer?"

"Doesn't matter what I want. What matters is what I'm given."

"If what I like matters, then what you like matters, too."

"I'm an inconvenience. I'll take what's provided."

"You're a *guest*, and it makes me happy to have you happy."

All the air in my chest abruptly vanishes.

She considers me a guest? Like an actual…wanted person in her home? Her life? What the fuck is wrong with her? Why! Why would she want me of all people here? Is it pity? Is it…obligation? Did she run over a bunny and thinks this will make amends for it? What inclines her to be so fucking nice to me when the rest of the world won't even look my way?

Unsure of what to say yet aware the mental spiral I just slipped down isn't it, I quietly state, "Water."

"Bottled?"

"Sure."

"Perfect!" She slowly backs up towards the doorway. "I'll see you at the table after you make your bed then?"

There's no hiding the surprise in my tone. "You want me to eat inside your home?"

"Yeah."

"With you?"

"Yes."

"At the same…," bewilderment stutters my speech, "at the same fucking table?"

"That is what those words mean." Her grin is teasing. "And words matter. Trust me. I'm a librarian. I know these things."

Okay, so wrong about the teacher shit. Sort of. If she is a librarian for kids, then that's really just splitting hairs.

She offers me another giggle, an over dramatic wink, and bounces away the way she came.

Why the fuck do I suddenly feel way in over my head?

It doesn't take long to unplug the pump or make the bed. Finding my way to the kitchen, on the other hand, feels as though two tours of duty are complete before I finally arrive to find her placing down plates on opposite sides of an island that doubles as a table.

I never understood the point of places this fucking big. Not sure I ever will.

My feet plant me a safe distance from where the food is being served. From her. "Where do you want me?"

While the question isn't meant to sound sexual, the flushness her face suddenly grows indicates she wishes it was.

Which makes two of us.

Even if it shouldn't.

Jaye steals a small moment to compose herself prior to pointing to the space closest to me. "There's fine."

I nod in understanding of her order and slide myself onto the cushioned white stool. Now faced with the choice to focus my gaze at her as she fills her glass of wine or let my eyes wander around the wide-open space, I struggle to make the right call.

Do I want to hungrily stare at the way her middle finger slides into her mouth to suck off the drop of wine it caught?

Fuck yes.

Is it the respectful or gentlemanly thing to do?

Absolutely not.

See. You don't have tell me all the obvious shit.

I force my glare to admire the modern décor, the stainless steel appliances, and the strikingly strange fact the entire scene looks like something a person would stage for an open house showing.

Not live in.

What's that about?

"Feel free to eat as much or as little as you want," Jaye sweetly hums at the same time she slides onto the stool opposite of me. "It's not my favorite brand, but it's the one I buy."

"Why do you buy it if it's not your favorite?"

"Uh…" she innocently begins to contemplate an answer given the nature her face is scrunching.

"Is it because it's the most cost efficient?"

"Oh, definitely not."

"Is it because it's the one most often on sale?"

"Almost never."

116

"Then why?"

"Um…," a small, absentminded shrug presents itself, "Chris liked organic food, and this one fits the bill."

"I see." I do my best to grin rather than grimace and swallow the judgments jumping around on my tongue. "Thank you for dinner, Jaye." She begins to smile again pushing me to encourage it to resume to the full-fledged one it was before I started asking too many questions. "And thank you for the clothes. And the toothbrush. And the hot shower. And the warm place to sleep tonight. And um…*rescuing me* from the cops." Gratitude nudges me to add another line. "Your actual friends are lucky to have you watching their six, and I hope they fucking know that."

"I don't…uh…I don't *have* friends."

The retort escapes without my consent. "Is that what you want me to be?"

Mixed responses appear in her expression yet not a single one leaves her lips.

Of course not. This is all some charity case bullshit. I should've just let them haul my ass off to a cell again. It would've given me a warm place to sleep with a clear fucking conscience.

Instead of pressuring her for answers, I merely nod, lift my fork, and dig into the steaming pile of pasta waiting to be devoured. The first bite is by far the most incredible thing I've tasted in probably the last four years. And the second is just as incredible as the first spurring me to shovel the shit into my face by the largest forkfuls possible.

Logic doesn't hesitate to remind me pacing is everything but the fear of not knowing the next time I'll have a warm meal annihilates it.

Has me shoving hunks of bread back.

Popping cherry tomatoes from the side salad one right after another – practically not chewing, just swallowing.

Hell, it isn't until I look up to grab my bottle of water that I realize what an uncivilized savage I must appear to be.

I prepare to apologize for my grotesque behavior, to offer to eat in the garage out of sight, to even just wait until she's finished to keep going when she snickers. "Gah, it's like the scene from *Beauty & The Beast* where he has porridge all over his face."

Her laughter prompts my own, and I reach for my nearby napkin. "Is it really that bad?"

"The question is…is it really that *funny*?"

"Gonna guess the answer is yes."

"You are correct."

More chuckles fill the room during the wiping of my face.

I've barely finished when she sweetly speaks again, "Can I ask you something?"

"Go for it."

"Why me?" She carefully swirls the wine around her glass, eyes never breaking contact. "Why my house? Why my trashcan?"

Resentment rushes through me causing a sneer to cross my face. "Don't feel flattered, sweetheart."

"Yeah, I don't like sweetheart in *that* tone."

Her pushback stuns me momentarily silent.

"And I wasn't meaning to imply that I thought I was special because I know I'm not. I never am. I-"

"Enough."

This time it's my counter that catches her off guard.

"You *are* special, Jaye. I didn't mean to insinuate that you aren't. You are by far the most beautiful and funny and kindhearted person I've ever met. It's just that-" cutting off my own voice due to pride I have no business having briefly occurs, "I don't want you feeling good for false reasons. The truth is I do extensive recon when scouting new locations to survive in. You have the freshest trash in the entire subdivision."

"I wish I could say I was surprised by that," she mumbles more to herself than me. "Okay, then I have another question. Why did you leave me a thank you note? And a flower?"

"Why did you talk to me that first night?" Answering a query with a query seals her lips. "Why did you *offer me food* instead of hiding in your home? Sending me away? Threatening to call the cops?"

"You didn't need jail, you needed help."

"And you needed thanking."

She gingerly places her glass down and quietly proclaims, "I didn't do it for thanks."

"*I know.*"

The response sparks her smile to return and my eating to resume.

After her first bite, she pipes up once more. "Can I ask you another question?"

I casually nod while using a piece of bread to lap up the red sauce.

"What did you do before you became homeless?"

Forfuckssake, did she have to go right for the goddamn jugular? Is she actively trying to kill my willingness to have a talk or is she just the clumsiest conversationalist?

My lack of a reply leads to her cringing. "*Sorry*. That was probably super rude. And super out of line. And you should probably know I'd make a terrible spy or detective. I've learned over the last couple of years I practically have no-tact when you get me talking. Or not enough to *cleverly* get information out of someone. I could *never* be Jack Reacher's temporary partner, that's for sure."

"The...book guy?"

"You read those books?!"

"I've read some, yeah. In some fucked up ways, we have a lot in common."

"Have you always read…suspense novels?"

"I'll read whatever I can get my hands on. Whatever people have thrown out or the used bookstores didn't think they could get cash for. Can't be too picky when the shit's free, but I do appreciate the escape."

Jaye mindlessly swoons, *"Men who read are so sexy."*

Blushing can't be helped.

"And so fucking rare in my experience."

The heat in my cheeks deepens as I state, "I've always enjoyed reading. When I could *choose* what I read – during my time as a grunt – I preferred biographies. Presidents. Athletes. Musicians. That sort of shit."

"A grunt? Is that…Is that like a rock band thing?"

"What?"

"Metal band? I know there's a difference in the two, but I don't know *all* the terms. Is that slang for bassist? You being a bassist would make so much fucking sense to why I'm into you. Before Chris came along, they were totally my type. I was not so secretly that girl that liked guys in bands."

There's a shit ton of information to search through there; however, we're gonna start at the most important part.

Curiosity crashes into smugness. "You're *into* me?"

Being completely startled causes her to squeak and squawk and incoherently stutter until she lands on a half-ass concocted statement. *"Into getting to know you more."*

"Right." I ignore the niggling in the back of mind that informs me she's lying and explain, "Grunt is a slang *military* term. I was in the army."

"Oh!" More waves of embarrassment flood her face. "Oh, that makes way more sense. Especially considering the tattoos I saw earlier." Thoughts back to the moment seem to color her face yet again but aren't openly acknowledged by either of us. "How long were you enlisted?"

"Eight years. Straight out of high school."

"Wow." Her fork finally cuts another piece of the lasagna for consuming. "Why didn't you keep going? Why didn't you push to ten? Don't you get better benefits or bonuses or something at that point?"

My body instinctively tenses.

Strains to the point my muscles ache.

Typically, this is where I would switch subjects with someone, but unfortunately for me, Jaye isn't just a random *someone*.

She's…*different*.

And that fucking difference is what gets me to confess. "I was injured."

Worry for me that I've never seen on another individual – all foster parents included – springs on her face. "You're okay, though? Other than the limp?"

My non fork wielding hand grips the back of my neck and gives it a harsh squeeze forcing my head to fall forward in shame.

Fuck, I hate the fact that she noticed.

That it's *noticeable*.

That my weakness is so fucking exposed.

Anxious to get out of the spotlight, I abruptly declare, "I'm full."

"*Oh.*"

The dejection in her tone lands on my shoulders.

Chest.

Crushes my ribcage.

Vocal cords.

Makes it almost impossible to meet her gaze.

"Okay," Jaye sweetly backs down yet the gentle grin on her expression remains. "You can go ahead and get settled in for the night if you like."

"I can help with the dish-"

"Don't worry about those. I'll take care of them." She struggles to redirect her attention to a piece of food on her plate. "And I'll leave the light on in the guest half bath just in case you need to go in the middle of the night."

"Jaye-"

"Remember to turn the space heater off before you fall asleep," my hostess continues as though I hadn't tried to interrupt. "Don't wanna burn the house down. Police *and* firefighters in my driveway would be *a lot* for one day."

"Ja-"

"Once your clothes are ready, I'll fold them and leave them outside the door to the garage, so I don't wake you up. Assuming you're asleep."

Sensing that she no longer wants to hear from me, I quietly concede. *"Thank you again."*

She meekly nods, pokes her food, and doesn't bother watching me exit.

Look, I fucking tried, okay? My people skills are a little rusty. Fuck. Fine. Really fucking rusty but that doesn't mean I didn't try to be friendly or flirty. And I didn't mean to be rude. Or hurt her feelings. Or deny her the chance she desperately wants to be something more than the woman with the fresh trash and guy who eats it. I did my best and like everything else in my life, it wasn't good enough. I'm not good enough. I've never been good enough. To be adopted into a family. To be promoted high in the ranks. To be loved for more than the tags around my neck. Not once have I ever been good enough, so why did I think because some brown eyed beauty looked at me like I could give her the world that for a second I believed I could? I'll tell you why. Because hope is the most dangerous drug of them all. Far more addicting than any substance you could ever smoke or inject and much more fatal. I thought I'd given that shit up a long time ago.

126

Guess I made the mistake of having another hit tonight. Don't worry. I'll make sure to properly purge that shit from my system in the morning before I disappear out of her life forever.

Chapter 7

Jaye

You're not still fussing at me for letting a complete stranger spend the night in my home, are you? You should definitely just give that shit a rest! Seriously. I'm fine. I know I look cute and sweet and like I scream easy target, but I'm not. I sleep with my Beretta within arms' reach. I go to the shooting range with Dad for target practice every six weeks. And we clean our firearms together afterwards while cookies bake. I swear, I'm good in that aspect, but even if I weren't, it wouldn't have mattered last night. He didn't make a single sound after he closed himself inside the garage. Not. Fucking. One. Do I wish he had? Yes. Do I wish he had needed something else so that he had another excuse to talk to me rather than shut down? Ugh. I hate to admit it, but yes. And you wanna know what's the weirdest thing about this whole situation - putting aside of course the obvious portion of inviting some stranger to stay warm in my home. Last night's dinner was...ohmygod, I'm really gonna say this, aren't I? Okay. Last night's dinner was the best date – or date adjacent meal – I've ever had. Ever. Even me and Chris's first date – or date like situation – wasn't that smooth. Or smiley. Fuck, I couldn't stop smiling during pretty much the whole damn thing. What is wrong with me? Seriously. Am I just that...lonely? Am I just that afraid of turning into the nursery rhyme about the little old woman who lived in a shoe?

I've just finished adjusting the sleeves on my chunky, light gray sweater when my cellphone starts buzzing across my nightstand. Always happy to see my dad's face on the screen, I quickly answer it in a cheerful tone, "Good morning, Dad!"

"Good morning, sugar." The term of endearment warms me up further. "You doing okay after that storm?"

Huh.

I did better with it last night than I have in the past.

Was it because of Archer or am I reaching?

"Yeah. I'm okay. Gonna make some breakfast. Go in a little later than normal. Let the roads thaw a bit and get driven on first."

"I'm glad your boss understands your situation."

I have a hard time driving on icy roads since Chris's death. Period. You saw me last night. The truth is…most of the time, I won't even get behind the wheel of my car. Thankfully, Presley's completely aware of the situation, my discomfort, and added an amendment to my contract that allows me an automatic pass for life to be late or call in on such days without penalty. I do my best never to take advantage of her kindness. You know…sort of like Archer wasn't trying to take advantage of mine despite what you might think.

"Speaking of situations," the segue is swift, "how's the one with your friend?"

My lip slips between my teeth on a less than innocent hum. "Hm?"

129

"Pizza Dude?"

God, I am not good in a crisis.

"Is Pizza Dude still there?" There's a small rustling that informs me he's shifting his grip on his device. "Is he being...*respectful*?"

Not surprised that he knows or by his interrogation, I sweetly smile. "Yes, to both."

"Is he being *grateful*?"

"Extremely."

"Is he aware you're locked, loaded, and capable of lining up his organs alphabetically?"

Giggles helplessly fall free. "*Yes.*"

"Good." The short pause is followed by a warm sigh. "Promise me you'll shoot first and call for assistance later if necessary."

"*Dad.*"

"Sugar, I know my little girl. I know you would climb to the top of a mountain in your flip-flops to save a helpless rabbit if you thought it needed it. And maybe the rabbit does but that doesn't mean I want you to put yourself at risk to *possibly* save someone else."

"Are you aware of the irony in the statement, Lieutenant Jenkins?"

"I am," he lightly chortles, "however, I signed up to do that shit for a paycheck. You get paid to *read* books about rabbits, not save them."

In some ways Archer really is that rabbit. Trapped on top of a snowy mountain. Scared. Alone. Lost. I know all he needs is someone to care. I can see it. I can...feel it.

"*Jaye.*"

The realization I've been quiet for too long has me shaking my head to snap back to the present moment. "I promise to let you know if I need anything."

"Is that as good as that promise is gonna get?"

"Yup."

"Fine. Call me later? We need to plan a weekend at the range and *not* just because I feel you could use more target practice now more than ever."

"I don't believe you."

"Too bad that alone isn't enough to keep a suspect in holding."

"*Dad!*"

"Love you, sugar."

"Love you more."

Our call ends, and the device is tucked safely into my light blue jeans back pocket. Next, I exit my room and head for the stairs, butterflies fluttering frantically around my stomach the same way they do when a new shipment of books gets delivered to me.

You know Archer's kind of like a new book, too. He's got pages and pages and pages that I can't wait to read and understand and get lost in. I just...I just hope he lets me. I get keeping people at a distance – trust me, I really do – but I hope I somehow for some reason become the exception to that rule. It'd be nice to have...at the very least...a real friend again.

Upon my arrival at the garage door, I notice his missing clothes, which prompt me to politely knock as opposed to just barging in.

Again.

Although, between you and me, seeing him wet and almost naked was an amazing dessert for the eyes.

When there's no answer, I crack the door open just a bit to investigate the situation. The sight of his deflated bed and folded bedding has me swinging it wide just in time to see him getting ready to go out the open garage.

"Wait!"

My voice initially ignites a smirk, yet he banishes it for scowl.

"Where are you going?" Trekking into the cold air is done fearlessly and without a coat. "And why are you leaving?"

The mad rush of words out of my mouth prompts him to turn my direction and challenge, "Why would I stay?"

"Why wouldn't you stay?"

Bewilderment bumps him slightly backwards. "Why would you want me around any longer than I've already been?"

"Why wouldn't I?"

"Why are you answering my fucking questions with the same fucking questions?"

"Why are you asking these asinine questions to begin with?!"

"Why would you call them fucking asinine?"

"Because they are!" I mindlessly shriek, a little surprised at my pitch as much as my strength. "If I didn't want you around, I wouldn't have invited you in. And if I didn't want you to stay, I would've asked you to leave. And instead of constantly forcing me to defend the decisions I'm making, how about you just look me in the eyes and tell me they're just not the ones *you* want. That this isn't the place *you* want to be. That I'm not the person *you* want to be around."

Outrage rips through his gaze at the same time he takes a step towards me. "You fucking with me right now?"

Did I just poke a bear?!

"You think I don't *want* all that shit?! You think I *want* to escape the first real chance I've been given to be more than the homeless asshole the rest of the world spits on?!" Pain pierces his

134

green stare, pushes me to move towards him. To get closer. To comfort him. "That's the last fucking thing I want, Jaye."

"Then why leave?"

"Because I don't deserve that shit. I don't deserve *you*."

"I think you do."

"You don't know me."

"Then stick around. Give me a chance to get to know you better."

"*Why?*"

"Because I like you."

"*Why, Jaye?* Why do you like *me* of all people?"

"Because you're my person." Awkward cringing is immediate. "Er…um…*my kind* of person."

Despite his best efforts, I manage to see the smirk on his face.

"You listen when I talk. And you ask me things I wanna answer. And you tell me things I wanna know. And you make me laugh. And laughing…isn't something I get to do much of outside of work and my dad and binging sitcoms. It's nice to laugh *with* someone. And to just…*be* around someone that I *want* to be around."

To my surprise, understanding immediately seeps into his stare.

"And maybe I know what it feels like to have the entire world look at you one way and just wish for one second, one person, would see you *just once* a little differently, too. Maybe that's why whatever this is," my hand casually gestures between us, "*works.*"

Archer quietly coos, "How could anyone see you for anything less than amazing, sweetheart?"

My face heats to the point I swear I'm going to sweat off my mascara, yet I force my eyes to stay locked on his. "Breakfast?"

His lips tighten.

"I'll even let you help with the dishes this time."

Archer reluctantly caves on a small chuckle. "Fine. But I'm doing *all of them* tonight after dinner."

Excitement doesn't bother hiding itself. "You'll stay?"

136

"For one more night."

Mmm…we'll see about that.

"It's probably best anyway. I get the feeling the woman next door will be looking for *any way* to prove you were lying last night."

"But I *wasn't* lying." Folding my arms firmly across my chest, I plant a victorious smirk on my face. "You *are* my friend."

"You don't have to look so fucking smug about it."

"Oh, except that I do."

His laughter sparks my own further proving my point.

He belongs here.

Making me laugh.

Letting me make *him*.

Laughing together.

Even if we only end up as friends that's still better than nothing.

Archer creeps back inside, encouraging me to push the button to lower the door down behind. "She's probably so hyper focused on your life because hers is a shitshow."

"What makes you say that?"

"Because her husband is having an affair. Affairs *typically* mean shitshow."

"He's cheating on her?!" The gasp comes out of me is unintentionally dramatic. "What?! No. Seriously? *Shut up.*"

Baffled at the several phrases that just spewed out of my mouth has his face scrunching in confusion. "Okay that shit was a little hard for me to follow, sweetheart. Which of those am I supposed to answer?"

Slight embarrassment is followed by a small bite to my bottom lip. "*I meant*...how do you know that? How do you know he's cheating on her? Did you see him?"

"*Overheard him.* Plus, a person's garbage speaks volumes about their life."

Holy shit, does yours? Doesn't that statement now make you feel a little more self-conscious about what you throw out?!

Not wanting to know what mine says about me, I simply ask, "What sounds good for breakfast? Oatmeal? Cream of Wheat? Bagels? Oh! Oh! Should I make us coffee and *then* decide what we'll eat?"

"How much time do you have before work?"

"It's a late day for me, so quite a bit."

He pauses his movements rather than continuing to close the gap. "Why's it late?"

"I um…I don't like to drive in the sleet or recently sleeted roads, so typically, I go in late or not at all."

"It has something to do with Chris's death, doesn't it?"

There's no stopping the way I shrink inward.

Tense.

Struggle to nod.

"What happened?"

My fidgeting carries on in the form of rocking on my sock covered feet and flicking random curly strands away from my face and chewing on the inside of my lip, all the things that usually buy me enough time for a person to change topics, yet he doesn't.

He silently stares.

Waits.

Demonstrates patience and the willingness to remain that way like the long-lost saint of widows.

Wow. Guess this whole learn about each other's past thing isn't going to be a one-way street, huh?

"He was driving home on a night like yesterday about three years ago, about a week before Christmas," my voice slowly begins, "and in a typical Chris fashion, he acted as though he knew better than everyone else – the weather itself included. To my best understanding, he figured he could make it home from our downtown penthouse before the sleet got too bad. He drove like there was no real need to slow down. Like the roads weren't as bad they really were. According to the traffic report and investigation, he lost control of his Porsche on an icy bridge. Crashed." Tears threaten to stop me from talking, but I force myself to push past them, and the discomfort that comes from sharing the information with someone new. "I was coming home later than usual from work that night – he had a whole I couldn't bring the office home with me thing – and when I got here, my father – who was on duty that night – and his partner were waiting for me. Everyone in the local PD knew exactly who Chris was. He always wrote a huge check anytime they had any kind of fundraiser, plus he was dating a cop's daughter.

The officers first on the scene recognized the car and immediately called my dad. He showed up and simply waited to tell me in person rather than over the phone." Sniffling away my sadness is easier than expected. "So, yeah. I don't really like to drive on the roads like this."

Archer offers me a compassion-filled nod prior to a gentle joke. "I'd offer to drive you but no form of valid ID, remember?"

The playful jab exiles the remaining sadness prompting me to smile. "We're gonna have to do something about that."

"One thing at a time, Jaye." He casually returns to heading my direction. "Coffee, first."

"Breakfast next."

"Lending me a book to read to keep me occupied while you're working should be after that."

Holy. Fuck. Is it weird if the homeless man who was eating out of my trash turns out to be the man of my dreams? Huh. Yeah, I heard it, but I'm gonna pretend I didn't say it.

"That can certainly be arranged." Backing inside occurs at the same time I state, "I gotta stop by the grocery store when I get off – it's my designated grocery day. Do you have a preference on *what* you want for dinner? I'm pretty open to making just about anything or *Googling* how to make just about anything."

141

Archer shuts the door to the garage and pauses. "Would you mind if I came with you?"

"To the grocery store?"

He enthusiastically nods.

"Sure, but only if you promise me that it's not to stock up on supplies for a midnight escape from my garage."

Mirth quickly paints itself in his gaze as well as mine. *"Promise, sweetheart."*

The two-word combination causes the butterflies in my stomach to go berserk for the umpteenth time.

Geez, what the hell am I getting myself into? And more importantly, why am I totally, one-hundred and fifty percent, okay with it?

Chapter 8

Archer

Fuck, I don't know how we got here.

Yeah, obviously I know how we **physically** *got here. It was her idea for us to read on the couch side by side after lunch, but I didn't expect her to be passed out less than five minutes later with her feet in my lap. What I meant was I don't know how we got here. This...close? I guess if you break down the timeline, it* **might** *make sense? It started with coffee. One cup each. Both mugs bearing cheesy book phrases – mine said 'So many books. So little time.' while hers had a glass of spilled wine on it and the phrase 'Not so loud, I had book club last night'. This naturally led to her telling me* about *said book club, which was why she had come home later the night before. Learning about that preceded learning about her job – librarian at a private early childhood academy – over scrambled eggs, bacon, and toast. Not moaning during the whole process was by far the most difficult part of our morning. Watching her cook was a delightful sight in itself, the way her hips sway side to side while timing whatever needs to be timed but listening to her giggle over every joke I made – cheap puns and witty one-liners alike – was undoubtedly sexier. And hiding the wood I kept popping was ridiculously fucking hard – pun intended. After we finished our meal, which contained so much conversation about classic literature that I almost felt like I was in a community college course on the subject, she did something she apparently never does. She decided to take the whole day off. No, you heard me right. The whole fucking day. Even though the roads were thawing – thanks to the random spike in sun and heat – it was obvious there was still some lingering anxiety about getting back out there. And when I spotted the familiar tells of trauma, I encouraged her to take the time if she could afford it as to not trigger an episode or worse situation for herself. She seemed* *surprised I cared but took the advice. And then when I learned it was an option all along from her boss, I told her she should* always *take the day instead of risking her life no matter how much she loves her job. The last thing she needs is to be on an icy road, have her tires lose a little traction, and then spiral out into a full blown panic attack where she crashes or causes someone else to. She saw my very valid point yet instead of using it to explain to her my own situation, I bitched out. Buried how I could relate behind a brick wall and smug grin.*

Jaye's toes wiggle around unknowingly brushing my cock, calling it back to life once more.

If my dick could get the memo that this woman's every single movement is not a summoning spell that would be fucking appreciated. Almost as much as I appreciate being welcomed to have an actual roof over my head. By someone who...wants me around. Her words. Her. Fucking. Words. Pretty sure that's what really stopped me from getting up and bailing sooner this morning. It wasn't because of the weather or worry about the cops catching me...It was because in spite of what I told myself, I clutched onto that tiny bit of hope I was determined to throw out. I hoped she wanted to see me again, even if it was just to say goodbye. I hoped that she had enjoyed being around me prior to my conversational fails. And then hearing her vocalize exactly *what I was feeling was the last one-two combo I couldn't handle. And the reason I said only one more night here wasn't because I* want *to leave – fuck, why would I wanna leave someone so sweet – but because I need to. I need to get the fuck out before Jaye Jenkins becomes a causality of the shitstorm I call living.*

I clear my throat, divert my gaze back to my book, and do my best to ignore the curled legs I wish I could rest a hand on.

Friendship may be possible but anything more…that's just unfathomable even if I swear, she's been flirting with me all day. I'm sure that's just more of my being unsocial for too long bullshit. Can't even distinguish the difference between the two. Post breakfast and her call in to work, we watched a few episodes of a cop drama called Lawless Lives – she started it over from the beginning so I wouldn't be 'lost' – had lunch – haven't had a grilled cheese that good since I had something called an Irish Grilled cheese during my last leave – and crashed back on this purple cushion of glory to read for a bit. Like I mentioned earlier, her reading lasted all of five minutes while mine on the other hand is being done in between longingly looking at her and trying to figure out just how in the fuck I got here. Got so…unexpectedly fortunate. No. Not luck. I don't believe in that shit. Never have.

All of a sudden, a loud yawn escapes Jaye at the same time she rolls over onto her back. I expected fear to be the first emotion on her face considering the fact she's not used to having company in her house; however, the first thing I see is relief.

Followed swiftly by excitement.

Fuckin' hell, what's going on with this woman? She can't actually like me this much, can she?

"You're still here," she sweetly coos.

"I'm a man of my word. I told you I'd stay another night."

"*At least* another night."

145

"I didn't say *those two words*."

"No, but I did." Girlish giggles are followed by her tucking her hands behind her head. "I can't believe I fell asleep like that. Well, I *can*," she quickly corrects, "because I always do on this couch. It's the only place I get *decent* sleep, which is crazy when you consider the California King just eating up the middle of my bedroom, but I don't know. This couch just…feels…better. Could be because it's one of the only things in this house – besides all the books – that's really mine." Her pause isn't long enough for me to ask questions. "Sorry to fall asleep during book time."

"You don't need to apologize for that, sweetheart. You needed the rest. I'm glad you took it."

"Yes, but *you* needed me to explain how much Janet Evanovich's *One for the Money* made me feel like I could've been a kick ass bounty hunter in another life."

Smiling is done absentmindedly. "*Did I* need that?"

"Of course you did," Jaye laughs even louder, "*and* you needed to hear about how you're reading my original copy because I have a personalized copy Chris got me during one of his business trips locked away so that people can't even *look* at it, although now that I bring it up, I'm not sure I don't want people looking at it so much as I don't really have a place to display it."

My eyes cut around the enormous room we're occupying prior to poking. "You fuckin' with me?"

Bafflement instantly blasts itself in her expression. "Uh…no?"

"You live in mega mansion with four bedrooms and can't find space to put up one of your favorite *signed* books?"

"Four bedrooms, two offices, one game room, one living room, one loft, one formal dining room and one kitchen."

Her breakdown twitches my eyebrows in further confusion. "And there's not a *single space* in any of those places you could display the book?"

She offers me an absentminded shrug. "Chris would've considered it clutter."

"And Chris has been dead for three years."

The bluntness tumbles her jaw down and my own to tighten.

Fuck. Fuck. Fuck. See what I mean. Combat skills? Pristine. Fitness regime? Sharp. Social capabilities? Non. Fucking. Existent. I gotta learn to either say the right things or say fucking nothing at all. I'm leaning towards that one.

Softening my tone to the most apologetic one I can find, I start, "*Jaye, I'm-*"

"Right," she quietly chokes out before sitting up and forcing a grin on her face. "You ready to go grocery shopping?"

Hesitation to speak is hard to deny. "You sure you still want me to go with? What if I say something else fucked up on accident?"

Her feet suddenly disappear from my lap to be crossed and tucked in towards her. "Is what you're saying fucked up?" She lets a small bounce hit her shoulder. "Maybe? Words are strange that way. What one person hears as 'fucked up', another may hear as honesty. As tough love. As an attempt to *help*. And despite how uncomfortable it makes me to hear some of these things, I need them said. I *know* I need them said. And like the adorable children often in my care, I know I have to hear these things *repeated* in order for them to truly stick. So...worry less about saying 'fucked up' things on accident and more about receiving the 'fucked up' things I may someday say to you in an attempt to...*help*. Like what I'm about to for instance."

There's no stopping worry from crossing my face.

"You *cannot* keep wearing one outfit."

Bewilderment replaces the previous emotion. "What?"

"You need clothes. Ones that didn't come out of a dumpster, that were *made* to fit you, and will inevitably remind you that you

148

are a wanted part of this society even if you have convinced yourself you're not."

So sweet, so sexy, and so fucking wrong.

"We're gonna go by G-Street, the mega grocery store that has the clothing and house goods section too. It lets us get food *and* things for you to wear *and* new books for us to read *and-*"

"I don't think you've said and enough."

"*Andddddd* I get a discount there. The CEO or CFO or something close to those letters has a grandkid that goes to my school. All educators who interact with her have a special discount card, which comes in *super handy* considering how often I bake cookies."

"How often is that?"

"Um…few times a week." Her lips pull together to one side before she confesses. "I have a tendency to stress bake. And unlike a normal human who can make a batch, I have to make at least four, every time I bake."

"Why?!"

"The first batch is always weird shaped and then the next batch is overcooked and then the following batch is under because I second guess myself, so it isn't until that fourth batch comes out with all my mistakes nonexistent that I find that relief I'm looking for." She flashes me a small smile. "In other words, I hope you like the smell of cookies."

"Who the fuck *hates* the smell of cookies?"

"People I can't trust."

We exchange a few laughs, part our separate ways to get ready, and wander out to her car just in time to see Mr. Prescott arriving home with a large bouquet of roses.

Most likely an 'I'm sorry you caught me fucking around on you again' gift. Personally? I don't think flowers should ever be given as an apology. It shits on the sentiment meant to express love or affection or devotion. But what do I know? I've never been married, and my longest girlfriend fucked me out of so much money I barely had enough to eat when I got discharged.

Our car ride to the store is filled with unexpected music. While Jaye is upbeat by nature, her choice in tunes is quite the opposite. Every song we listen to has some pretty strong emotional undertones. Bands like Incubus and Nirvana are ones I'm familiar with; however, The Script and Georgian ArKtecture – Irish bands I'm told – are brand new. Sadly, Fall Out Boy is the most upbeat shit we listen to, yet even the ones that come across her playlist have tragic themes.

Maybe this shit is like therapy for her? I know it's how St. Clair used to work through some of the horrific shit we dealt with.

150

Parking takes forever, and as my stare roams around the busy lot, I helplessly zone in on the weakest shoppers.

The one whose basket would be easiest to grab a box of crackers from.

A two litter of soda.

Perhaps a precooked meal that simply needs to be heated.

Sometimes that's really more recommended than required.

In spite of my best efforts to stop the train of thoughts, I can't. Instinct to always be prepared and ready to take what is necessary to survive another day ruthlessly kicks in. Leads me to glaring. Judging. Shaking my head at how careless and gluttonous some people are.

Fuck, they don't have a clue how good they have it. At least Jaye seems to have some grasp of that concept. Afterall, she's temporarily housing me.

Inside the building, my attitude doesn't get any better. I'm immediately blinded by the bad lighting, annoyed by the people talking loudly on their phones, and unable to ignore the number of individuals who scoff at the very sight of me.

How could they not? Fucking look at me. I don't belong here. I don't belong at her Real Housewives of Highland Mansion. I don't belong anywhere but in the shadows. In the unseen. Fuck, why did I ask to come to this place? Why did I think in doing so that maybe I would be momentarily seen as human by the masses instead of subpar. Fuck, this was a terrible idea. Come to think of it…us being friends or anything related is a terrible goddamn idea. What if she starts to see me like they do? What if she begins to become embarrassed by the sight of me? Is that the real reason she wants to get me new clothes? So that she hates staring at me less?

Jaye's just finished guiding us away from the area they keep the carts when I offer, "Maybe I should just wait in the car?"

"Why?" My eyes don't find hers until she waves a hand in front them to assist in redirecting. "Why would you *ask* to come and then wait in the car? Doesn't that defeat the whole purpose? *Plus,* how am I supposed to buy you clothes you like when I don't know what those are because we've never been shopping together before?"

I prepare to argue when the sound of a woman gagging from one glance at my tattered backpack ceases my ability.

Hey, I know the shit is old and used and worn, but it's the best I can do. It's the best I've been able to find.

"Archer, look at me." Her commanding tone reminds me of an officer naturally forcing my body to respond to the instruction. "If you wanna wait in the car because *you're* uncomfortable, okay. I will respect that choice. You are a person whose feelings matter, and you, too, should have your boundaries respected. However, if you think you need to wait in the car because *I'm* uncomfortable, let me

152

make this *Cat in the Hat* clear for you." An unexpected stern expression crosses her face. "I don't give a shit about what others think. I know better than to just judge a book by its cover. And people are exactly like books. We all have stories. We all have chapters. We all have pages that some are interested in exploring while others miss out. And I will *choose* to continue going on adventures with you for however long I can."

The sentimental nature of her statement swells my chest in indescribable ways.

How can one person be so fucking...compassionate?

Sweet and thoughtful and affectionate responses eagerly bounce around my brain waiting to be picked yet like my mouth has a habit of doing, it speaks playfully without consent. "You're *really* into the idea of touching my spine, huh?"

Jaye blushes, loudly snickers, and teasingly swats at my chest. "For that, *you* can push the cart."

"Was gonna ask to do that anyway."

"Uh-huh," she good-naturedly brushes off prior to pointing to the left. "Clothes are that way."

Getting to the men's section is thankfully an easy feat that includes an odd amount of breakfast cereal discussion during the process. All conversations regarding our shared secret love affair for the types with the most sugars – which we both weren't allowed to indulge in often as kids – are immediately stopped and exchanged for much more intimate ones.

I've never been shopping with a chick before. My ex – yeah, the one that fucked me over – never did anything like this with me or for me for that matter. Fuck, she never even bought a shirt for a gift.

"Ohhhhhh," Jaye enthusiastically squeaks holding up the fourth thick, turtleneck in a row, although this sweater is green instead of white, "what about this one?!" She presses the material against the front of my chest forcing me to choke down a moan from her light touch. "It says warm but fashionable."

"It says Ken Doll."

Her face instantly frowns at the comment. "It does not."

"It does."

"It does not."

"*It does.*"

Another small cringe occurs as she moves the sweater back to the rack. "Maybe like an army Ken Doll…"

"You mean G.I. Joe?"

154

Her gaze cuts over to see me smirking prompting her to grow one too. "You don't have to be a G.I. Jerk."

I can't help myself from wincing at the terrible joke, which thankfully only makes her giggle again, a sound that's almost too beautiful to be heard by the masses.

"Okay, so is that a no to *all* sweaters or just *these* sweaters?" She turns her frame to completely face me once more. "Do you hate sweaters? Would you prefer button downs? Polos? Long sleeve polos?! Graphic tees?" Jaye folds her arms across her chest. "What do you prefer?"

"I don't."

She tilts her head in a challenging nature.

"Warm?"

The firm expression remains.

"Sweetheart, I haven't had to buy clothes in…" my speech drifts off taking my eyes with it. "Fuck…forever?" Another uncomfortable feeling roots itself in the pit of stomach pushing me to make eye contact again. "Look, whatever you wanna buy me – or don't buy me – is fine. Ken Doll accessory shit included."

Her slow headshake stirs the feelings in the worst ways. "*No, Archer.* We are going to get you something *you like.* You've had plenty of what fits and what's available. What is something *you* want to wear? To be seen in?"

"Seen fucking where, Jaye?! Your living room?!" Realizing how harsh my outburst unintentionally was has me rushing to do what I get the feeling I'm going to be doing a lot. "Fuck, I shouldn't have snapped at you like that. I'm-"

"Dinner."

The initial response stuns me silent.

"Or the movies."

Seeing her shoulders push back as she straightens her spine to stand up to me...*for me*...is almost too incredible to process.

"Or – let's be real for a sec – one of the many, *many* bookstores in this city. Or maybe bowling. Or to see holiday lights. Or to grab a drink. Or hell, I don't know, maybe *grocery shopping.*" Her hand waves around to underline her point. "I've answered your question. Now, answer mine."

The firmness in her tone causes a part of me to get firm in the wrong way.

"*What* would you like to wear? Pick something and two pairs of jeans and one pair of sweats."

"That's too much." When there's no effort to redact part of what she suggested, I release a heavy sigh, "Jaye, I don't need-"

"To keep fighting with me. You're just slowing down the dinner making process, and I'll be totally honest. The longer it takes me to grocery shop, the more likely I am to order delivery versus cook."

"*I'll cook.*"

"And you'll wear…"

Sensing that she won't cave, I reach for a couple nearby flannel shirts, "These. And I'll grab a pack of long sleeve tees."

"And jeans."

"And *one* pair of jeans."

"And *one* pair of sweats."

I reluctantly surrender. "Fine."

She struggles not to squeak in glee. "Fine."

Strolling away is attached to a quiet grumble, "You're too fucking sweet for your own good."

"Like my cookies!"

After grabbing the items and tossing them into the cart, I resume pushing only to be stopped almost immediately.

"You need boxers!" She doesn't wait for a response. "Or briefs...Or boxer briefs. Or you know whatever you prefer."

With the opportunity to lighten the mood back up, I playfully poke, "You don't like me going commando?"

The redness that rips her expression is instant. "Uh...um...y-y-you can – If that's wh-wh-what – I just thought that-" Her inability to finish the sentences receives a loud laugh which causes her to deliver another teasing swat to my chest. "Go grab whatever underwear you wanna wear or pretend to wear. We're gonna go by storage next. We need something to keep your stuff in. Maybe a set of those plastic drawers or a couple of totes. Whichever you like more."

My mouth twitches to argue, barely being caught before a single sound can leak free.

What the fuck do I need that shit for? What am I gonna do, stop by for visitation of my pants? Yeah, I know I can't – or shouldn't – say that shit to her. I should just let her live in her weird fucked up friendship fantasy for a while longer. I'll make sure she keeps the receipt so she can return all this shit when she comes to her senses.

Traveling from clothes to the organizational area is completed in silence; however, the minute we arrive in the section, another wave of enthusiasm busts free from Jaye as she Vanna White's various options for me to choose from. The sight in itself is amusing, but the continued implication I am staying longer than just one night is uncomfortable.

And that unease has me shuffling my feet.

Grinding my teeth.

Balling my fists not to say something else dickish to the woman I'm slightly convinced might be a little insane.

How else do you explain wanting to let a stranger to basically live in your garage?

Jaye begins to grab the three-drawer plastic piece and I promptly take over the task of retrieval. After rearranging the awkward piece at the bottom of the cart near the squeaky front wheels, I'm quickly reminded of something I forgot to mention earlier. "Since we're here," rising back to my feet is slowly done, "can we grab some WD-40?" Resuming my position to push the basket is done next. "I noticed a couple of your kitchen cabinets squeak and so does the downstairs half bath door."

All of sudden, she swings herself in front of the cart to cease our movement. "That's it!"

"What's it?"

"That!"

"WD-40?"

"My brilliant idea!"

"I don't think you invented that shit, sweetheart."

"Huh?" She shakes her head, realizing what I've said doesn't have anything to do with what she's thinking. "No. No, this isn't about the WD-40. This is about how we get *you* to stay with me."

I don't like where this is going.

"You can 'rent' my garage space – not because you're not welcomed in the house but because I know you won't accept the offer to sleep in one of the guest rooms – in exchange for fixing stuff around the house!"

160

"Like a live-in handyman?"

"Exactly!"

Her excitement has me hesitating to retort. "Yeah, the thing is, I don't think you really need one, Jaye."

"Yeah, and I think it's best for this arrangement if you don't pre-emptively know just how many things are broken at my house."

Laughter instantly bounces back and forth between us.

Fuck. Me. I need her to be less irresistible.

"Come on, Archer! This is a win-win scenario which are everyone's favorite. *You* get a warm place to sleep, fresh food to eat, and the chance to add a new job to your résumé – whenever you're ready to fill one out – while I can stop having my dad fix things at *two* houses instead of just his one. *Plus*, I get a roommate that's also a friend who can talk about books with me and TV and eat the leftovers I feel guilty about chucking."

I can't stop myself from shaking my head. "That's a terrible idea."

She gleefully claps. "That's a brilliant idea!"

"Clapping doesn't make it true."

161

"And frowning doesn't make it not true."

My lips press tightly together to prevent from spewing another word.

"Look, if it were totally up to me, you wouldn't do *anything*. You would just accept all the help I'm trying to give because I care about you, move your shit into one of the spare rooms, and make yourself at home however you saw fit, but we both know your clouded conscience – for some reason – won't allow that, so this is an alternative solution. We *both* get what it is we really want, which is *you* out of the cold, safe, and somewhere I can find you when I need you."

Warmth rapidly spreads throughout my chest. "*Need me?*"

"Want you."

The heat swiftly moves to lower regions as I ask, "*Want me?*"

"Err…um…" Her face starts twitching and cringing in winces while searching for more appropriate phrasing I honestly hope she never finds. "You uh…you know what I mean."

I'm not sure that I do.

But I'm not sure that I want to.

162

She shouldn't get attached to me.

Just like I shouldn't get attached to her.

And yet I'm pretty sure we both already are.

Why didn't you stop this shit from happening?!

Tightening my grip on the cart, I cautiously investigate, "For how long?"

"How about we don't try to eat the whole elephant at once? How about we take it one bite at a time?"

"Who the fuck eats elephants?"

"Lions. Hyenas. Crocodiles. They all go after baby elephants or the sick ones in the herd."

"Why do you know that?"

"I know a lot of random things about a lot of things. It's a blessing and a curse of reading so much."

Offering her a warm grin can't be helped. "Just a blessing, sweetheart."

The faintest amount of red touches her cheeks prior to her adding, "Anyway, the phrase isn't about actually eating elephants. It's just something my dad has always said to me about dealing with big problems or issues. It's something *his dad* said to him. And *his dad* said to him. And something I hope to say to my own kids someday."

"You will."

My reassurance is met by a bashful grin.

What? She will. I didn't correct her to say* our *kids, which would be a reason to blush. Huh? No, I don't think we'll have kids together someday. Fuck, I don't even think we'll be friends longer than a couple days. Clearly, you're just as insane as she might be.

After ditching the organizing area, we grab the aforementioned oil and a couple of other house maintenance items I think we might need for this arrangement. Meandering through the book section is next with both of us grabbing a couple new books. Jaye grabs fiction novels – one romance, one young adult contemporary – and I grab two non-fiction – one autobiography, one biography. Eventually, we find ourselves in the food selection, the area we should've been in long before now. I do the best I can encouraging to grab items *she* likes or wants only to be met by the insistence we *both* pick out things. From what I gather by the comments she makes, this is new. Typically, she has always bought what Chris wanted. Liked. *Preferred.* And when he didn't have a preference, she either didn't get it or referred to her mother's choice.

164

Repeatedly hearing how she's lost her capability to choose even the simplest things hurts in unpredicted ways.

Maybe because I hate how it sounds like she was bullied into being someone she's not.

Or maybe because I've lost my own ability to have choices too due to survival needs.

Both? You think it's both.

Our cart gets overrun with what I believe to be more than we need and during the check-out process, the jaw-dropping bill just further confirms it. I do my best to casually insist we can put some things back to which Jaye playfully brushes off to me *and* the cashier. My attempting to assist in bagging the items is also blocked by my new landlord yet before leaving the building she manages to get an application for the store that swears they're always hiring.

Her victorious strutting back to the car is equally irritating and sexy.

She *should* always have this much confidence to her.

She's brilliant and kind and curvier than a 1962 Tuxedo Black Chevrolet Corvette.

Still.

165

I don't enjoy having someone rub their triumph in my face.

Definitely not when I want them rubbing something else in my face if you catch my drift. And yeah, I know I have no business fantasizing about that especially now that we're going to be living together. Holy fuck, we're going to be living together.

"*No, Jaye,*" I firmly state after a small chuckle. "We're not *ordering in.* You just dropped a shit ton of money on food. We're gonna cook it."

"But grocery shopping is so exhausting," she continues to good naturedly whine while spinning on her heels to face me again. "It takes so. Much. Energy. I really don't think I have any left for cooking, which is why having *Dos Mamas* delivered is the only solution to that problem."

"You mean it's your *preferred* solution." Smirking mindlessly occurs. "*Words matter, sweetheart.*"

Snickers slip free as we arrive at her car.

"I said I would cook. And I'm going to cook. I swear it'll be edible."

She flashes me a playful pout at the same time the trunk pops open.

"If it's not edible and you *actually* hate it *then* we can order in."

"*Dos Mamas.*"

"Gonna guess that's Mexican."

"Yup."

"You're in the mood for Mexican?"

"I'm always in the mood for Mexican, especially if you add extra cheese."

"Cheese enchiladas it is."

Her eyes widen in newfound excitement. "Do we *have* stuff for cheese enchiladas?!"

Lightly laughing can't be helped. "You don't even remember what we bought?"

Guilt briefly flashes itself prompting my laughter to get louder.

And deeper.

And livelier until a car at the opposite end of the lane fiddles with their lights creating rapid flashes, I'm unprepared for.

The stun grenade sends me plummeting to the hard ground like the enemy wants.

Expects.

Bullets wiz by forcing my frame to stay low while fighting through my disoriented senses to find my team.

Where the fuck is my team?! Where's Hiltz?! Where's St. Clair?! Were they hit?! Fuck, were they hit!? Answer me!

Harsh scrapes collect along my forearms while high pitched screams and barbaric last cries have me unsure of which way I should go for my next move.

Left? Right? And where are those women we saw earlier? Were they in on this? Were they innocent victims killed by a stray bullet?! Were they decoys? Are we decoys?! What about the child?!

"...*Archer?*"

Archer?

That's my…that's my first name.

We don't go by our first names.

Just our last.

Always our last.

Especially during a mission.

The soft, delicate voice calls out again, like a siren my mind ruthlessly insists we follow, "*Archer…It's me. Jaye. Can you hear me?*"

Jaye?

I don't know a Jaye.

A small twitch of my entire frame is swiftly followed by a huge headshake.

Of course I know Jaye.

Jaye is now.

"Jaye is now…" I force myself to state as I squeeze my eyes shut, determined to bring myself back to the present.

"I am now," she warmly echoes at the same time her hand lands on my shoulder causing me to flinch. However, she doesn't remove her grip. Doesn't relocate it. Doesn't even consider how dangerous it might be to keep it there. *"Jaye is now."*

Her grip tightens and instinct has me jerking.

Away.

Towards.

In place like a junkie in need of a hit.

And I am.

A hit of sanity.

Fucking clarity.

Where am I?

Pop music blaring from a nearby vehicle have a new question piercing my mind.

When am I?

Then?

Now?

"*Archer*," the feminine voice softly coos, summoning the answer out of me.

"That was then…this is now."

My palm aggressively lands on top of hers only to have her other sandwich it. "*Jaye is now.*"

"Hiltz was then."

"*Jaye is now.*"

"*Jaye is now,*" is repeated again and again and again until I'm dragged back to the proper point in time.

The one where I'm sprawled out on the concrete of a grocery store parking lot being watched over by a woman whose life I can't endanger.

Won't endanger with this bullshit.

It takes longer than I care to admit for me to steady my breath and rise to my feet. People stare and gawk, yet Jaye keeps all of her attention on me. Dusting away rubble. Checking for new marks. She even places two fingers on my pulse, overly concerned about the way it races.

Once I'm completely composed, she quietly suggests, "Why don't you go ahead and get in the car? I can unload this stuff on my own."

There's no hesitation to bite, "You don't want me to embarrass you again."

"I'm not embarrassed. I'm worried."

"About your precious fucking groceries?"

"About my precious fucking friend that's still trembling!"

Her counter isn't the one I'm expecting and hearing someone give a damn about me when I can barely manage to draws tears to my eyes that I'm not accustomed to having. Unbearable emotions swell in my throat, clogging my vocal cords, causing the words I manage to croak to be ragged and broken just like me. *"Please let me do this."* I use the back of my hand to banish a small sniffle. *"I need to do this. I need to…be useful."*

172

Brown eyes I don't deserve to have in my life instantly soften with understanding. She sweetly nods, touches my scuff covered cheek, and whispers, "I'll get the car warmed up."

Rather than think about my own shame or the pending shame that's waiting for me inside the vehicle, I focus all my energy on transferring the contents from the basket to the trunk where they belong. It requires some shifting and rearranging – we really did overbuy – and I'm honestly grateful for the time I'm left alone.

Left to finish…*recovering* myself.

The instant I'm settled in the passenger seat I brace myself for the swarm of questions or lecture on why the earlier proposed scenario can't work – *won't work* – but am surprisingly met by silence.

Calm.

Eerie.

Silence.

Guess I should go first?

"I completely understand why you have to take back your offer."

Jaye shifts herself in her seat to properly face me. "I don't."

The expression on my face instantly becomes skeptical. "*Jaye.*"

"*Archer.*"

"It's not…It's not a good idea for me to be around you. Around anyone. Especially not when I get like that. Not when I'm…having a fucked-up episode."

"You suffer from PTSD."

"Most of Uncle Sam's mercenaries do."

The bitterness in my retort receives an eyebrow lift of question.

"It's…really not uncommon to comeback from duty with some…*damage* – mental as much as physical. I was no exception. Just like when I got lost in the cracks of government paperwork that could've helped me when I fucking needed it the most." One hand runs across my face in a desperate attempt to remain cool. Collected. "Flashing lights *sometimes* trigger a response in me. They take me out of this moment and place me back in one where-" not ready to explain that situation has me shaking my head rather than continuing. "In the beginning, I would self-medicate like many others do. I didn't like it. It didn't always work. And sometimes it made it worse. And it's expensive. And drugs like that are always addictive. And it fucks up the body's system. And I don't need any

174

more fucking damage while I'm just out here trying to survive." I briefly look away before adding. "Look, like I said, it doesn't *always* happen, but when it does I'm typically alone where I can't hurt anyone but me."

"You weren't gonna hurt me, Archer."

"You don't know that, Jaye."

"I know what I *saw*." Her challenge threatens to have to look elsewhere. "You weren't reliving combat. You were reliving trying to stay alive. Getting to others who needed you. And while I want *all* the details of that situation, I won't push for them. Not until you're ready."

"Jaye-"

"And you having an illness – that you haven't been able to receive proper treatment for might I add – isn't a reason to revoke my previous decision to move you in. You need help, which I know you hate to hear and accept, but you do. *Help, Archer.* Not hatred. Not rejection. Not abandonment. Just. Help."

Pride infused with self-disgust has me shutting my eyes and growling. "I. *Don't. Need. Your. Sympathy.*"

"Then it's a good thing I'm just offering you my kindness."

The words fill the rims of my eyelids against my own volition.

Fuck, I hate having a body that doesn't listen to me.

"Buckle your seatbelt, please." Her instruction is spoken as though nothing between us has changed. "What kind of enchilada sauce did we buy?"

I lift my lids to complete the task, to focus my stare on anything but her for the time being.

"Was it red or green? Please tell me it was red. I've never really liked the green one, but Chris always preferred it, which may be why ordering *Dos Mamas* has always been my go-to for Mexican food at home because it was the only way we could both get what we wanted."

"You deserve to get what you want, sweetheart." Still unable to meet her gaze, I quietly add, "And I plan to do everything within my power to make that happen for you no matter the case."

All of a sudden, her hand stretches across the short space to rest on top of mine.

Protectively.

Compassionately.

Adoringly.

Unlike her, I don't deserve anything good that's coming my way. I don't deserve the money or time or effort being spent to keep me alive. I don't deserve someone to listen to me. To care. I deserve a pine box and an empty funeral. Nothing more. How can I make her understand that? How can I make you understand that? When will the two of you fucking get that?

Chapter 9

Jaye

I can't believe we're really about to do this.

Gah…*should* we be doing this?

Is it sanitary?

What? No! I'm not talking about living with Archer. I'm talking about Goat Yoga! My gym has been hosting the new trend once a month for the past year, and I've really wanted to give it a try. They're just so cute! Archer was actually the one who really encouraged me to give it a go this weekend. Insisting that I have nothing to lose. He even offered to try it with me, which may be why I went ahead and decided to take the plunge today. Not because I can't work out alone – um obviously I can as I have for most my gym membership career – but because it means he'll finally leave the house again. He hasn't since the episode at the grocery store almost two weeks ago. He says it's for safety. I say it's from embarrassment. Nonetheless, me wanting to do downward dog with a baby farm animal seems to overthrow any of his lingering reluctance to being out in public once more. Honestly, his incident didn't scare me as much as it scared him. I can't imagine what it's like to not know where you are or who you are or who you can trust. I can't imagine not getting the help you need or not wanting help anymore at all. However, despite his huffle puffle, I am *going to help. Hell, I'm already doing everything I can to! I read books about the disorder on my lunch break at work – never in front of him because I don't want it to accidently conjure up more shame, which I don't think he should feel at all – and I've casually had my mother pulling me information, slyly spinning the truth of it having to do with a discussion brought up by someone at work – which is technically true since my boss asked me about what I was reading one day during my downtime. Knowledge is the best weapon in a person's arsenal, and I am getting locked and loaded. Ugh. Forgive the terrible metaphor. I watched a cheesy 80's cop movie with my parents last night, and I've been using themed phrases ever since. Archer laughed so hard at the one I did during breakfast he almost choked on his coffee. Hm? Oh, no. I don't mind leaving him here by himself. I mean I do because I think he'll get lonely and needs to socialize but not because I think he's going to steal from me. Please don't start on that. Gwenith makes snide marks about that shit every chance she gets. And I'm not too trusting. I just…I go with my gut. And my gut says Archer Cox is a good man. One that I'm glad has walked into my life. One that cooks – some of the best macaroni and cheese from scratch I've ever had – and cleans – the maid even made a comment about not needing to come as often – and organizes – he started fixing up the area around Chris's model cities, throwing away old dried-up paint containers. Besides all that, he makes me laugh. All. The. Time! We laugh at scenes from books and shows and movies and even each other. What can I say? He makes me very punny! I'm like one long, poorly constructed, kid joke with crazy curls, I tell ya.*

The feeling of my phone vibrating in my white and purple tie dye yoga pants stops me just two steps from my bedroom door. Retrieving the device exposes me to an unknown number yet ignoring the call isn't done.

My mother has been warning me like fucking Paul Revere that 'the doctor will be calling'. I wanna tell her it's been two weeks. If the man hasn't called me by now – which is fine by me – he probably isn't going to. I know how these setups work.

I swipe answer and politely speak, "Hello, this is Jaye Jenkins."

"Your mother's right," the smooth male voice declares from the other end of the phone. "You *do* have a beautiful voice."

Naturally smiling at the compliment occurs at the same time I state, "Dr. Dmitri Chappell, the very single, very ready to mingle, pediatrician."

"Is that how your mother seriously introduced the subject of me?"

"Almost verbatim."

"Wow," he lightly chortles, "that's um…that's a new one."

The sound of his laughter encourages me to grin wider, yet I don't.

Can't.

Something about it just doesn't do it for me like Archer's does.

Now, he has the most incredible laugh I've ever heard from an adult. Only innocent, bliss filled kid giggles can beat it. And that's barely.

"Let me start by expressing my apologies for not calling sooner. It's not that I haven't been interested, it's just that I haven't exactly had the time. We're a bit short staffed at the practice this month. I've got one doctor leaving for retirement, another on vacation, and one who caught the flu last weekend, so I'm kind of a one-man magician at the moment. This isn't me making excuses, although I can hear how it sounds exactly like that," another small chuckle, "but it's meant to explain why I would wait so long to contact someone I think I might be a great match with. It wasn't really my choice, just my responsibility. Your mother's a doctor. I'm sure you understand how that goes."

"I do."

And between you and me and the bumble bee on page three, I don't like it. I don't...know that I **want** *someone who puts their career before me all the time again. Chris did it and asking him not to – even for something as simple as to celebrate my birthday – was like having to read The Polar Express for the thirty-fourth time during the Christmas season. Utter. Torture.*

"I would love to meet up sometime this week for a cup of coffee or maybe even a drink after work?" There's a small pause prior to him adding, "That is if you're actually interested, and I haven't lost my chance to some other guy. And if I have, I hope the son of a bitch knows how fortunate he is."

Smooth Operator indeed.

"Nah, you're still in the running," I playfully reply, grateful when the response receives another chortle. "I'm actually headed out to the gym at the moment-"

"I appreciate a woman who isn't afraid to take care of herself."

The new compliment doesn't settle quite like the first.

I knew what he was trying to convey but what's so wrong with someone who enjoys a monster cookie eating marathon and a re-read of Bridget Jones's Diary by Helen Fielding?

"Why don't you check your schedule and text me what nights are best for you, and we'll see what we can make work."

"Absolutely."

Ending our call happens immediately after cordial goodbyes. I tuck the device back where it originally was and resume my trek to the downstairs hall closet where I keep the yoga mats. To my surprise, Archer's already waiting and ready to go on the bottom step.

Not grinning from ear to ear just from the sight of him is impossible.

And not swooning over how sexy he looks in gray sweats would be impossible too if it weren't for my top teeth clamping onto my bottom lip like the jaws of life.

Let's just say, I totally understand sweatpants season, friends, and I am. Here. For. It.

"You look good," I thoughtlessly coo only to quickly try to cover my tracks. "*Ready.* I meant you look *ready.*"

He cockily leans on the stair railing and flashes me a sexy smirk. "Did you?"

"I meant *both*, but you don't have to look so fucking smug about it."

"Oh, but I do, sweetheart." He theatrically winks in reference to when it was said to him.

Loving that he's a flirt yet hating that I'm not sure if he's flirting, flirting or just friendly flirty leads to me batting away the butterflies that probably have no business hanging around in my stomach. "I gotta grab us mats. Wanna get the car warmed up?"

"Can do."

And with one last toothy grin he disappears to complete the task.

183

Look, I know I'm working on not comparing every little thing he does to what Chris did, but can I just say that I love there's no resistance to help out with something as a simple as getting the car toasty? Yes, I have auto start, but Archer doesn't trust that someone won't slip into my backseat to try to steal the vehicle from me because I have a tendency to forget to lock my doors. He goes out every morning while I'm getting ready for work, starts up the car, makes sure everything is defrosted, and that I have a fresh cup of to-go coffee in the cup holder. I appreciate that he cares so much. It's...refreshing.

An idea hits me upon my locking the door prompting me to excitedly scurry to the car to pitch it. Unfortunately for me, rather than finding my friend inside where it should be warm by now, I find him with his hands surrendered in the air, trying to calm down a screeching Mrs. Prescott.

This. Fucking. Woman...

"I'd like to report a theft in progress," she snidely says into the phone while jabbing the edge of a broom Archer's direction. "Yes, he's a white male, green eyes-"

"Gwenith!" I loudly shout, interrupting her call, nearly causing her to lose her grip on the device altogether. "What the hell do you think you're doing?!"

"Saving your car from this thief!" She jams the cleaning tool at him again. "You should be thanking me! I saw this filth about to drive off with it – like the scumbag he is – and rushed out here to stop him."

184

"And I politely told the woman wielding the weapon at an innocent man that I was *asked* to warm up the car."

"You weren't."

"He *was*," I swiftly reassure on a heavy sigh. "Now, would you please put down the broom? We have a fitness class to get to."

She ends the call and places the object at her side, stare planted on me. "I *don't* trust him. I know the truth about your little," her sneer has me wishing I were a more violent person so that I could punch her in her face, "*act*. And one of these days, I'm gonna prove it. I'm gonna get him in jail where he belongs, and you kicked out of the neighborhood-"

"Because I don't belong, either?"

The racial implication I suggest has her hurrying away in a tizzy.

Is it wrong to hope the woman her husband is having an affair with is not white? Just to add an extra sting to the mean-spirited stitched together hag.

Archer unlocks the doors granting us both access inside and swiftly apologizes. "I'm sorry I-"

185

"Don't even," I huff, tossing the objects in the backseat before taking the keys. "None of that was your fault. Her behaviors are not your fault. Her attitude is not your fault. I think she's just so deeply unhappy that the mere *thought* of someone else being happy upsets her."

"Probably because her husband has learned to be happy *without* her." We begin fastening our seatbelts. "I mean I doubt its *her* he's using that warming lube marked for his and her pleasure on. Or those nipple clamps."

There's no stopping me from squeaking. "Nipple clamps?!"

My housemate nods like it's no big deal. "He left the instructions in the box. Found it in the recycle during my rounds." A small shrug is wedged between statements. "I told you. Your garbage says a lot of shit about you."

Does mine say I haven't had sex once since Chris died? Would we just assume that by the different vibrator packages that I've put in the recycle? Ohmygod, has he seen those?! How long has he been digging in my trash?! Should I ask what he knows?!

"Why's your face turning so red?" he cautiously inquires.

I do my best to play it off while fiddling with the defroster. "Is it?"

"And why is your voice so squeaky?"

186

The pitch hits an even higher level. "Is it?"

"Squeak toy level," Archer lightly laughs and gently nudges my leg to collect my gaze. "You're thinking about sex shit, aren't you?"

"Why would you say that?!"

"Those are your tells."

"I have tells?!"

"Most people do." His smile remains. "Spotting them has been necessary for my survival – during and post service."

Flicking away the curls that missed the memo to stay in my messy bun, I quietly confess, "I didn't even know I did those things."

"Maybe you just do them with me?"

So not the thing I wanna be doing with him.

"Maybe you're not comfortable talking to *me* of all people about sex."

His accusation instantly banishes the embarrassment. "And what is it you're trying to say?"

"That maybe talking about sex with the homeless vet that lives in your garage makes you uncomfortable because you don't really trust me as much as you think you do."

"Or *maybe* it's because talking about sex with the ripped, single hottie that lives within boning range makes me uncomfortable because I know he's not attracted to me the way I am him."

Archer's stare suddenly darkens in a delicious nature. "Oh, he's *very* fucking attracted to you, sweetheart."

The new information has all the air in my lungs exiting.

And the muscles between my thighs dampening.

Okay…so…that happened?

Tension-filled silence fills the first stretch of our drive and songs like "Closer" by Nine Inch Nails – one of Archer's favorite bands I added to our shared playlist – don't exactly help to deescalate it. He struggles to casually adjust his crotch while I wiggle in my seat hoping to secretly do the same. Less than coy glances are repeatedly exchanged and the idea of testing my flexibility in new ways flies to the front of my mind.

***What?! I know it's not classy to fuck in a parking lot but
like…I've always wanted to try it.***

With the gym sign finally in sight, the thought I had earlier –
pre-Mrs. Prescott – barrels back to me pushing me to bark, "Right!"

My passenger jumps in his seat, accidently hitting his elbow.
"Fuck!" The brush off of the pain is immediate. "What? What is it?
What's to our right?!" He begins a frantic visual search. "Gunman?
Sniper?"

"God, I hope not," I reply and begin looking with him.

Archer angles his face my direction to showcase a small
smile. "What made you scream?"

"You should be the one making me scream" damn near
leaves my mouth instead of what actually does. "It was just an
exclamation over a returned idea I had that I hadn't gotten to express
yet."

He nods his comprehension. "Go on."

"What if we get you a job application from the gym?" The
light turns green indicating it's time to accelerate. "And this isn't me
pushing you to get a job, to get you out, to force you to do something
you're not ready to do. This is simply just me…*suggesting*…we grab
you some from nearby places that are easy for carpooling so that
when you *are* ready you can apply."

"I can just walk."

His defensiveness is expected but the type isn't.

"I'm used to walking."

"And you walking along the highway in the dead of night or the ass crack of dawn or middle of traffic gives me *A Bad Case of Stripes*."

Perplexity pierces his face. "Fucking what?"

The smallest cringe crosses my face as I pull into the parking lot. "Sorry, it's a kid's book by David Shannon." Guilt graces itself next in my expression. "I should probably make less literary references, especially child-based ones."

"No, you should just keep being you, and let others adjust if they want a place in your life."

Swoon for me too, please.

"How about we focus on just getting applications first? Figure out the other bits like hours and carpooling or bussing later?"

Archer allows a small smile to slip onto his face. "Roger that, sweetheart."

We park near the entance, grab our gear, and hustle through the front doors with me determined to get a good spot. Getting Archer checked in as a guest, unfortunately, requires more effort than we were prepared for. His lack of ID requires them to take his photo and fill out additional liability paperwork. The whole process is long and tedious yet convinces me to just add him to my account as to skip all this shit in the future. On our way to the back studio where the class will be taking place, he expresses his displeasure with the situation. Gripes about being a charity case. Complains that I already do too much for him. However, all of his grievances are immediately lost upon me the instant my eyes set focus on a brown and white baby goat.

They're so adorable!

Finding a place to toss my mat down is swiftly followed by a black and white creature wandering over to me. Its front two feet brace themselves on my thighs while it nudges against my sweatshirt covered chest in a silent demand to be petted.

Loved.

You know Archer is a lot like this baby goat. He basically just walked into my life and gently looked for attention.

Our instructor, Kirra, explains the very simple process of how class will unfold. We're instructed to follow her guidance but to connect to the creatures however and whenever we see fit. The little

191

farm friend wanders away to someone else when I move for the first position and by the time we're taken on a third, it's Archer who has a furry friend.

One that is a caramel brown color and directly in front of his face in our downward dog position.

Unsure what either will do, leads to me studying the situation rather than transitioning to the uttanasana pose like the other class members.

For just a moment, Archer seems annoyed.

Irked that the thing meant to bring him joy is standing in the way of completing his mission.

Yet one glance my direction and his demeanor shifts.

He lowers himself to his knees.

Keeps his attention on the four-legged friend until he realizes that *I'm* like the goat.

I'm not going anywhere.

You can be gruffy and huffy and scruffy, but I'm going to stick around and give you the love you need.

The love *he* needs.

Whether it's reciprocated or not.

In a hushed voice, the man to my side playfully grumps, "She put you up to this, didn't she?"

I lightly giggle and bend my body into the pose just as he begins to nuzzle the goat head-to-head.

"I like you. I really do," my stubborn friend quietly states to the creature, eyes shutting during their continued nuzzling, "just like I really like her."

Those pesky butterflies I can't seem to permanently banish go wild in the pit of my tummy once more.

I really like him, too. And I really like whatever this is that we're doing together.

Chapter 10

Archer

Steering the basket around the slow Sunday shoppers crowding the aisles of Harry's Hardware, I unhappily grunt, "You're very pushy about this fucking topic."

"And *you're* very circumventy."

"You may be the word expert, but I'm pretty sure there's not supposed to be a y on that."

"I *am* the word expert because I conduct words for myself and others," the playfulness in her tone successfully sparks a smirk, "therefore I declare that it's an adjective now."

Faking a gasp occurs at the same time I stop our cart in the area for paint. "What would Webster say?"

"It's actually *Merriam-Webster* – which, fun fact, is the oldest dictionary publisher in this country – and none of those people would say anything because they're dead and they've been dead and if the dead start talking, we have a *Warm Bodies* situation on our hands that I'm ill prepared for."

"I'm not." The casualness of my counter receives an eyebrow lift. "I've read my fair share of survival material over the years –

mainly while I was serving. I wouldn't say I'm a bushcraft expert, but I think based on the skills I've adapted and perfected, we could make it through at least the first few waves of a zombie apocalypse."

Jaye tucks the sleeves of her warm caramel colored sweater into the palms of her hands and girlishly giggles. "Is it weird I find that oddly comforting?"

Leaning into the beautiful sound is accompanied by me resting my arms on the edge of the basket. "Nah."

What? It's not any fucking weirder than me finding comfort in that sound. Or the way she always put out a coffee mug for me in the morning no matter how busy she gets. Or the fact that we're out shopping for things to make the house feel like our home rather than her dead fiancé's. Okay, yeah. That last one is still pretty fucking strange.

"We're making you a DMV appointment *and* a doctor's appointment. Both *are* happening. I already put them on the calendar for this week – the one in my phone *and* the one in the kitchen – so you can keep being evadey and dodgey and flighty-"

"You're just adding ys for the fuck of it."

"-all you want, but we are doing those things whether you grump and grumble like the Pigeon or not."

"The Pigeon?"

"From the Pigeon Series by Mo Willems." Her face slightly cringes in its typical fashion. "It's a kid's book series-"

"I figured that."

"And the Pigeon is the main character. He goes through emotional pout spells sometimes *especially* when he's being told he has to do something he doesn't wanna do. *Hence* you being the Pigeon."

"I'm not a pigeon."

"You are for the sake of this conversation."

The glower on my face expands.

"Now, can you *stop* being the Pigeon long enough for us to pick out paint for your bathroom."

My displeasure swiftly deepens. "It's not *my* bathroom, Jaye."

She sassily folds her arms across her chest. "Do you shower in it?"

"Yes, but-"

"Do you brush your teeth in it?"

"Yeah, but-"

"Do you keep your soap, deodorant, razor, and other toiletries in it?"

"I don't like the word toiletries."

"But don't you love *having* them?"

Fuck me, I really do.

As if she could hear the retort I didn't speak, she gleefully grins. "Exactly. And that place you keep them is *your* bathroom."

"It's the *guest* bathroom."

"No, housemate, it's *your* bathroom and you should get to have it catered to a style you enjoy rather than staring at framed photos of Chicago, Seattle, Boston, and Manhattan skylines. Those were Chris's choices in décor. *His* favorite cities. *His* favorite places. But like you keep reminding me, he's *not here* anymore."

For fucks sake, why can't I be gentler about saying that shit to her?

197

"It's okay…that…things…change."

The words lack the strength they should prompting me to reach over and gently cup her arm. "Sweetheart, we don't have to change shit until *you* are ready to change. Everyone moves the fuck on at their own speed. Don't let me push to do shit you're not wanting."

"That's the thing…," excitement unexpectedly blooms in her gaze, "I *do* want these things. And I *do* want a house that feels like a *home* versus a museum I sleep in. I'm tired of living exactly like other people dictate. Doing things just because that's how they've always been done. I want these changes as much as I need them."

Thoughtlessly my thumb strokes the area under its grasp.

Jaye softly whimpers at the contact, and I have to force myself to remove my touch.

You think I **don't** *want to hear her making those sounds? What are you, fucking crazy? Of course, I want to hear that shit. And her moaning. And crying out my goddamn name. But that, my friend, isn't happening. Or going to happen. We're…as much as it pains me to say…friends. And fucking…roommates. And neither of those have the word naked before them. I keep trying to tell that to my dick, but he still seems to think if he keeps popping up enough that may change. Unfortunately, it won't.*

My tone remains gentle. Tender. "I just don't want you wasting money, especially on me."

"Please stop worrying about money."

The expression transposes to a sardonic one.

"I swear, the shit is really not an issue."

"Trust fund kid?"

"Not...exactly."

It's my turn to lift my brow in question.

"Chris owned and operated a multibillion-dollar cyber security company. To my understanding – which honestly isn't much – he created a program to show you the biggest weaknesses in your system that you might not have seen before. Places where more skilled hackers might be able to penetrate. He made *most* of his money in the private security sector, which is why when he died, I sold it outright to Haworth Enterprises. Upon his death, not only did the majority of the shares in his company fall to me but so did all of his investments – domestic and foreign – his savings – domestic and foreign – and the trust fund his parents had planned to give him when *they* died which he instructed that they he will to me instead, although we all agreed to keep that locked away to send my theoretical children to college someday."

There's no preventing my jaw from tumbling downward.

"Basically, I could never work again, buy the castle from *Beauty & The Beast*, fill the entire thing with all the books I've ever read and want to read, hire an entire staff to maintain it, and *still* have more money than should be humanly possible left over."

Wow. I really, really don't fucking belong even breathing the same air as her.

"So, how about we ditch the dollar worries and focus on the paint ones?" She clears her throat and sashays her way around me to the wall of samples. "What type of color are you thinking? The current shade is this one." Her finger extends to point to the paper. "White Opulence."

"Surprise fucking surprise," I mutter under my breath at the same time I position myself beside her.

"I don't really like white," Jaye causally informs, "and he was…almost *obsessed* with it. Like all of our – er – *my sheets* are white. I even asked once would it be okay to get some *gray* pillowcases just to spice shit up and was met by a look of horror that belongs in a Stephen King novel." Her headshake is followed by her stare lifting to mine. "They were just pillowcases!"

"So, we'll get some."

Her brow crinkles in confusion.

"After we're done here, we can go to wherever it is you go to get some and get you whatever color shit you like."

She presents me with a slow headshake. "You don't really wanna spend the whole day shopping."

"I don't, but *you* obviously *need to*, so I'm here to tag along." The smile on my face is warm. "*Happily, roomie.*"

"No," Jaye playfully shakes her head again, "I prefer sweetheart."

Me too, honestly.

"Oh, you're the only one who can add the y sound to shit?"

"Correct." Her smug nod is attached to an arrogant snicker. "What do you think about maybe a green?" She gestures towards a very light shade. "Mint-chocolate?"

"Are we painting or picking dessert?"

Giggles precede another point elsewhere. This time towards a white blue. "What about morning mist?"

"Mist or piss?"

More laughter escapes, although this one is accompanied by a playful elbow to the side. "Be helpful."

"Is that not helping?"

Her gaze soars to mine alongside a mirth-filled scowl.

"Alright, what about…" my stare slowly starts to sweep the colorful choices in search of something better, only stopping when I have a viable suggestion. "This one. Taupeoca Pudding." The eye roll that follows can't be helped. "Who the fuck came up with these names?"

Jaye giggles again yet gravitates closer to me.

Has her side brushing my side.

The heat from her jean bearing frame practically melting a hole in mine.

She's right within palm's reach.

My reach.

Maybe I should drape my arm around her shoulder?

Reach for her hand?

Lean over and…

Nope.

None of that.

And where were you to stop that train of thought from leaving the fucking station?

The woman at my side lifts the sample and nonchalantly nods. "I like it. It's kind of earthy. Kind of moody."

"You and those ys today," I playfully jab.

She teasingly bumps into me again, this time swaying my figure a little more than expected, prompting me to wrap my arm around her waist to latch my hand onto her hip to assist in keeping me upright. My reaction is instant yet removing my grip once it's landed is reluctant. Having her tucked tightly against me feels like all the pieces in life are right where they're supposed to be despite the fact that I know those same pieces will never really belong here.

Or get to stay here.

That I'll never do anything that could earn them the right to be here.

I begin to pry my fingers away only to be met by her body inching towards me.

Wordlessly requesting I keep them where they are.

And the doubt in the front of my mind that that's what she's asking gets aggressively slammed to the back when she peers up at me while less than innocently biting her bottom lip.

Um…okay. This uh…happening?

"What do you think about…uh…an uh…," getting my brain to focus on words rather than having her glossed lips on top of mine feels impossible, "um…the edges?"

"Huh?"

Her cluelessness causes my ability to speak correctly to go back into place. "The trim." I clear my throat and continue the conversation. "What color should we do for *the trim*?"

"Oh!" She whips her head back to the wall, free bouncing curls slapping more sense into me. "I think anything in the white family should do. I don't really *like* white like I said, but I think it meshes well for a trim. Maybe something off white? More beige? Something that will blend better?"

"Most of those were questions, sweetheart."

Jaye noticeably lights up over the nickname yet doesn't outwardly acknowledge it. "I know. I'm just throwing things out there. Seeing what *you* want." Her gaze meets mine as she adds. "What *we* want."

Hm? Yeah, now would be a great time to be like us naked and banging on that bathroom floor, but I'm not gonna say it, just like it's not gonna happen.

"I think an off white-shade is a good idea."

Us, on the other hand?

Not so much.

She resumes browsing her options while I investigate other areas of renovations. "I know we need to get some shit for me to fix the towel racks that are a bit wobbly and that small leak under the sink, but do you wanna look at anything else while we're here? Cabinets? Toilets? Lighting?"

"That's a lot of different things," Jaye stops mid movement of grabbing a piece of paper to meet my gaze again. "You really know how to do all that?"

"Mostly, yeah." The expression on my face struggles not to fall. "I grew up in foster care and learned early on, the more useful I could make myself, the longer I might get to stay. I picked up tidbits of basic shit as early as eight, so by the time I was sixteen, it was a lot easier to do more of the complicated shit my last foster father was eager to teach me about."

She doesn't hide the heartache that appears in her eyes. "You know you don't have to be 'useful' to stay with me, right, Archer?" Her body presses firmly against mine robbing me of the breath I didn't realize I had been holding. "I want you around regardless of if you do any of this shit or not."

Fuck, I know it, but it feels damn good to hear it.

I offer her the only thing I'm capable of.

A tiny nod.

Jaye quietly and cautiously inquires, "What happened to your parents?"

The question fills me with dread – even all these years later. "The man responsible for helping create me beat my mother to death in front of my own eyes with a baseball bat. And had the neighbor across the street not been as nosey as she was, he might've done the same to me too instead of me being carried away by the first responder who found me hiding in the pantry."

One hand covers her mouth to try to catch the gasp that escapes.

"That's actually the reason I originally *wanted* to be an EMT, but that shit costs and money wasn't something I had much of considering how I was bounced around the system. At graduation, the choices were go to the military or move out on my own, which we all knew I didn't have the funds for. I'm just grateful they let me stay until basic." Uncomfortableness about a subject I rarely speak on has me anxiously fidgeting. "I thought about being a field medic, but truth was, I really only wanted to help people the way I had been helped, ya know?" A small shrug slips in between statements. "I eventually believed I could do that for my own country on a grander scale which is bullshit I bought into when I joined only to realize that it was indeed bullshit and that a lot like the system I had come from, it was broken, too. The difference was…being a grunt gave me more *stability*. It gave me *brothers*. It gave me…*hope*." Disgust causes me to sneer and unwind myself from the female beside me before I can tarnish her. "And then all that shit was taken away by the same people who gave it to me when they let me become another form they forgot to file."

Jaye's entire face falls, "*Archer-*"

"Hey," anxious to change the subject as well as create breathing room for myself, I retreat myself back to the cart, "what if I pick up an application here? Put some of that knowledge to use?"

It's obvious it pains her to leave the emotional bomb I just dropped at her feet; however, she does. She chooses to do what's best for *me*, something I can't verbally appreciate enough. "Think you can handle working *and* renovating at the same time?"

207

"*If* I get a job, I'll just work on the bathroom when I get off at night or dedicate my time to fixing it on my off days. I don't start anything I can't finish, sweetheart."

Her bottom lip tucks itself out of sight, clearly linking the statement to something else.

Something *less* platonic.

Less innocent.

Something we both shouldn't be thinking of.

You see what a fucking disaster I am. You know I'm right.

I fight every urge in my body to allow anything other than a friendly statement to leave my mouth. "What do you say we take the samples over to the paint counter and go look around lighting while they mix the shit up?"

Redness finally flees from her face on a nod of agreement.

The instant she's turned around again, I release a low, heavy breath.

Fuck. Me. Hopefully renovating something will be the healthy distraction I need. The one that keeps me from thinking of an exit strategy to take from this situation and how I'll have to survive without the little luxuries I'm beginning to become accustomed to. And I'm not just talking about running water or a warm bed. I'm talking about having someone in my life who actually gives a shit about me as a person versus what I can do for them. That's definitely the shit I'll miss most when Jaye comes to her senses and asks me to leave. Until then? I'm gonna do my best to relish in it.

Chapter 11
Jaye

I lean back in my barstool seat at No Need to Wine, the wine bar where I met Dmitri two hours ago, on another airy laugh. "Seriously?! You love that book, too?"

"Who doesn't love *Where the Wild Things Are*?" The Patrick Dempsey doppelganger playfully pokes back. "Do those people really exist or are you just trying to get me worked up?"

"Oh, they exist." Pushing my empty wine glass away is done to provide me better space to rest my elbow. "I'm not sure I *trust them*, but they definitely exist."

"I wouldn't trust them, either," he laughs once more, smile blindingly bright.

What? Why are you judging me? It's just one drink. One drink that I'll have you know we have scheduled and rescheduled and rescheduled six times over the past three weeks. First, he had to work and then his doctor friend was in town from Applecourt for a conference and then there was something I didn't quite understand about a seagull and after that I just kind of assumed it was never going to happen. Which I was totally fine with! I wasn't exactly looking for a date; however, when he texted this morning while I was getting ready for work, swearing not to cancel, I didn't even have the chance to decline before my mother was calling me to tell me I had to go. How she knew he had sent the message is still a question I don't have answered.

Dmitri rests his arm on the bar in a similar position to mine. "It's gonna sound like a total line, but I really like getting to talk about kids' books with you."

The smile he's offered is playful. "It *definitely* does."

"Too bad it's the truth." He grins wider. "I kind of collect then. Some I donate to the hospital; however, the others are the ones I cycle through reading when I'm volunteering."

Surprise cakes over my face. "You volunteer with not just animals but children as well?"

"Weekly, which contributes to the conflicting schedule issues we've been having but asking a woman to come down to a local battered family shelter and listen to you read *Pirates Don't Change Diapers* before offering free medical exams doesn't exactly make for the greatest first date."

Swooning should be stopped yet can't be.

God, can Mr. Perfect For Me really get any more perfect for me?!

"Maybe for our next date we could hit up a local bookstore?" His fingers that are dangling near mine lightly brush them. "You could recommend me some librarian approved reads to add to my shelves?"

The idea alone should fill me with inexplicable joy.

I mean that's like...*an ideal date* right there.

What woman in her right mind wouldn't want to go to the bookstore?!

It's just that...I know *he's* not the one I want to go to the bookstore with.

He's not the one whose spine I want to touch.

Pun so intended. And let me just say, touching it in my fantasies at night is so not enough. Oh, don't get me wrong...It's enough. Size. Shape. The way it strokes at just the right speed so that I always get off. No, I mean not getting to experience the real thing is torture. Not nearly as much torture as falling for someone that you're pretty sure has no interest in ever seeing you as anything other than a friend. A non-naked friend at that. A non-naked friend who happens to tell you her shameful secrets and guilty pleasures and the things she's read about sex in romance novels but hasn't ever had the courage to try. A non-naked friend who you cook for and tuck in on the couch when she falls asleep during a TV show and who you bring hot chocolate to while discussing the choices for next month's book club with her. Look, I'm really happy to have Archer in my life. I am! It just sucks a teeny tiny bit that I can't have him in the one way my heart keeps telling me I should. You can't make someone want you. Trust me. I spent way too much time trying that shit in the past.

All of sudden, the tip of his finger is lifting my chin up that I didn't even realize had fallen. "Why do I get the feeling you want that date, just not with me?"

I helplessly cringe. "*Dmitri-*"

"It's okay." His hand lifts to politely stop the sentence in its tracks. "I knew it was a long shot that I hadn't missed my chance."

The words slip free at a muted tone. "I didn't think you had."

"But now you *know* I have?"

Garbled words clump together forming an incoherent slew for an answer.

He lightly chuckles, lifts his hand for the check, and teases, "How about in English, next?"

Embarrassed snickers proceed a more understandable response. "*It's complicated.*"

"Why?"

"He's my roommate."

"You have a roommate?"

"Housemate?" Realizing that doesn't sound much better has me rushing to explain. "He's a friend that fell on hard times, and I moved him in to my garage to help get him back on his feet – only because he didn't wanna live in the house – and we've grown close-" Dmitri shoots me an incredulous stare in the middle of my rambling. "Okay. *Fine.* We've grown *really* close. So close that we're practically dating, but we aren't actually dating, which is why it's okay I go on other dates with other people because we're not dating no matter how much I wish we were dating, and the truth is we will probably never date, so it's all really just a moot point."

Dmitri offers a nod of thanks to the bartender for the bill before inquiring to me, "As the weird consolation prize in this whole thing, can I offer you some advice?"

Ohmygod he is, isn't he? The like 'Thank You for Trying to Date Normal' giftbag from the 'My Mother Won't Stop Setting Me Up Gala'.

"Sorry," I whisper on an awkward cringe. "I didn't mean for that to come out that way. That's not what I wanted my words to infer."

He fishes his wallet of his suit pocket, smile never wavering. "First off, there are worse things to be than some sexy librarian's second choice in dates, Jaye."

*Am I sexy? I thought I might be in this shorter than normal purple plaid winter mini dress and these brown thigh high boots, but I didn't know I was **that** hot in it. Score for me!*

"And second, instead of just assuming this guy is not interested, how about you tell him how you feel?" The debit card lands on the receipt. "I'll be honest. Most of us out here are…pretty fucking dense when it comes to women or what they want. Some of us are just better at faking that shit than others."

Both hands cup my mouth to keep in the giggle.

"Tell this guy the bluntest version of the truth that you can. Don't leave any doubt for what you could possibly mean because let me be the first to say if you do, then you'll both get screwed over." The bartender takes the bill into his possession while Dmitri explains. "My ex said I work too much – which in fairness I do – and that she needed a big gesture to prove to me she mattered just as much as work. *I thought* she meant planning us a couple's vacation to Disneyworld. *She meant* a 2ct princess cut diamond engagement from That Ring You Do."

A loud hiss is attached to a wince.

"Yeah. However, I will say going on a couple's vacation solo *wasn't* so bad. There was a little magic to be found with a bridesmaid at The Magic Kingdom. She was desperate to getaway from the bridezilla she called a sister, and I was desperate to stop looking at those princesses the way Mr. Mouse did *not* intend."

More laughs spring loose from parted lips.

215

"*My point is*…leave no room for miscommunication." The smile offered next appears genuine. "If you're right, and he's not interested in you then it'll be easier for you to move on. Preferably with a fairly attractive, *still single and ready to mingle*, pediatric doctor."

Warmth remains in my tone as I reach over to give his leg a friendly pat. "You're a great guy."

My statement is met by a slightly defeated shrug. "Just not the *right* guy."

No.

Not for me.

Post signing the receipt, Dmitri and I spend a little longer freely chatting mostly about the organizations he volunteers to with me making mental notes to donate to them. Afterward, he walks me to my car, kisses me goodnight on the cheek, and wishes me luck with my housemate.

And I need all the luck I can get.

I'm not always the *best* with words.

Maybe because I know how powerful they can truly be.

Seems like an obvious concept, right? But it's not. Words reaaalllyyyyy matter. Whether they're on the page or being spoken, how we put them together can be the difference between life and death, pain and pleasure, unrequited love and undying love. Hm? Okay, fine, maybe I'm being a little dramatic, but what do you want from me? Reading a Sloan Mathers romance novel always does that to me.

Getting home doesn't take nearly as long as normal considering it's well past rush hour. I collect my workbag, my change of clothes bag, the bottle of wine I can't wait to share with Archer tonight while we watch a couple episodes of *Lawless Lives*, and hustle to my front door the fastest that I can, hating the cold that's nipping at my overly exposed thighs.

The instant I've closed the door behind me I'm greeted by Archer descending the stairs, large hands being wiped by a white towel, tattooed muscles glistening for the gawking.

What?! If he didn't wanna be ogled, he should've put on a shirt! Oh…yeah…I hear how questionable that sounds. Do you think I had too much wine?

His grin grows too arrogant to deny that I'm doing anything else.

I allow myself another moment to indulge in all the places my anxious fingers are literally twitching to touch prior to pointing out the obvious. "You're covered in paint."

"Believe it or not there's more on the walls than on me."

"Good thing we bought you *specific* paint clothes, huh?"

He rolls his eyes over the reminder.

By we, I, of course, mean me. I bought them right after he forwarded me an article of 'What to Expect When Renovating'. He wanted me to be aware of the noises I'd hear and possible damage and why he would be showering elsewhere for some unknown amount of days. I took it as a reason to buy him paint clothes and protective eye gear and earplugs. Ohhhh. That would be the miscommunication thing Dmitri was warning me about, huh?

The towel in his grip gets tossed casually over his shoulder. "I *finally* finished the bathroom."

"All of it?"

He slowly nods. "Every single bit."

I wiggle my bags off my shoulder but maintain my hold on the bottle. "That sounds like cause for celebration!" Holding it up, I dangle the object in a playful fashion. "What do you say, I pour us each a glass and then we can go up to marvel at your amazing handiwork together?"

"How do you know it's amazing?"

218

"Because *you're* amazing."

Archer's cheeks slightly redden on a bashful grin.

"Is that a yes, Mr. Fix It?"

"That's a fuck yes, sweetheart."

Excitedly, I start towards the kitchen area with him trailing behind me. "Have any problems today?"

"Just painting behind the toilet. That area's such a bitch."

Placing the bottle on the island is done at the same time I meet his stare again. "I'm sure it's fine. No one ever looks there. And if they do look there, the bigger questions are *why* are they looking there, and do we really want them in our house?"

Archer lightly laughs while inching over to retrieve the glasses. Once they're near the wine, he casually asks, "Is this why you're home so late? Stopped at the liquor store?"

Guilt struggles not to gloss over my gaze. "Um…not exactly."

"Not…exactly…" He slowly echoes the words on a cocked head motion. His eyes sweep my frame from head to toe prior to noting. "That's not what you wore to work today."

My mouth twitches to move, yet the most I manage to do is shake my head.

"You'd *never* wear something like this to work. The dress is too short. Way too fucking short. You'd flash an entire preschool class acting out *The Crayon Box that Talked* in it."

He's not wrong.

"And those boots are all wrong. Sexy…Very fucking sexy, but wrong. You don't wear boots to work of any kind. Just flats. You like to slip them off under your desk or while you're in the reading circle or playing and hide and hunt the book."

*Gahhhh, can we stop for a minute and appreciate how much he knows about me? I mean **really** knows? Chris couldn't even remember the name of the academy I worked for.*

Displeasure deepens in his expression at the same time he folds his arms protectively across his chest. "Where did you change?"

"Work."

"*Why* did you change?"

"I um…," a nervous bite is taken out of my bottom lip, "I had a date."

There's no missing the way his frame stiffens at the new information. "*A date.*"

"Really it was more like just a drink."

"*A drink.*"

"One glass of wine, no food, and lots of talk about books!"

For some reason the mention of our conversation topic seems to spark more outrage than anything else. "*Books.*"

"It wasn't like that!" I defensively squeak, although to be honest I don't know what I'm arguing against since he hasn't done anything other than repeat the words I've spoken. "See, Dmitri is a pediatric doctor-"

"Of course he fucking is."

"-that works in the same hospital as my mother-"

"Because of course he fucking does."

"And she's been trying to get us together for *weeks-*"

"Weeks?" Missing the hurt in his croaked question is impossible. "You've been…You've been trying to go out with this guy for *weeks*?"

Shit! Wrong words! Wrong words!

"Archer, I-"

"No." He interrupts, voice now devoid of any emotion. "It's fine. You don't owe me an explanation."

"But-"

"You owe me nothing."

"But-"

"I'm your housemate, not your boyfriend." His crisp nod hurts as much as the emotionless tone. "It's none of my business who you go share wine with or have dinner with or put on dresses for."

"*Arch-*"

"You know, I'm not actually in the mood to celebrate." The grimace on his face doesn't waiver. "I think I'm just gonna crash early. It's trash day tomorrow, and I like to sweep the area before Mrs. Prescott comes outside to remind me of what a worthless human being I am."

My mouth bobs to speak, but he leaves no opportunity.

"Enjoy your wine. There's some homemade chili in the crockpot if you're hungry."

The airiest squeak escapes.

"I'll do the dishes in the morning."

All I manage to do is repeat the sound.

"Night, Jaye."

Being given his sweat-caked backside to say goodnight to rather than his face tells me everything I need to know.

I screwed this up.

Someway.

Some fucking how.

I *fucked* up my chance for us to be more.

The sound of the garage door being slammed shut has me squeezing my eyes closed.

Well, there goes that whole spill my guts plan. I guess the only thing left to do now is drink an entire bottle of red. Alone. On the only thing I like almost as much as him in this house. My purple couch.

Chapter 12

Jaye

What's a woman to do when she can't sleep? Well, reading is the obvious answer, but what am I supposed to do when that doesn't work? Oh. I mean…yeah…I could do that to see if it helps, except I'm not in my bed. I'm on my couch. My very comfy, very feels so much better when I'm sharing it with Archer, couch.

Rolling over onto my side, I check the time on my cell again.

I wish I could time travel. While time traveling novels aren't my favorite – the rules are just so shitty in most – I did really enjoy The Time Traveler's Wife, although sometimes it was more heartache than I wanted.

Two minutes.

Two whole fucking minutes have passed since I last looked.

Hey, I guess I should be grateful, it's not going backwards?

Unlocking the device reveals to me the silly selfie of me and Archer hiding our faces behind books during one of our reading sessions.

Sometimes after dinner instead of TV or air guitar rock battles or card games, we'll have a book date – er – session. We'll have dessert – typically cookies I made earlier in the week – and hot chocolate – homemade usually – cuddle under the same blanket and just read, stopping only to gush to the other one about a scene that we love or a topic that we wanna discuss. Do we usually get very far in the books? Nah. However, we do talk. And talk. And talk for hours sometimes. I love talking to him. It's so easy and natural. There's only one other person that's ever been that easy to talk to in my life.

With that fact in mind, I hit the number two button on my speed dial.

You know number one is voicemail. That's default setting shit.

There's a single full ring before my dad's voice is flooding my system with a much-needed feeling of tenderness. "Hey, sugar."

"Hey, Dad."

"What's bothering my little girl so early this morning?"

I keep the device pressed tightly to my ear as I close my eyes. "And how do you know something is bothering me? How do you know I didn't just call to ask you a cop question related to the Alex Cross novel I'm reading?"

"Because I know you," he casually states. "Because I know book calls start with an exclamation like 'Ohmygod' or 'You won't believe this' or a long drawn 'Dadddddddd'. Because I know frustrated work-related calls have you huff and the sound of cookie pans getting slammed around is the background. Because I know the only time that I get a 'Hey, Dad' is when you're sad or unsure about something."

A heavy sigh thoughtlessly escapes. "Why are you such a good detective?"

"I credit my skills to Columbo and Shaft."

Giggles can't be stopped from joining the conversation. "Those are *very* different people, Dad."

"You asked."

More laughter springs loose, shifting some of the tension out of my system.

"Now, you knew I would be up working on paperwork, because when your mom's on call at the hospital, I take the same hours here at the precinct-"

"So that you can be closer to her if she needs you."

"So that we can be on the same sleep schedule," he playfully tries to hide the truth.

227

They've always hated having to be away from one another for long periods like that. Ever since they first started dating – according to Mom. I've always thought it was cute and sweet. Hoped I'd find a love like that. Maybe I have? I do…hate to be away from Archer for too long. I miss hearing his voice or hearing him laugh or hearing him grunt in unhappiness. And God, when I'm away do I miss his face. That sweet smile. That smug smirk. Even the bashful grin he gets when he's been complimented. You know it kills me that I can't text him in the middle of a workday like a normal person? I hate that I have to call my housephone and hope he answers or shoot him an email to the account we set up for potential job offers. Hm. Let's put get him a cellphone on this morning's errands list, too.

"You knew I was available to talk, sugar." The sound of his squeaky office chair indicates I have his full attention. "Talk."

"Okay, well, there's this…somewhat, slightly, *unorthodox* situation I'm currently in," I awkwardly fumble out.

"Does this have something to do with Pizza Dude?"

"It does."

"Is this something I could solve if you would just tell me his name or email or social security number?"

"No."

"Can you tell any of those things anyway? That would solve *my* issue with the strange man I know in my gut is now living in my daughter's house."

"*Garage.*"

Dad grumbles over his confirmed suspicions.

"And no. I don't think he's ready to have you prying into his past yet."

"*He's* not ready or *you're* not ready?"

Ugh. Damn detective.

When I don't retort, he releases his own weighted breath. "Fine. I will – as much as it pains me to do this – let that shit go *for now* and back burner my plan to arrive unannounced in my uniform with my taser ready."

"Thank you."

"What's the problem occurring in your unorthodox situation with Pizza Dude?"

The hesitation to respond has him doing it for me.

"You're into him."

"Uh…erm…well, we've become um…*good friends*."

"You're falling in love with him."

"I – Um – See – I don't think-" Cutting myself off is quickly done yet collecting my composure is slower. "Dad, we haven't even been on an official date. I think using the L word is a bit like trying to swallow the elephant whole."

He lightly chuckles prior to stating, "Then how about starting with that official date."

"I didn't think he wanted that or anything like that, but then I went out on a date with another guy tonight-"

"Dr. *Grey's Anatomy*."

"-and he flipped out. Okay, flipped out might be an exaggeration. He didn't Thanos smash the island or anything. He just…looked…*upset*."

"Upset like the woman he's into yet probably will never feel good enough for went out with another man while he was at home waiting all day to see her for dinner because he knows it's the closest, he's most likely going to get to an actual date?"

Guilt of new portions prompts me to whisper out. "Maybe…"

"Look, sugar, let me preface this by saying I know how your mom feels about you and dating. I know how she's been pushing you to replace Chris in your life for the last few years with her handpicked candidates. I know she thinks you're not trying to move forward and are simply lingering in a love lost."

That's the thing, though. I'm not.

"However, no one asks me my opinion on the situation, so I keep my mouth shut. But if you were to ask me…if you *wanted* my thoughts on you and dating and Pizza Dude…I would say you shouldn't keep going out with the wrong men in an attempt to refrain from upsetting anyone – I.E. your mother – and that it's okay to do what's best for *you*, sugar. Which means, *yes*, you should confess how you feel to your houseguest and give him a chance to tell you how he's into you too versus continuing to assume he's not. Or you coming to the wrongful conclusion that maybe he does like you for more than a roommate but that it's just a result of Stockholm Syndrome, something that isn't possible since you've *invited* him into your life and aren't holding him captive."

The deep groan that escapes is followed by a grumped question. "Why are you such a good detective?"

"I told you. Kojak and *Action Jackson.*"

"You said Columbo and Shaft!"

231

"Did I?" He teasingly taunts. "I think it's late and you're hearing things."

This. Man.

"Hopefully you heard the *right* things from about what to do regarding your self-proclaimed unorthodox situation and will be texting me pictures soon that *include* Pizza Dude's face and not just his impressive handiwork."

The bathroom is fucking gorgeous. Between the new cabinets and the new lighting and the nature-themed book décor, I kind of wanna switch where I shower.

"Get some rest, sugar," Dad warmly insists. "You know where to find me if you need me."

"I love you, Dad."

"I love you, too."

Our call ends and to no surprise, it feels as though a weight has been removed from my chest, allowing the butterflies that had been dormant to swarm again.

First thing in the actual morning I'm gonna tell Archer how I feel. Just rip it off like a price tag instead of peeling at it like a price sticker. Ugh. I hate price stickers on books. Way to ruin covers or back covers. And it takes sooooo fucking long to

232

carefully remove it to not damage the book. Hm? Oh. A little off track but you see the comparison, right?

After managing to get a couple hours of sleep, I shoot my boss a text to tell her that the half day I was going to take will be a full day and get the coffee pot going the instant I hear Archer slip into the downstairs guest half-bath for his morning routine.

Trying to not slam the cabinets closed due to my overly anxious disposition fails poorly.

Rather than launching us a peaceful start, banging and clamoring and shouted swears from dropping things echo throughout the entire residence prompting Archer to appear at the edge of the kitchen with a concerned expression. "You okay, sweetheart?"

Just hearing the nickname has my entire frame melting.

"It's sounding like that scene from *Chicka Chicka Boom Boom* where they all fall out of the tree except in high-def." He folds his arms across his white t-shirt covered chest. "And in our kitchen." His wince is followed instantly by a correction. "*Your kitchen.*"

"No, I like *our* kitchen better." The lower of his jaw in surprise has me abandoning the well thought out speech I had prepared for something more natural. "Because it's accurate. This is *our* kitchen, Archer. This is where *we* cook. Together. Separately. This is where *we* have coffee in the morning or wine at night or cookies on Saturday after the gym."

233

His lips press together firmly rather than arguing.

"And this is *our* home. It's where we read and talk and spend so much time together but…"

The word at the end of the statement has him slightly leaning forward.

Brow creased.

Eyes overran with fear.

"But I want us to spend time together *not* at home."

Confusion causes him to quietly counter. "We do."

"I mean, yeah, we…*technically* do. We go to the gym. And Harry's. And the grocery store. And the drive through of Loca Mocha Casabloca. And today we've got that appointment at the DMV to finally get your license, oh and we're also gonna swing by the cellphone store to get you a phone – yes, I just decided that this morning, and no you can't talk me out of it – but what I'm trying to say is that I want us to go out and do other things like a normal…" My mouth slams itself shut before the wrong words can spring free.

Dad said love and I told him that was swallowing the whole elephant yet here I am calling us a couple – which we are clearly not – instead of asking for a real date. Isn't that me still basically

234

deep throating my problem instead of just completing the first task?!

Rather than let me off the hook, Archer takes a single step at the same time he cautiously pushes for the answer. *"A normal what, Jaye?"*

I can't say it.

Okay, I can, but I clearly shouldn't.

Won't.

Nope.

His eyebrows lift in a silent command for a response prompting me to blurt in a frazzle, "Couple!"

There's no flinching over the increased volume.

"And I know *technically* we're not officially a couple, but we do almost everything together like one. And the parts we *don't* do, God, I *want* us to do. The dating-"

"You wanna go on a date with me?"

"Dates." The franticness of my speech remains. *"All of them.* To the movies. To the park. Bowling. Dancing. Fuck, I don't know. Maybe indoor skydiving?" Tossing my hands in the air is attached to a dramatic shrug. "Whatever it is *we* wanna do for dates!

"Jaye-"

"And I want us to hold hands. And I want you to put your arm around me like you want it there or need it there or have been thinking about it being there for as long as I have. And I want you to touch me. And I want you to kiss me. And I want you to touch me again *in other ways.*"

This time his face noticeably flushes on a slow lick of the lips.

"I like you, Archer," I loudly confess over the thrumming in my ears. "Yes, I love that we're friends – and I never wanna lose that – but I'm fucking tired of pretending that it's not *you* I wish I was going to bed with every night. And that it's not *you* I wish was texting me about our plans for the night. And that it's not *you* I wish was sitting across from me at some fancy smacy wine place talking about how Harmony read her first book to me all by herself-"

"Brown Bear, Brown Bear, What Do You See?"

"Ohmygod, you remember?!"

The bashful beam I was thinking about earlier makes an unexpected appearance. "Of course, I remember, sweetheart. I

236

remember everything that matters to you. You're my-" His mouth abruptly makes the same motion mine made earlier.

Excitement and hope push my bare feet across the floor a couple steps in desperation to eventually close the gap between us. *"You're what, Archer?"*

He slowly shakes his head, obviously fighting himself.

Fighting the situation.

"Say it!" I command like on a stomp of the foot. "Say what I am!"

"You're fucking *mine* is what you are," the man I'm crazy about begrudgingly professes. "And you belong with me. And you belong in my goddamn arms. And the fact you went out with some other asshole last night is shit that should've never happened and probably would've never happened if I wasn't so fucking chicken shit about just telling you how I feel."

Gotta play it cool.

Gotta play it cool, Jaye.

Keep reminding me of that!

My toes impatiently drum the floor beneath me. "Which is?"
237

"I want the same shit you do, Jaye."

Yes! Yes! Yes!

"But…"

No! No! No!

"I don't wanna risk the first *real* friend I've had since Hiltz and St. Clair died." Another slow headshake occurs. "Losing you…losing what we have if things didn't work out the way we think they might…It's not something I think I could survive."

My heart pounds harsher against my ribcage causing my argument to be airy, "Yeah, well, I don't think I can survive *not* taking that risk when I know we both want more."

His stare retreats from mine, dropping to his sock covered feet.

Realizing what I've done, how far I've pushed, how right yet incredibly wrong I was leads to me briefly shutting my eyes again. I squeeze them tight to banish the idea of crying from a different type of lost love and stomp down the lump of sadness swelling in my throat.

We both knew the shit was a long shot. It's fine. It'll be fine. I'll cry into a book in the bubble bath later and um…I don't know. Guess give Dr. Perfect a chance? I've already done the whole significant other who works too much thing. It'll be like riding a bike. Hm. Perhaps I'll pick out Duck on a Bike for him to add to his collection on our next date.

"I'm being dramatic," I mutter to myself, opening my eyes, although I don't meet his. "Forget I said anything. Let's just um…Let's just go back to-"

Warm lips are unexpectedly smashed on mine exchanging whatever the end of the sentence was planned to be for a soft whimper. The impact alone is moan worthy, yet the first swipe of his tongue against mine has me practically muffled screaming. Instead of focusing on getting it together and acting as though I've been kissed before – because I really have been – I lose myself to the aggressive strokes. Clutch onto the edge of his tee and succumb to the desperate and wild whirling. Surrender to the way one large palm is wrapped possessively around the nape of my neck while the other is helping itself to a handful of my ass. My body is pitilessly pulled to him and pinned there as I'm redirected backwards towards the island where our coffee mugs are waiting to be filled. Bumping into the edge should break his hold; however, the opposite occurs. It deepens. His mouth…*my mouth*…both open wider and grow more determined to devour the other. To taste every single drop, we've denied ourselves to have for weeks. In spite of logically knowing we should slow things down, I hastily do the opposite. I chase his restless tongue around. Instantly submit whenever it demands. Whine when it draws away. Allow the hand cupping my backside to slide down the side of my thigh and hoist that leg around him. Wetness steadily soaks the thin fabric of my pajama bottoms pushing me to grind myself against him and wordlessly beg to have them be yanked down.

Turned around.

Taken from behind – a position that I've never experienced but wanted to.

Two fingers curl around the edge of his sleep pants prompting him to pull back and pant, "*Wait.*"

Is he serious right now? I'm wetter than a fucking Slip 'N Slide, and he wants to stop?!

Through chopped breathing, I ask, "Did I do something wrong?"

"*Fuck. No.*" A small nip is stolen of my bottom lip. "Sweetheart, you and wrong don't even belong in the same goddamn sentence."

I smirk and prepare to tip my lips back towards his.

"No." The word sounds as painful leaving his lips as it does hitting my ears. "We gotta stop."

"But we just started."

"Yeah, but if I don't walk the fuck away right now and go take a cold shower, the only mission on my mind will be doing everything possible to have you coming from this moment until first

240

thing tomorrow, and I only say that because I know we gotta stop for me to make you coffee and you to go to work."

Holy shit, talk about endurance! Can my nether regions handle that? Can yours?!

I poorly swallow the urge to whimper over the idea of a sex-filled day. "And that's *bad*?"

A fierce, sexual groan I absolutely need to hear more of instantly falls from his mouth. "Not bad, sweetheart." His mouth lightly teases mine. "So far from fucking bad." Before my tongue can successfully touch his, he adds, "Now's just not the time."

My pussy clenches in objection.

Outrage.

Mutiny.

Not pouting suddenly becomes the most impossible action I can think of. "Don't I get a say in that?!"

Archer's answer is smug and blunt. "*No.*"

The squeak of irritation that escapes receives an arrogant chortle alongside the lowering of my leg. More salacious snickers slip loose as that same hand gently glides itself up the back of my thigh to settle comfortably on my cheek once more. I immediately beam brighter at the cupping and bite my bottom lip in anticipation for what's next.

Archer's other hand relocates itself to my hip. "Where does my girlfriend wanna go for our first date?"

His simple question attached to a loving smile render me momentarily speechless.

Is this really happening?! Is this actually real? Is this a dream?! Fuck me, is this like one of those books where everything gets really amazing and then you turn the page to find the whole thing was a hallucination?! I hate that shit. I really do.

"Keep in mind, I've only got like forty bucks," he playfully informs, "and that you gotta drive until I get my license." Laughter leaves us both, yet it's him who speaks again. "Is it just me or did that shit sound very broke guy junior promish?"

Loud giggles flood the kitchen at the same time I wrap my arms around his frame. "Broke or not I'd let you take me to prom."

Archer coyly smiles.

"Where'd you get forty bucks?" I curiously inquire.

"The neighbor across the street, Ada, gave me a couple twenties for returning her cat that got into our garage while I was tossing the empty paint cans. I told her it wasn't necessary, but she basically started to cry when I refused."

Grinning widely can't be helped. "I love hearing you say *our*."

Another sheepish smile precedes his next statement. "I don't love only having forty bucks to take you out."

"You don't have to ever have *any* money to 'take me out', Archer. Us going out like a couple is all I really want."

"I got that, sweetheart; however, it doesn't change the fact I *want* to pay for shit. For you. For me. For *us. Our home.*"

More urgency to get him into bed is ignited, yet I ignore it to provide the comfort he needs. "One bite at a time, remember?"

I'm given a slow nod in return.

"How about I make us some coffee and breakfast and we can spitball ideas for what to do *after* the dreaded DMV and cellphone store?"

Archer settles both his hands at the small of my back. "Counteroffer. *I* make us coffee. *I* make us breakfast. And *I* talk you out of this cellphone nonsense before we discuss our date."

"Declined."

He struggles not to laugh at the retort. "Can I at least make coffee?" His grip grows unexpectedly tighter. "I really like making it for you every morning."

Swooning can't be denied, and neither can his request. "Dibs on the Bookdragon mug."

The corner of his lip kicks upward in a playful fashion. "Only because you're my girlfriend."

Giggles immediately fill the air, increasing in frequency courtesy of a chaste kiss and a gentle pat to the ass.

I love the way that label sounds. And something tells me I'm gonna love the way it feels even more.

Chapter 13

Archer

The DMV is awful, but at least I get my license out of it. Paper for the time being yet knowing it'll be mailed to Jaye's house – *our house* – does fill me with a sense of…belonging. Having a place in this world again. And that is something I haven't felt in far too long.

Between you and me, not completely comfortable calling it our house. Come on. Yeah, I live there and I fix shit and change shit and organize shit, but that doesn't make it part mine, right? What? Why are you agreeing with her?

The cell store is somehow *worse* than the fucking DMV. I'm not entirely sure if it's because they seem extra smug when using tech terms, I'm unfamiliar with or because my girlfriend and I – fuck, I can't believe I have a girlfriend again – not so quietly won't stop arguing about my need for a stupid phone.

Do I need one? No. If she needs to reach me, she can call the house phone or email me on the tablet she's practically given me. If there's an emergency the landline works just fine. Would it be nice to text her or get texts? Sure. But it's not fucking necessary no matter how hard she pouts that it is.

Leaving the store with the cheapest smart phone possible is the best compromise we manage to reach. She hates that it's not something more recent while I hate having anything at all. We're both unhappy; however, we're still relieved the other person is somewhat satisfied.

Paying for an early dinner from Piggy Bank, a bacon themed food truck, and eating at a nearby picnic table lifts my spirits back the level they were before all the errands began. The ability to be able to buy her a meal – just one fucking meal – feels like a medal of honor has been pinned to my chest. Like an accommodation from the highest powers has been given. Maybe I can't take her to fancy fucking wine bars or high-priced steak dinners, but I can do *something*. And being able to do something beats the fuck out of being able to do nothing.

I'll look into other neighborhood shit to make a few quick bucks here and there while waiting for a real job to pan out. Walk dogs. Rake leaves. Build birdhouses. Whatever. Whatever it takes to start financially contributing to this relationship, I'll do it. And let me just say one more time, fuck...I can't believe how good it feels to be in one.

Sharing an ice cream swirl cone on our way to a local bookstore wipes out the last of my funds, which leads to Jaye insisting she'll cover whatever we decide to buy in the shop, swearing she doesn't mind.

She loves purchasing books.

For her.

For the students.

For random literary charities.

246

Me.

I hate that she spends her money on me. I really fucking do, but yeah, I like getting to pick what I read versus just what others don't. Doesn't matter to me if it's new or used. It's just so fucking nice to choose to read a mystery or fantasy or a sports scandal.

As we prepare to enter Crack That bookstore – located in Highland's very trendy Cloud District – I momentarily halt our movements to inquire about the place next door. "Have you ever eaten there?"

Jaye's head tilts up to read the quirky Little Soup of Horrors sign to herself. "That's a negative." She swings her stare back my direction. "Chris was *really* picky about his soup. Taste. Texture. *Temperature.* I learned *pretty early on* to just avoid places where that was the only thing they served."

I slowly nod my understanding prior to asking, "Do *you* like soup?"

Confusion crinkles her brow.

It shouldn't.

It was a simple fucking question.

I didn't ask her to solve a calculus equation.

Fuck, I didn't even ask if chowder is technically a soup, a definition challenge that would excite her because words always do.

No.

I merely asked did she like a certain food.

Something I know no one else has probably asked her.

It irks me that no one seems to put the time in to get to know this woman.

Almost as much as it pisses me off that she's let herself just become a compilation of other people's preferences over the years.

The *real* Jaye, though?

The one that eats Skittles in the color of the rainbow and belts Gym Class Heroes songs while folding laundry and tries not to cry every time she watches – or rereads – *A Walk to Remember* is the person I've come to know and fall for against my more responsible judgement.

There's just something about her that does that to me.

Makes me forget that I'm less of a man than others.

Less of an unworthy human.

And learning everything I can about the real version of *that woman*…that curly haired, smells like cookie dough, brown skinned female is my main mission in life.

And I don't plan to fail it.

Or her.

Ever.

We clear?

"Sweetheart, I'm not asking for the ingredients to your *favorite* soup – however, I am open to making it for you if you like." The offering shifts a smile back onto her face. "I was just trying to see if you liked soup at all."

She drops her hands onto her thick, off-white sweater dress covered hips on a loud hum. "I guess I don't really know anymore. It's been so long since I've had any. Dad prefers chowders because they're thicker and heartier and have more meat, but Mom rarely ever makes those, and I honestly can't remember the last time she even thought about making soup."

"Maybe we could try that place on one of our future dates?" The question is followed by my hand finding hers. "You know when I can afford a bowl."

Jaye sweetly smiles and gently tugs us towards our actual destination. "We'll start a list of places to go together and keep it on the fridge." I'm shot a sweetly scolding expressing. "And who will be picking up the tab for those dates will *not* be included."

Inside the bookstore, we're immediately given a warm, loud welcoming. The people behind the counter enthusiastically yell, "Crack That!" and those in the store shopping happily reply "Spine".

Did not expect that shit.

Jaye giddily giggles as she leads me to the right, the direction of children's books according to the dangling from the ceiling street style sign. "I fucking *love* this place. The energy. The excitement. That *smell*." She suddenly sucks in a giant gulp of air. "Plus, they have the largest section of diverse books – for both kids and adults – in the entire city. This is my go-to choice for every specialty topic that comes up. Whether I'm looking for books to acknowledge or celebrate the differences in cultures or how families are shaped or built or even something emotionally specific like building self-esteem – shout out to *Giraffe's Can't Dance* for assisting in that one – *this* place is perfect. They have a whole team of buyers who *specifically* aim to keeping the shelves stocked with more than just 'basic mainstream' shit for both children and adults."

Fuck. Me. Is there anything sexier than listening to her excitedly go off about something? Nah, I don't think she's rambling. I just think she's passionate.

250

"I'm sold." The grin that grows on my face is bright and genuine. "Show me around, sweetheart."

Correct choice of words I guess given the way I'm instantly rewarded with a hot, sloppy kiss that makes walking around the kids' section a bit awkward for the first two minutes.

Jaye ardently points out the different sections, pulls various random books to browse, asks my opinion, and slowly turns me into a walking bookshelf as she stacks new "must-haves" for her personal collection as much as the school.

Eventually, we escape the jungle themed area to explore the next which is the hobby section. Its décor is tailored to that of a workshop, and to my surprise, I rather like it. We discuss different types of hobbies; however, instead of focusing on the ones we know the other likes, we search for ones that perhaps we don't, leading to Jaye adding a book about Toy Voyaging for her and Upcycling for me.

Before I can be guided elsewhere, I swing back by the front to grab an actual basket and meet her in the romance section making sure to steer clear of the War & Military section on the way there. The whole territory is bright and bold. Decorated with zebra print and tiger stripes and random lip stick kisses – both stickers and painted on. Oversized chairs and beanbags are available for lounging, creating a come one, come all and stay vibe, yet it's the way that my girlfriend is mindlessly stacking everything that catches her attention for longer than a minute that draws me in. Rushes me to her side. Assists in stacking the books carefully inside.

Guilt grows in her gaze after she glances at the growing amount of materials we've collected. "Maybe we should go to a section *you* like now? I think we've got me covered."

"Sweetheart, if you wanna keep shopping for books for *you*, keep shopping for books for you. We've got all the time in the world."

"We really do," she swiftly coos. "They don't close until midnight – unless of course they're hosting a book slumber party. They even play the chime that Cinderella rushes away to in the movie to let you know they're closed."

"Did you say a book slumber party?"

Her head frantically bobs. "I've never been, but I *so* wanna go!"

"We'll add that to the list then."

Jaye squeaks in joy, plants another kiss on my lips that has me having to hide my hard on with the cart, and leads us away from the romance section after snatching up two more books. Browsing the classics section is followed by thumbing through a few in the fiction section; however, the minute she makes an attempt to pull me into the area I want to avoid, I suggest we check out mystery. Suspense. Distract her with questions about nonfiction novels and hone our attention there. Under her insistence, I add a couple of sports history reads by Jeff Pearlman and encourage us to check before she can redirect us to the area that I'm anxious to evade.

It isn't until we're back in the car that she actively decides to investigate what I thought I was being sly about. "Do you always avoid military related things?"

Keeping my stare on the process of fastening my seatbelt becomes my primary goal.

"I noticed you wouldn't look at *any* books related to the subject. And I started thinking about it a little harder only to realize you always change the channel if something comes on or leave the room if the show focuses on it for too long. You don't even display your dog tags despite the fact you now have a place to."

"Why would I want another reminder of the horrific shit I've seen, done, survived, and am constantly haunted by?"

My eyes lift just in time to see her lips pull to one side on a tiny head bob of comprehension. "It wasn't *all* bad, was it? I mean…why cover yourself in tattoos of something awful?"

The innocence in her tone defuses some of the tension in my system. "No, Jaye. It wasn't *all* bad. I got a lot of shit out the military I didn't even know I needed." She begins to smile prompting me to stop it. "But for everything it gave, it took twice as fucking much." Her expression falls once more, and a heavy sigh precedes me ending the subject. "Can we let this shit go?" Jaye's mouth twitches to argue, forcing me to quietly beg, "*Please.*"

At that, she sweetly nods.

253

Starts the car.

Plants a hand supportively on my leg once we're out of the parking lot.

Maybe I'm an asshole for how I handled that shit, but I don't care. I don't wanna talk about it. I don't…need to talk about it. And if we talk about it then the chances of a fucking episode arriving increase rather than decrease, which is the wrong goddamn direction. Especially in a new relationship. She doesn't need to be reminded that I'm damaged goods. That's the last shit she needs.

Our drive home is thankfully smooth. We sing along to classic rock, and she tells me little stories about bonding with her dad over certain bands. Bringing him up always fills her with happiness yet diving into anything related to her mother, a bit of sadness.

Not really sure why their relationship is so strained, but I get the feeling nothing Jaye does is ever good enough for the woman.

Once we're home, I announce that I will be unloading our goodies all by myself and for her to get inside where it's warm. Jaye decides that means to not only change into her pajamas but prep the couch for TV time. Ignoring Mrs. Prescott's suspicious peeking through her blinds is ten times easier when I know that the woman of my dreams is waiting for me braless in a thin lavender sleep top and matching short shorts.

Our haul is left in the entryway – per my girlfriend's command – for proper sorting tomorrow, and I don't bother putting up a fuss about it.

The sleep pants she first gave me are the ones I definitely wear the most and seem to be perfect for our first night on the couch as more than housemates.

More than *friends*.

Fuck. Me. Remind me to take this shit slow. Yeah, we sort of passed go, collected our two hundred dollars, and went straight to buying property on Boardwalk, but I know physically speaking we should pace ourselves. She hasn't been with anyone since Chris – a little fact she let slip out on accident about two weeks into our situation – while I haven't been with anyone since pre-physical therapy which means I've been celibate even longer than her. I'm way out of fucking practice. And her finding that out on our first official night together isn't exactly something I want. Understood?

Stretching ourselves out lengthwise to fit side by side lying down on the purple couch requires the removal of the back cushions yet the instant it's done, getting comfortable under a shared blanket is effortless. Jaye's soft, curvy, figure curls itself against me so that her ass is pressed to my front, leaving me with no choice but to chomp down on my inner cheek to keep all the groans it conjures up inside. I do my best to focus on the show *Unbreakable* that we started binging together a week ago instead of how tiny the shorts are that she's wearing.

How I can pinpoint exactly where they stop.

Her bare ass starts.

Yeah. Bare ass as in she's not wearing any fucking panties.

I force myself to zone in on the TV screen rather than how the palm of my hand is resting comfortably on the smooth skin of her stomach with hers lingering on top of it. "All his training looks so fucking real."

"According to an interview the author did in regard to the show, the guy that plays the main character, actually *does* train like an MMA fighter, to stay in shape *and* in character."

Smiling over the trivial bit of information can't be helped.

"*And* the author worked one on one with each of them to *really* develop their characters wanting them to be as close to the book as possible."

"Do you think they are?"

"So. Fucking. Close," Jaye squeals and wiggles in excitement.

Yeah. Don't fucking need those wiggles. Not now. Not if my dick is ever going to go down again.

All of a sudden, the worst possible thing begins to happen on the huge screen.

In fucking stereo.

You've got to be fucking kidding.

Slowly, the MMA fighter whose name I can't remember now for the fucking life of me, starts to fingerbang the very girl he's been trying to resist since the show started.

Why is the fucking series mocking me?! What type of bullshit is this?! Did I do something to deserve having to suffer through watching the very thing my hand is breaking itself not to fucking do?!

Jaye follows that surprise with one of her own. She begins to grind her ass slowly against my cock back and forth.

Back and forth.

Back and forth.

The motions alone are enough to get me groaning but hearing her breath become choppy each time she brushes my shaft has me airily huffing.

Burying myself in the crook of her neck to grumble for mercy.

Permission.

Both.

The weak whisper of my name damn near causes me to come in my shorts. *"Archer..."*

"Yeah, Jaye?"

A breathless whimper escapes as she angles her head over her shoulder to face me.

Relocating my lips to hers is done like an automatic response that can't be stopped. Determined to capture that deliciously maddening sound, determined to suck it straight out of her into me like it's the only thing that's going to keep me alive, has my tongue roughly rolling around hers, searching every inch of her mouth for where that cock-swelling sound could be hiding. More muffled moans encourage me to dive deeper. Search harder for the sources to the audible treasure. Momentarily disregard the way her legs are parting. Thighs spreading. Hand guiding mine lower.

The instant my finger skims the outside of her bare pussy, my mouth fumbles from hers to confess, "Once I start, sweetheart, I won't stop until you fucking finish."

She heavily pants against my lips in response.

"And you know I'm a man of my word."

Her hips anxiously rise leaving no reason to further deny myself.

Fighting my instincts to rush through the moment requires strength I didn't even know I fucking had. The determination to give Jaye the best experience possible works double time to override the selfish nature that's tempting me to skip exploring and get straight to handing out orgasms. Allowing my fingers to gently brush the outskirts of her wet, lower lips, tracing them, teasing them, taunting them, receives hitches in her breath.

Trembles her thighs.

Causes her to grab a handful of my tee shirt and tug me closer.

Gliding the edge of my finger around her clit in gradual circles is done next and thankfully, the response is even better than before.

Those hitches become huffs of need.

Those trembles transpose to couch shaking shudders.

And the tugs at my shirt transform into untamed scratches attached to desperate pleas, *"More, baby."*

Whatever gentleman code of honor I was following is hastily tossed out the window. Dipping one finger into her soaking wet heaven elicits a loud whimper of my name but replacing one with two and curling them in tandem receives the type of moan I thought people had to pay to fucking hear. Withdrawing the dripping digits, just to harshly thrust them back inside, results in my girlfriend's head dipping backwards.

Her back arching like its possessed.

Pussy thrumming in warning that it's unprepared for whatever I'm capable of.

I repeat the motion again and again and again, growing more barbaric with each passing pump. Her slick muscles ceaselessly swell, sucking the pair in deeper, wildly riding them while my thumb brazenly works the slippery nub in desperate need of rubbing. I fight the urge to bury my face in her neck knowing that I don't want to miss a single sexual offering being submitted to me yet can't stop the craving to mark the exposed skin.

Leave behind a bite.

A hickey.

Anything that will remind her when she looks in the mirror of what our first night together was like.

Being driven by the desperation increases my speed.

Intensity.

Has me fucking her like it's my cock as opposed to my hand and her throwing herself into every thrust like an untamed creature begging to broken.

Wanting – fuck that – *needing* to see the sight has me growling closer to her ear, "Let me see you come for me, sweetheart." I give her clit the slightest bit of extra pressure. "*Show me that fucking pussy's mine now.*"

There's no holding her orgasm at bay any longer. Jaye explodes on a sharp curse and shoots upward towards the ceiling. Her muscles pulsate uncontrollably, striving to sever my fingers from the rest of my hand, while her voice quivers like every euphoric shiver is happening on a sexual sob. The combinations of feeling and seeing and hearing and fuck, even smelling, her undoing, the undoing *I* caused, the undoing *she* begged me for, has my balls tightening to the point of pain.

No. No fucking way. I'm not gonna bust a nut in my shorts from watching my girlfriend come. I fucking refuse.

Jaye struggles to catch her breath and bearing, and I arrogantly watch.

Relish in the fact I'm the reason her eyes are still hooded.

Her body still twitchy to even the gentlest touch.

Carefully removing my fingers is followed by slipping them into my mouth to taste my reward.

Her brown eyes suddenly widen in surprise yet rather than investigate the response, I simply allow her the opportunity to observe. Study the way my tongue works around them and sucks. I let her get lost in the fantasies her mind can conjure while creating my own to jerk it to later.

Just because she got hers doesn't mean I have to get mine. I've never been that prick.

The freedom from my clutches makes it easier for her to roll over.

Face me.

Wrap an unexpected hand around my cock and purr, "*My turn.*"

On the other hand, if she's willing to offer, who I am turn her down? What kind of shitty boyfriend would I be? However, now that we're here, let's just pray that I last longer than thirty seconds. What? I told you it's been a really, really *long fucking time...*

262

Chapter 14

Jaye

You know I've always read in books and seen on TV that the first part of relationships is all about sex and talking and sex and talking and more sex; however, in my personal experience, that's never quite been the case. Even when I first started dating Chris there wasn't exactly an abundance of either. There was some talking but very little sex. We were together for three months before I finally just took the initiative to make it happen. I know. Very unlike me. But what can I say a girl has needs, too! He had a whole could take it or leave view on sex, which was interesting to me. And let me just stop you there. No. Chris wasn't secretly gay. He just...didn't see the high and mighty appeal of sex. At all. His focus was typically on making money or getting to people who could make him more money or his mini constructed cities. Sex was more like trips to the gym. He did it. He enjoyed it while he was there. Yet he didn't go out of his way to add it to his schedule if it didn't fit. I kind of think living in that *frame of mind is why I'm hesitant to take the plunge with Archer. I mean what if it wasn't Chris, ya know? What if it's just me? What if men just don't like sex* with *me? Chris wasn't the first to not be that into me, but in my defense, the one before him* was *gay, and the one fling I had during that summer of high school to college was a virgin too, so his overenthusiasm could've just been chalked up to that. My point is...it's been about two weeks since we first got handsy – literally – and I'm a bit nervous about his feelings changing if we start adding mouths or connecting bodies to bodies, if you catch the scene I'm typing. Right now? The man is like a fiend. One touch or rub in a naughty way, and I'm the only thing he's focused on doing until I'm screaming to the high heavens and shaking like a wet poodle in winter. I don't want that to change. You think it will?*

Archer's teeth gently scrape the side of my neck as I remove the last treat from the baking sheet. I thoughtlessly moan and melt against his flannel shirt covered front, eyes shutting on instinct. My boyfriend delivers a tiny nip to my ear prior to whispering, "I know you taste better than those cookies, sweetheart."

The smallest smirk slips onto my lips.

"You sure we don't have time for me to have you while those cool?"

I could make time...No. Wait. Wrong thing to say!

I let my hungry gaze find his over my shoulder. "Not unless you want my dad sending a squad car by the house to commandeer these."

My boyfriend backs down with a small chuckle. "I don't think that would win me any points in the Lieutenant's file."

"What makes you think he has a file about you?"

The sarcastic expression I'm shot receives a loud giggle. "Good point. But it's probably pretty empty since he still doesn't have more than just a few basics."

Not for lack of trying though.

265

"Why don't you go put your shoes on while I package these up and then we can get going?"

He offers me a warm grin at the same time he untangles his frame from mine leaving me feeling emptier than expected. "I hope you're prepared to lose, sweetheart. I used to be a bowling *king.* All balls bowed down to me."

"I don't think that sounds nearly as intimidating as you think it does."

Archer immediately frowns and leans his frame against the edge of the island.

"Go finish getting dressed, *Lord of the Balls.*" It's impossible not to snicker. "It'll only take me a couple to finish up here."

"*Lord of the Flies* is actually one of my favorite classics."

"That shit was so dark."

"Yet such a fucking amazing allegory. One that's sadly always been relative to my life."

The pain in the statement hits like a ton of bricks to my stomach.

Do you have any idea how heartbreaking that is?

"I like that it's okay to tell you that." Archer offers me a half-hearted smile. "I also like that you've read it, so I don't have to spend forty-five minutes explaining it to you like other people I've met."

Grinning is naturally done. "Typically it's *me* who is explaining to *you* books for forty-five minutes."

His hand waivers from side to side. "We're getting to a point where we spend more time *discussing* rather than explaining."

I mindlessly coo, "God, I love that."

"I love that, too." He tosses me a wink and slowly backs out of the room, not breaking eye contact until he absolutely must.

I also love him, but I am not dumb enough to admit that out loud. At least not yet. Probably not until after we've had sex, right? No. Wait. I don't wanna be one of those women that says I love you after sex like she equates love to sex. Ugh. Why is being in a relationship so complex?! And why didn't I face any of this shit with someone I was **engaged** *to?!*

After boxing up the white chocolate, cranberry cookies, dropping off a batch around the corner to Mrs. Tippet – who asked for some at the last HOA meeting *and* hired Archer to help in disassembling as well as assembling a new bookshelf she had delivered for her husband for an anniversary gift – and delivering the

267

remaining amount to the precinct to assist in distracting Dad from prying further into my love life, the two of us finally begin our Saturday date night out.

*We're open to going out any day of the week – perk of being the only one who has to go in to work each morning – however, unless it's dinner or the bookstore, we typically save "big outings" for Saturdays since Sundays typically consist of running errands – gym, grocery store, hardware store – or making appointments – like the physical exam we fought about him having and my routine eye appointment that became **our** routine eye appointment. What?! He needs his checkups. Yes, I'm aware he's not a cocker spaniel. And I'm not dealing with him like a fucking pet. I'm treating him like a man I give a shit about and just need to know he's okay. Inside and out.*

Archer treats us to grilled sandwiches from Mo's Mo's – using the cash he earned from Mrs. Tippet – before we head on over to Pick a Lane, the new car themed, eighteen and up only, bowling alley.

Due to it being Saturday night, there's a small wait, which prompts the two of us to hang out in the bar area while we wait.

We try to keep the mood light but my habit of wondering out loud if they're hiring sparks the unpleasant argument that we don't have to get him an application from every place we visit.

Apparently, that's patronizing rather than helpful?

To my surprise, a very unexpected face drops by our table, beam just as bright as ever, when it interrupts the bickering. "Lovely library lady."

Archer's arm protectively flexes around my shoulder at the same time I greet him, "McCoy."

"You know they don't have books here, right?" He good-naturedly jabs.

"Give me ten minutes, and I bet I could prove you wrong."

Laughter escapes us both while my boyfriend shifts around uncomfortable in the booth seat beside me.

Ohmygod, is he...jealous? Is that what a jealous boyfriend does? I mean I've read that this is what he does, but I didn't think it happened in real life!

As if he's noticed, my co-worker extends an open palm toward the man beside me. "McCoy."

Archer immediately grips the hand tight. Shakes. "Cox."

Okay, so do men just not use their first names with each other?

"Nice to finally meet the reason my favorite librarian's been smiling a shit ton lately."

"McCoy!"

Archer arrogantly chuckles, kicks his chin a little higher, casually confesses. "She's the reason I smile a shit ton, too."

McCoy adjusts his backwards black baseball cap on a cocky smirk. "Yeah, my girl does that to me. I get it."

"Is that what you're doing here?" I interrupt, cheeks so red I look like a zit that needs to be popped. "Who you're meeting?"

"Nah," he casually brushes off, "otherwise I'd call her over. Have us all hang out. She likes you." His grin grows wider. "You speak her language."

"Classic lit?"

"That too." He rolls his baby blue eyes in a familiar fashion. "I meant cop dad."

The grin on my face thoughtlessly grows wider. "Right! Her dad's The Commissioner where you guys are from."

"You're dating a cop's daughter, too?" Archer slyly joins the conversation. "Got any tips?"

270

His mouth cringes prior to answering. "None that are probably useful to your situation."

Wonder what he means by that.

"Anyway, I'm here to cash in a favor." His eyes cut the direction behind us. "And I see favor has just arrived." The mischievous smirk he lets slip into place is both sexy and unsettling. "You two have fun." He gives me a playful wink. "Private bathrooms are in the back if you wanna have *too much* fun."

More redness explodes in my expression, yet Archer merely chuckles.

Public sex?! Did he really just suggest public sex?! Is that something a lot of people do?! Do you? Have you? Should I?

The question leaves my mouth before I can stop it. "Have you ever done that?"

Archer quirks an eyebrow in question at me as he reaches for his beer. "Care to be more specific?"

"Bathroom sex. Or public sex? Or sex in a public bathroom?"

Rather than bring his mug to his lips he pauses to reply. "Yes."

"To which one."

"All."

An unexpected wave of jealousy washes over me that I know I have no business feeling.

He's allowed to have a past…I logically know this. Illogically hate it.

"Sweetheart," he begins, gently nudging my arm for my eyes to return to his, "don't start planning for battles that there's no need to fight. We have enough."

The statement pulls my lips to one side in hopes of keeping my composure.

"You wanna know about my exes, I'll be an open book, but if you're looking at the shit that happened between me and them like a research guide, don't waste your energy. What *we* have can't compare. Fuck, Jaye, our relationship isn't even in the same *section* of Crack That as the bullshit I've had in the past."

There's no stopping my gray sweater covered shoulders from relaxing.

"Roger that?"

"Roger that."

"Good." He leans over to let his tongue momentarily dip into my mouth, slide aggressively across mine, only pulling back once he's successfully made me whimper. "Now, tell me more about McCoy. He's the in-house paint guy?"

Explaining McCoy's position at the school naturally leads to us discussing what's been going on during the week. We chit-chat about some of the pending school events including my ideas for the next month's book club but cease the conversation when our buzzer summons us over to our lane.

From Archer's very first turn, it's clear I'm in trouble.

Nothing slows the man down.

Not the godawful shoes – that only I seem to be slipping in.

Not the easy to be distracted by music – kudos to them for finding so many songs that are "car" related.

And not even his limp that had been hurting him so bad last night he had to soak it in my master bath's tub.

Loved that we got bubbles everywhere. Didn't love mopping them up.

Another successful spare occurs prompting my boyfriend to throw his hands in the air and smugly state, "King of the balls!"

Pressing my lips tightly together is done to hold in my giggles.

"Fuck, yeah, I hear it." His open mouth laughing encourages my own. "It sounds better in my head."

"I go through *that* shit all the time."

More snickers slip from him at the same time he flops into the space next to me. "I love hearing whatever you have to say." His arm stretches back around my seat while the pins are being restacked. "No matter how weird or accidentally pornographic it may sound."

Our additional laughs are suddenly overpowered by the evening DJ making an announcement. "Let's do a disco minute! Everyone up on your feet for this next one!"

The main lights immediately lower to allow disco strobes to begin right before the unforgettable notes to "Car Wash" by Rose Royce flood the speakers. Excitement to get up and groove with the rest of the crowd that's already clapping along, however, only lasts for a split second.

Seeing Archer's head twitching to the left, over and over and over again as though trying to be taken away by something redirects all of my attention.

My focus.

Knowing this is an episode or about to be an episode pushes me to act yet being unfamiliar with what to do in the situation leaves me hesitant.

So much of the material I have read is contradicting. Some insists you let the moment just play out and be there for them when they snap back. Others swear that trying to pull them out before they get in too deep is better. And then there are the ones that say its harmful to make a generalization versus playing to an individual's need. Yeah. See! I don't know exactly what I'm supposed to listen to and since he refuses to see a therapist or go to group therapy – both of which could possibly give us tips – I feel like my cluelessness will continue on.

Unusual coughing and gasping ensue pushing me to do the only thing that makes sense to me.

What worked the last time we were here?

I cautiously state, "*Jaye is now.*"

The simple statement seems to cut through the fog.

275

Momentarily stop the twitching.

The choking.

My hand gently lands on his leg next and his slams down on top of it in a way that indicates he's not sure if I'm a friend or foe, in the past or present. *"Sweetheart is now."*

"Sweetheart," he murmurs, grip transitioning to loving. *"Sweetheart..."*

"Sweetheart is now, Archer."

"Archer..." Echoing his name is followed a long, deep breath. "Hiltz was then."

"Sweetheart is now."

"St. Clair was then."

"Sweetheart is now."

"That mission was *then*."

"Bowling is *now*."

"*Bowling is now*," Archer repeats during a frantic head nod. "*Bowling is now*." The bobbing motion continues alongside a slow rock that I simply gently stroke his leg through. Eventually, his green eyes locate my brown informing me he's back in the present yet the sadness that's glazed over them screams shame. "I'm sorry. I'm sorry for embarrassing you like this. I'm sorry you can't take me places without worrying about this shit. I'm sorry I'm-"

My fingers pinch his jaw in a loving, firm fashion. "*Enough.*"

He immediately stops.

Seals his lips.

Shrinks into himself.

"I am *not* ashamed of you or these moments. I'm not *scared* of you or these moments. What I worry about is you never *healing* from them. And you not getting the help you *need* for them. And as much as I wish I knew what they were about, what you were reliving, I know you'll tell me when you're ready. And just so you know, whenever that is, *I* am ready. Just like I'm ready to be there for you as you tell a doctor about your limp and your nightmares and whatever else they need to know for your quality of life to continue to improve."

Archer's head slowly shakes at the same time he airily croaks, "Why won't you give up on me?"

"You don't give up on people you care about."

277

Tears fill his eyes forcing them to briefly close. It takes what feels like lifetimes for them to finally open and meet mine once more. "The last mission I served killed everyone on my team except me."

There's no catching the gasp that leaves my lips.

"*Yeah*." Archer's jaw trembles as he lets his head fall forward as though facing me during his recounting is too painful. "It was a simple order. Clear the area. Get in. Get out. Retrieve the target."

Desperation to hear more pushes me closer.

Has my hand tightening tighter in support.

"We knew they used women and children as decoys. We'd been briefed numerous times on the subject, but that little girl didn't *look* like a threat. And I know what to look for in a fucking threat. I've been trained on that my entire life. From my father to predators in foster homes to the asshole you run into getting a slushie at the gas station. I *know* what a threat looks like, Jaye. And unlike the women we had sent out of the area, she didn't look suspicious." His eyes cut up to mine. "She looked genuinely *scared*. Fucking terrified to be in the middle of a fucking combat zone." Regret or remorse clogs his vocal cords. "There was...a bright flash. Then another. Quick. One right after another."

The rapid lights that trigger him.

278

"They were blinding and the bang that followed deafening." More head shakes arrive. "I don't *consciously* remember much more after that. I know there were bullets flying. I know it was hard for us to find cover. I can practically still hear the screaming and see my best friend bleeding out while I did the same."

"Ohmygod!"

"I don't really know how I survived. Fuck, the rescue team didn't either when they finally arrived on the scene." A slow, shaky break is expelled. "I had a severe concussion. Memory loss. Cuts. Bruises. A broken finger. Fucked up knees. And some shrapnel in my leg. I was furthest from both blasts but not completely out of the radius. And you know how that happened? Because instead of being in the front with my boys, my best fucking friends, my goddamn brothers, I was in the back. Concerned about our six. Concerned about that child that I didn't want to die from a stray gun shot." His jaw trembles, and I can't stop myself from reaching out to cup it for just a second. "From *my* gun shot."

"Baby..."

"I had to look Hiltz's pregnant wife in her face when she came begging for answers, pounding on my door to know what happened and tell her more than the bullshit classified line I was instructed to. And as if the dying howls of her husband I had somehow crawled closer to weren't enough, I then had to live with *those* nightmarish cries. Listening to her blame me. Saying it should've been me instead. Swearing to me I'd never see my goddaughter again – which I haven't."

279

"She was just…grieving."

One shoulder slightly bounces. "And if all that shit wasn't enough, mental and physical therapy sucked every dime out of me that I had. Turns out that wasn't very much because the chick I had been calling my girlfriend while on duty had replaced me with some bartending asshole and *wiped my account* damn near clean."

"Bitch!"

"One minute I'm just trying to learn basic functions again, and the next I'm out on my ass because I'm lost in a fucking jungle of paperwork with no guide, no mercy, no fucking clue how to get the help it's obvious I need. I don't have any money. I don't have any family. I don't have any ties. I don't have anywhere to go because all the programs designed to supposedly help men like me require more hoops for you to jump through than the fucking Olympics." Resentment suddenly rages through his stare. "I gave my goddamn life for this fucking country. For these…fucking people who make more money than God by exploiting our vulnerabilities, our need to fucking belong, our need to *contribute* to society yet when the tables are turned, when its *us* who need *them,* they can't fucking give back? They can't – *at the very fucking least* – help make the process of getting vets the assistance they need *less* complicated or have *less pitfalls* for us to fall into? They can't help us from becoming just one more case number in an endless line in their flawed fucked up system? Can't they see we really need fucking help?" Ignoring the tears on his cheeks is impossible. "Can't they show a little more…fucking compassion?" Hearing his sniffle has my hand leaning over to wipe them away. *"Like you did, sweetheart."*

Heated hatred promptly fades into pure anguish of a broken man.

Geez, I can't blame him for being the withdrawn and grumpy type knowing that. Can you?

Once his face has been rid of the clearly unwanted tears, I quietly state, "Maybe having the compassion of *one* can be enough to help you let go of not having the compassion of *many*."

"*Maybe.*"

I run my hand slowly over until our fingers can fold together. "You don't have to keep fighting by yourself. Not the memories. Not the emotions. Not the paperwork. None of it. We'll eat the elephant together, baby. One bite at a time." The expression on my face softens. "You're not alone anymore, Archer. I'm here for you. Day and night. And you know what? I'm not going anywhere."

He squeezes my hand but doesn't say another word.

Honestly, I don't need him to. As long as he heard me, that's what matters. I was already determined to prove that I can be here for him; however, now that I know just how deep he really needs someone, I plan to double my efforts. Show him the world isn't just the cruel place he's come to know. Like I said. We'll take everything on together. *Day by day. Nibble by nibble.*

Chapter 15

Archer

I make my last trek to the recycle bin for the night, thankful that this part of my project is finally fucking over.

Don't get me wrong. I love renovating this house – our house – but putting together Jaye's fancy fucking weird shaped desk for her new home office was a goddamn nightmare. So many little pieces. So many strangely shaped parts. Oh, and the fact some asshole forgot to pack a set of English directions for the fucking thing didn't help either. Watching tutorial videos on YouTube from my phone was somehow both helpful and infuriating. Maybe because I didn't think the stupid thing should've been so complicated or maybe because the dude was drinking a beer while he did it like the shit was far from difficult.

Letting the last of the boxes fall to my feet while I open the gate to the area occurs at the same time that I hear a door slam shut from the neighboring house. Training myself not to even look there wasn't exactly a hard habit to create; however, keeping my mouth shut during Mrs. Prescott's tangents regarding how useless I am and how my attending HOA meetings with my girlfriend is a disgrace to the entire community has been a whole other beast to battle.

And I don't wanna politely continue to eat that elephant. I wanna fucking scream at it. Put a mirror in its face. Show it where I can see the wrinkles and crows' feet and say some asshole shit like no wonder why your husband is fucking someone else.

Unusual feminine giggles have me cutting my gaze the direction I know to avoid just in time to see Mr. Prescott pull the blonde-haired woman by her barely covered ass against him. "Come on, Justine. Don't be pissed at me. I brought you here, didn't I?"

Justine dramatically pouts on a bounce that jiggles the tiny tits spilling out of her corset top. "You told me we could stay."

"I know, Ju Ju," he tucks a strand of hair behind her ear, "but Gwenith is coming back from her mother's earlier than expected, so we can't."

See. I told you he was cheating.

Resuming my discarding of the trash unfortunately doesn't make it any more difficult to overhear their conversation.

"Then I wanna stay at The Frost Luxury Hotel."

I fold the boxes to fit better in the bin as he caves, "Whatever my little Ju Ju wants."

"Roses."

"Done."

"Champagne."

"Two bottles."

"Room service."

"We'll put it on the company card."

She squeaks in excitement prompting me to shake my head and work a little faster.

Why fucking cheat on your wife? Yeah, Mrs. Prescott is a raging bitch; however, there's no need to pretend to love her while banging someone else. I'll be the first one to say, I believe she deserves a lifetime of obnoxious podcasts about karma and a long overdue session in the self-help section of a bookstore but not this. No one deserves to be cheated on. Some people never come back from that shit. And some of us…well, for some of us, it takes a fucking miracle to heal. And I guess in a lot of ways that's exactly what Jaye is. My own little miracle.

Back inside the house, I wander towards the kitchen island where Jaye has been working on her children's book for most of the day since the office isn't quite ready yet.

She says no rush, but I want her to have a space that's hers to create in. I think she needs it more than she realizes. Before renovations and reorganizing, this place was Chris's house that his fiancée lived in when he wanted. Now? Now, it's beginning to look like a couple resides here. I've done everything I could not to have much of a say, yet Jaye refuses to accept 'whatever you want' as an

284

answer. The results? Copper style cookware. New shelves as well as hooks in the laundry room. And a new rug for reading on in front of the fireplace, which is something we'll probably do later tonight.

I brace one hand on the edge of the island and lean over to plant a supportive kiss on the exposed portion of her shoulder.

The action receives a hum of gratitude followed by another panic spiral I am assuming are just part of an artist's creative process. "Maybe I should do a book about owls? Or foxes? Those can't be that hard to draw, right? Maybe teeth? Should I do a tooth book? What about something involving doctors or the doctor's office? You know remind kids that the place isn't that scary? Oh! Oh! Maybe something about *therapy* offices?" She swiftly peers up at me. "You know there are a shit ton of children who have appointments there, too? Maybe it would be comforting to have a book on the subject to help the transition?"

Inching myself around so that we can be face to face, I ask, "You're still thinking about my appointment from earlier this week, aren't you?"

She poorly hides the truth in her expression. "No."

"*Jaye.*"

"Okay, kind of!"

Her outburst threatens to tug a smile to my lips.

285

"But I'm not worried about *you*."

The counter receives a sarcastic head tilt.

"*Fine*. I'm not worried *just* about you. I know your physical results weren't *stellar* but taking into consideration how you've been living for the past few years, I agree with Dr. Giambrone – and not just because she's my doctor too. Improvements to all your basics *will* happen due to your change in lifestyle – aka living with me – and the stress and strain on your leg will have a better chance to heal and be more manageable now that we have a physical therapy plan to begin."

Doctor's offices are one thing I didn't miss, and over the past few weeks, I've been to more than my fucking share. And you know what? It'd be nice to get a little credit where credit is due. I'm pretty fucking healthy, all shit considered. Plus, I'm disease free, which for the record is impressive shit considering the less than safe self-medicating methods I used in the beginning of my forced relocation for living.

"And I trust Dr. Giambrone's recommendation of Dr. McMahan who you seemed to have a good first session with! I have no doubt that the medication you've started to take will do its part in helping you with your condition, it's just that…"

Her trailed off statement has me gently nudging her with my foot. "Just that what, sweetheart?"

"It's just that…," the heavy sigh that escapes shakes her entire frame, "while I was in the waiting room I couldn't help but notice all the literature they had lying around for both adults *and* children. The way the practice is split to cater to both types of patients I think is brilliant, especially when both parents and kids need to go, but I kept thinking and wondering were there illustrated books on the subject to help the younger ones understand what therapy *is*. And why they shouldn't be afraid. And why talking about your feelings is okay. And why having feelings is okay. And that there doesn't have be to be a stigma around getting help. And how mental health matters no matter your age or financial state or race. I couldn't stop thinking about creating a fun, educational tool that projected these things in an easy way they could relate to that would also allow their parents to discuss it."

This time I let a small smile slide onto my expression. "You found inspiration while waiting for me."

"I mean…sort of?" Her awkward cringe I can't get enough of makes a predicted appearance. "I also got an idea while picking up your meds to do a book about pharmacist since there are a billion books on doctors, but I don't know. I just…shouldn't I *know* by now? What I wanna write?"

"Is this an actual question or are you being rhetorical?" My arms fold firmly across my Alice in Chains t-shirt we got from the thrift store last weekend. "You know I don't like not being able to distinguish the two. That's how I end up saying something fucked up. That's how I end up accidentally hurting you and you know how much I really fucking hate that."

My people skills are…improving; however, they're still not good enough to decipher if she really wants to know if something

287

looks good on her or if she's just brainstorming out loud and I should keep my mouth shut. Oh, don't give me that fucking look. She looked Tweety Bird in that sweater and not in a cute way. I didn't know I wasn't supposed to say that out loud!

Jaye sweetly beams up at me. *"Yes, Archer.* I would like some *actual* feedback right now. And preferably not from my mom because her texts about just giving up to take on another hobby are starting to sound really, *really* good to me."

For fucks sake, I swear that woman **lives** *to make her child a nervous wreck.*

"You're not a quitter, Jaye." The statement is given in a firm tone. "That's not who *you* are. And that's not the woman you ever wanna be, so first and fucking foremost, put that bullshit out of your mind."

She sheepishly nods.

"More importantly, stop putting so much pressure on yourself. You don't need it. This project is all about what *you* wanna contribute to the world of literature. A world *you* love. And however you *choose* to do that, with whatever topic you *choose* to put on paper, is going to be right because it's coming from a place of passion. Loyalty. Love."

Seeing the flicker of a smile pushes me to add more.

"I won't tell you what to write, sweetheart or what you 'should' be writing. I will simply support the notion of you doing it and give you useful feedback on what you create. From what I know…the more you ramble about something, the more passionate about it you tend to be. Maybe *that* should be your guiding light going forward."

My girlfriend takes a small bite out of her bottom lip while bouncing her head from side to side.

"And who knows. Perhaps having a real creative space to work on this book may help get the juices flowing."

"When you're around, they're always flowing."

The double pump of her eyebrows not only receives a chuckle, it causes my entire face to redden.

No, we're not fucking yet, but God do I love everything else we've been up to. I've been coming so often and so hard lately my balls literally ached. I was…lowkey grateful we had to pump the breaks for a couple days at the beginning of the week due to her period – which she insists means all of sexyland shuts down – because I needed the breather. Don't get me wrong. Finger fucking and mouth banging her until she's screaming my name at the top of her lungs are two of my favorite things in the entire world, but I've been out of the game a minute. I lack the fucking stamina I once had in the sack. Need to perfect that shit before we get into bed, you know? Plus…we're not really in a bed together. She has hers. I have mine. And when we sleep together, which is happening more and more often, it's done on the couch or the floor beside the couch. We should probably deal with our sleeping arrangements before our fucking ones, don't you think?

It takes an extra minute to battle away the heat in my cheeks. "Wanna come see your new desk?"

Excitement launches her out of her seat. "You're finished?!"

"*With that.*" Offering her an open palm is done at the same time I proclaim, "There's still a shit ton of things for me to do in there. Painting and building your desk were just the beginning."

And considering the fact that no one wants to fucking hire me, I welcome the project to keep me distracted from the bleak truth that I'm fucking hopeless. Not worth the goddamn ink I spill on the applications or paper they're printed on. I wish I could say some shit like this is all because I'm being picky about pay or position. I wish I fucking had that type of luxury. But I don't. I've applied for everything I possibly can from custodial staff at the gym to loading dock supervisor at Crack That. I haven't gotten a single. Fucking. Hit. Jaye keeps saying these things take time. Her fucking optimism is obnoxiously infectious. It's how we ended up living together in the first place, remember?

"I can't wait 'til it's totally complete!" She gleefully exclaims as though she didn't hear a word I said. "Can we paint quotes on the wall or is that too much? Should I go simpler? Maybe just *framed* quotes?" A large gasp escapes during our stepping into the entry way. "What about if I hire McCoy to come over and do an elaborate mural?! He does that type of shit on the side, you know."

"Can we hold off on contracting my *only* job out to another man for a little longer?" I playfully tease while we begin ascending the stairs. "Not sure my ego can survive that fucking hit."

My girlfriend giggles and squeezes my hand in support. "Whatever you do in there is going to be amazing. I just know it."

We slowly climb towards the top passing framed photos of us placed staggered on the wall.

Her idea. Which…I won't lie. I fucking love it. I love seeing photos of us together smiling or laughing or kissing whether I'm coming or going. I fucking love that our…relationship is the first thing you see when you step into our house. Our world. Our…sanctuary. Having our pictures on display proves that her saying this place is ours, isn't all talk. Jaye is definitely a woman not afraid of actions and as someone who isn't the best with words, I hope my own are reflecting my shared mindset. What I don't *love is the empty hook that's waiting for my dog tags. The last thing I want is that fucking haunting horror among my happier moments. She thinks they deserve respect and celebration despite the unfortunate circumstances while I'm not so quickly sold on that death before dishonor bullshit I once was.*

Our strolling down the opposite hall of my bathroom – fuck, I can hardly believe I have my own bathroom – exposes two different stacks of boxes for explaining. I start by pointing to the left. "Those are filled with Chris's personal belongings. Awards. Accommodations. Degrees. Framed milestones." My free finger is tossed the other direction. "Those are filled with supplies you might wanna look through for yourself or donate to a local school. Pens, paper, stationary, and equipment – like his fax machine, copier, computer monitors, ect."

291

As we creep closer to the room at a very slow pace, she inquires, "Did you find anything more personal? Like something I would wanna keep? Like old photos of us? Or a trinket that reminded him of me? Maybe the receipt I had framed from our first date? I have a box filled with that sort of stuff and just wanna make sure it all stays together."

Fuck me. This is uncomfortable.

I can barely keep my voice from straining itself during the answering. "No."

"Oh."

Fuck, that sound hurts.

And I'm not even the one who's clearly feeling discarded here.

Unsure of how to properly comfort Jaye about her dead fiancé who clearly didn't give a fuck about her like she believed he did, I do my best to force on a polite grin and redirect her attention to something more positive. "I really like the purple accent wall. Goes really well the gray."

Her warm smile returns yet is cut short by a huge gasp the instant we're in the room. "This place looks incredible!"

292

Grateful to have Jaye happy again, I release her hand to allow her the opportunity to freely explore the space. "You picked it."

"You painted it."

I casually cross over to the desk, the only piece of furniture in the room at this point and rest my ass on the edge.

"And you polished the floor." Her open palm dramatically slaps her chest. "Look at it! I can basically see myself in it."

The complimenting receives an amused headshake.

"You gonna do the lighting next?" She nonchalantly walks the space, fingers caressing territory I get the feeling she's never really been granted the chance to in the past. "You think the fixture I picked out will match or should we exchange it and get something different? Something louder? Bolder? More subtle?"

"I think you gotta trust that gut instinct of yours about shit *besides* people."

She sassily spins on her heels to shoot me a teasing glare.

"Now, what do you think of your desk?"

Jaye joyfully struts over, stare swiftly sweeping the strange piece of furniture, "It looks even better than it did on the display!"

Remind me to warn others that this fucking thing may look like a dream come true for the occupant but is a goddamn nightmare for the person building it.

Her fingertips lightly run the length of it while humming to herself. "I can't wait to pick out a chair."

"Can it be a little less complicated than the desk, please?"

She lightly snickers and while circling around to check out the drawers on the other side. Her scrutinizing suddenly comes to a stop, informing me she found the small surprise I left inside the top one. Rather than immediately remove the framed photo of the two of us, she simply meets my gaze. "How did you get this?"

"I know how to use our printer."

Swinging my frame around to the other side, I allow mirth to linger in my tone. "Mrs. Buckley – the world-renowned oboist that lives a couple blocks over – saw me coming back from the mailbox on Thursday and asked could I help her out with walking her poodles because the dogwalker had unexpectedly called in sick, and they wouldn't stop barking long enough for her to practice and she *really* needed to practice." An innocent shoulder bounces my shoulders. "She needed help, so I helped. She gave me some cash – in spite of my insistence I didn't need it, that I was just trying to be a good neighbor – and I used it to buy the frame. There's a corner store at the opposite end from our pizza place, so on Friday after you left for work, I walked there, picked out the nicest one I could, walked

294

home, and put the surprise together *before* I started touch up painting."

Her entire body seems to puddle at the explanation.

"You can um…put a different picture in there if you want." Slightly uncomfortable with the overwhelmed expression of adoration she's bearing, pushes me to bashfully look at my feet. "I just uh…it's the one that's the background on your phone and *my phone* and I guess I just assumed you really liked that picture, but whatever. It's up to you. Change it if you want. Or don't. Or-"

Lips become unsuspectingly smashed against mine ceasing the spiral I had started.

What can I say? She's not the only one who sometimes fucking rambles.

Jaye pulls back after a single swipe of her tongue to whisper, "It's perfect."

The corners of my lips curl upward in pride.

"*Thank you.*"

My mouth moves to say the appropriate response yet is pounced once more. Distracted by the haste of the slippery muscle that's gliding around territory meant for only it, I struggle to register Jaye's hand curling around the edge of my sweats.

My boxers.

I don't even realize what's happening until she's lowering in tandem with them.

Cool air caresses my cock causing my balls to momentarily constrict; however, the warm, wet confines of her eager mouth waste no time creating a different type of contraction. Her right hand curls around my shaft to assist in the process of working me from base to tip and the combination of the two has my bare toes crossing one other in content. Each savage suck has her slipping further and further and further down my dick until her hand sinks itself to my balls to gently squeeze while her throat takes over the job of stroking me. Gagging sounds bounce from wall to wall, worrying me that it's too much, pushing me to wind my fingers through her curls to yank her off, encouraging me to remind her she doesn't have to go so deep, but just as those things begin, Jaye tugs my balls and drives my cock a little deeper.

Proves she can handle more than I believe.

More than I'm ready to believe.

Spit leaks past the corners of her mouth, dribbles along the edges of my dick, and drips down into the palm of her hand where it's immediately smeared along my sac. Watching her head bob around steadily grows damn near impossible for me as my own lolls back, lost in the knee wobbling swallowing I know I can't take too much more of.

"*Jaye...,*" seeps out like a warning at the same time I curl my fingers around the edge of her desk.

Instead of heeding the announcement, she propels herself to the brink.

Chokes.

Forces herself to endure every.

Last.

Inch.

The heat of her exhaling while struggling to stay still effortlessly becomes my undoing on a barked curse. "*Fuck!*"

Scorching hot, short bursts splash themselves in the deepest depths of her throat only to be swiftly slopped down. Gorged on like some new fucking cookie flavor that she perfected yet doesn't plan on sharing with anyone else.

Aches rip through my legs, extra agony in the damaged area demanding I adjust my weight and commanding we rearrange before new destruction can be done but ignoring it to watch the prideful way my girlfriend guides herself off my softening cock is so worth it.

Jaye delivers an additional roll of her tongue around my sensitive tip prior to arrogantly humming. "Guess I'm getting better at that, huh?"

One hand abandons the desk to lovingly cup her cheek. "Sweetheart, you've never been *bad* at that."

"You know I haven't had a lot of practice."

"You blow me practically every other day. Anymore practice and I don't know that I'll have the strength to keep working on renovations."

She girlishly giggles on an eye roll.

Not exactly exaggerating. The chick likes to give head, and she's really fucking good at it. How Chris didn't appreciate this shit or cash in on it more often is a mind fuck I'm still trying to figure out. Was he secretly gay? Even if he was, gay guys still like to get their dicks touched, so...what the fuck was his deal?

"How about I get dinner started?" Jaye beats me to the punch of pulling my pants and boxers back up. "Feed you something tastier than cock?"

"Is there anything tastier than your cock?" she salaciously flirts, stealing a stroke over my now in place sweats.

"*You*," I hungrily retort and drift my fingers away from the desk to graze her clothes-covered pussy. "In fact, why don't I have *my dinner* while you decide what you want for yours?"

The mixture of a moan and whimper is promptly muffled out by my mouth latching itself back onto hers.

If you'll excuse me. I have a little unfinished business to get through before we inevitably cave and order delivery. Huh. Maybe we'll play that game where I see how many times, I can make her come on the stairs while waiting for it to get here. She really loves that one. And I'm grateful as fuck that I'm the only man she'll ever play it with.

Chapter 16

Jaye

"Isn't Daffy just as cute as a button?" Mom shoves her cellphone across the table my direction. "Just look at how precious she is with that big bow on her head."

Is that big ass red thing to distract us from the fact she looks like a baby Elmer Fudd or that her nickname is almost as bad as her actual name, Daffodil. You heard me correct. She's named after a flower while her mother is named after a color. Vyolet. Oh, the dad? Cedar. And the grandmother, who is in my mother's cooking club? Ruby. Nope. Not making this shit up. Although, part of me wishes I was. I'm struggling with character names for my book.

"I can't wait to have grandkids," she coos, pulling the device back to her to stare at it further. "And to be the one to show off *their* pictures at cooking club."

Yes. Cooking club. She's not really the type to play Bridge – she prefers Spades – or knitting – needs her hands nimble and uninjured for surgery – however, her, Chris's mother, Caroline, and a few other women they've collected from other social events, started their own cooking club. One woman hosts and cooks, the others eat and take the recipes they love. Always changing. It happens about once a month, and they pick the monthly type of cuisine out of a cookie jar. Yes. An actual cookie jar meant for storing cookies not paper. Have I gone? I actively try to find every excuse in the book to not go. You think my mom's bad without an audience? Get her in front of those Golden Girls inspired personalities and suddenly, she's one thick mustache away from becoming Belle's father from Beauty & The Beast, open to the idea of letting me live locked away with a werewolf man for all of eternity as long as it means she gets grandkids. What? Of course, I know that wasn't exactly how the story went. I was being dramatic for entertainment's sake. No reason we both have to be bored to tears listening to stories about kids I'll probably only see once a year at guilt-trip forced functions.

"Ruby mentioned that Vyolet and Cedar were looking into the private academy where you work yet couldn't even get on the schedule for an appointment to tour it for four months," Mom states in what can only be labeled as disbelief. "I didn't realize your school was so prestigious."

How could she miss that information that I've given to her every time we have an argument about what I do for a living?

"Do you think you could possibly get them in sooner?" She optimistically asks.

Picking out the green onions from the teriyaki chicken bowl she learned at club this week is done at the same time I answer, "No."

"Why not?"

All of sudden, Dad's bowl slides across the table to crash into mine. When I glance up in confusion, he points with his fork to relocate the little green irritants into his food rather than the tiny pile I started on my napkin.

"Because I don't have that kind of pull, Mom." I slowly begin to drop the round pieces into their new home. "And besides, Presley runs shit pretty fairly as opposed to favoritism among families, so if there's no room on the schedule for a few months, that really means there's no room on the schedule, not that she's using it like a power play. There's a reason some people start trying to get their kid enrolled before they're even pregnant. Employees are the only exception to that and even then, you're not *guaranteed* a spot, just more likely if you're open to signing a longer employment contract."

The huff that comes out of her is not only loud but aggressive. "*What* are you doing?"

She receives a questioning glance from me.

"With your food, Jaye."

"Removing the green onions."

"I can see that," she snips in a snarky fashion and picks up her wine glass. "*Why?*"

"I don't like them."

"That's new," my mother insists on a small sip.

"It's not." Resuming clearing away the last two pieces is followed by me announcing, "I've never liked green onions or chives."

Dad pulls his bowl back to himself. "I fucking love 'em."

He's offered a smile that's unfortunately cut short by a loud sigh from his wife. "If you don't like them, why have you always eaten them?"

Valid question.

And for the first time I can recall, I'm okay being honest.

"Because I have people pleasing problem."

Her eyes as well as Dad's widen.

"Instead of doing things that please *me*, I have a habit of doing things that please *others*, so that I don't upset anyone because I don't *like* upsetting people. And I don't want people to *not* like me. However, I am learning – with some emotional support and a couple of self-help books – that it's really okay to not be the book everyone wants on their shelf. That's it okay to write or *rewrite* the details on my own pages."

Dad's grin grows impressed on a slow head nod, filling me with excitement, yet the look of almost horror in my mother's swiftly kills it.

Probably shouldn't have said that, huh?

"Isn't being emotionally healthy one of the ways to prevent emotional eating?" I casually point out to defuse her shock. "And you're always telling me that the reason you think I eat so many cookies is because you think I'm unhappy, so really, this is the type of progress you *want* for me, right?"

The proclamation shakes lose her momentary stone like state. "You're right."

"And I have been eating less cookies." A forkful of food soars towards my lips. "But baking about the same."

"Who's eating my cookies then?" Dad curiously pokes on a quirked eyebrow.

I know what he's doing. I know exactly what he's doing. However, I...I don't know that I should tell them. I mean maybe? Is the right time to announce not only do I have a boyfriend but he's living with me and has been living with me for months? Should I wait?

"I can tell you for a fact it isn't Dmitri." Mom's gaze forcefully latches onto mine. "What exactly happened? You kept brushing off the subject when I asked for more details. I think now is a good time for them. I mean he seemed so *devastated* that you two never went on a second date."

304

"*Devastated*," Dad dramatically echoes, chuckling to himself afterward.

Holding back a smirk requires skill.

See why I love him.

"Was he too pushy? Too brainy? Too self-assured? You know there's nothing wrong with a man who has confidence, Jaye."

Archer has confidence. He just also…has insecurities. Like me.

"He just…wasn't…the right…*person*."

Okay, Jaye. Now. Now is the time to tell them.

"You're never gonna *find* the right person at the rate you're dating," my mother berates causing me to shrink down into my seat.

"*Mags*," Dad promptly scolds, "that's enough."

Both our sets of eyes swing to him.

"Whatever *dude* our daughter invites into her life and falls in love with will be done at the speed and pacing that's best for *her*.

305

And what's best for her may not be what you *think* is best for her. Just like me wanting to do a background check on the *dude* which I *know* is best for her, might not be what she *thinks* is best for her."

Yeah, I see what he did there. All *of what he did there.*

"Since when do you say dude?" Mom scoffs in obvious disgust. "Is that new, young detective with the Mahershala Ali *True Detective* style rubbing off of on you?"

His eyes hit the ceiling on a slow headshake of astonishment regarding her takeaway from the statement.

He should really know better by now. I mean...he is married to her.

"And now that we're on the subject of detectives," Dad sighs, stare falling back to me, "I grabbed you some of the old training manuals for reference purposes like you asked. They're on my desk in the study."

Excitement immediately tears through my expression. "Thank you! The kids – both the younger ones and older ones – *love* real life examples versus just props or toys. It encourages a more realistic connection between what they're learning and how it relates to the real world."

Both of my parents smile warmly.

Thankfully, the conversation that proceeds focuses less on my dating life directly – or what my mother believes to be lack thereof – and more on it *indirectly*. They ask about the progress of my home office – something I evidently should've had a long time ago – yet in doing so they seem to have difference stances on the subject with Dad believing I have every right to commandeer a space that once belonged to Chris and Mom appalled, I would be so disrespectful to him like that. As if the discussion isn't awkward enough, it only grows more so when I let it slip that I've been thinking about offering Chris's parents the model cities he built to have more room for other projects in the garage.

Archer has totally gotten into upcycling and creating recycled art! He's come up with some really interesting pieces – including the owls that are on display on our bookshelf in the living room – and the therapist believes that the creative outlet will be good for him as well. His sessions right now are twice a week, which is more than he wants – and why I don't push harder on group therapy – but they're what he needs. And Presley has been so incredibly understanding about me taking a longer lunch break one day a week to get him to and from his appointment. Part of me wonders if maybe she gets it on a more personal level.

Dinner doesn't end well, nor do I get enough to eat. Temptation to stop for something fast is strong but getting home to the man I haven't seen all day due to leaving early for an employee meeting is definitely stronger.

The moment my two feet cross the threshold into our house, Archer warmly shouts from the other room, "Welcome home, sweetheart!"

I silently swoon to myself over the greeting at the same time I drop my workbag on the floor.

Every night. This is how he greets me. Every. Night. Maybe that's not wild or crazy to you but considering Chris usually just mustered up a smile – especially if he was working on his models – I find this amazing.

"Hey!" I call back on my way to the kitchen. Once I'm there, seeing him look over from where he's lounging in front of a roaring fire fills me with relief, I'm not sure I could find anywhere else. "Nice fire."

Warmth floods his green gaze as he rises to his feet to come my direction. "Today's supposedly the last cold night of spring, so I figured why not try the reassociation assignment, I *know* Dr. McMahan is gonna ask if I've done tomorrow."

Nodding at his point is followed by me leaning against the edge of the island. "Where'd you get wood?"

"Oh, sweetheart, thanks to you, I've always got wood."

His eyebrow waggle successfully sparks a toothy smile.

"Did you mean for the fireplace?"

He arrives directly in front of me at the same time I reply, "I did."

"It's one of those magic log things." Archer delivers a sweet, chaste kiss to my lips. "Ran into Dane on my way back from getting the mail. Got to talking. Told me he was gonna light a fire and roast marshmallows with his kids since it's his weekend. I asked if he had an extra one that I could have, and he did."

"Dane?"

"The recently divorced guy that lives next door to Ada. You know the one Mrs. Prescott *swears* watches her out his window during her morning jogs."

"The Marine."

"Yeah, the jarhead."

"Why'd he put his head in a jar?!"

"You just don't know *any* military nicknames?" Archer can't stop himself from chuckling. "You're honestly telling me they don't use *any* in the romance books you read?"

"They probably do, and I just don't remember." Knowing better than to linger on the subject for too long, I make my way over to where we keep the bread. "And since we're on the subject of reading-"

"Aren't we always?"

"What were *you* reading when I walked in?"

"The book club pick for the month."

"Have I mentioned how much I love that you read those even though you don't attend?"

"You have," he playfully grins, "but I'm always open to hearing how you love the things I do."

This wiggle of the eyebrows receives a giggle.

"Finished listening to the audio book about Gretzky while installing shelves earlier, so I figured it was a good time to start *The Girl on the Train*. I know you're dying to talk about it."

"*Ohmygod, I am.*" My overdramatic gushing is accompanied by me grabbing the unopened loaf from its counter space. "We can start discussing what you know and how far you are while I make myself a sandwich."

His brow instantly crinkles in confusion. "Didn't you just come from dinner with your parents?"

"I went to dinner there." The confirmation is given on a fake, chipper grin. "Yes."

"Was there...food?"

Tossing the bread on the island happens on my way to grab other ingredients. "Yes."

"Was it edible?"

"Actually, yes." My hand wraps around the fridge door handle yet rather than pull I meet his stare. "Minus the green onions."

"You hate those as much as you hate chives."

See. He knows me.

"Could you not pick around them?"

"Oh, I did."

"And then what happened?"

"The Spanish Inquisition."

His wince is expected.

"It started with my feelings *on* green onions and continued into my dating life, my house choices, and of course couldn't end without discussing my physical changes. Although, she did compliment my skin as glowing right before she told me how *Humpty Frumpty* I look in this polka dot top."

"Do *you* like the shirt?"

"I did until she said that."

"Come on, Jaye. We've talked about this. If *you* like what you're wearing, if *you* feel comfortable or sexy in it, that's all that fucking matters, sweetheart. Your confidence starts with you."

It's impossible not to let my body slump at the reminder.

"And what's she asking about your dating life? If we're still together?"

This isn't about to go well, is it?

My lack of retorting causes him to fold his arms across his chest at the same time he states, "She doesn't know we're a couple."

Guilt convinces me to abandon the fridge and face him.

312

"Does she know that I live here?"

More shame scrunches my face.

"Does she know that I exist at all?"

Remorse barely has time to drop my jaw before he's seethingly asking, "Does your dad?"

"He definitely knows you exist!"

"That I live here?"

"I think he...*suspects* that you still live in the garage."

"Does he know that we're fucking dating?"

"Again...he has his *suspicions*, but I have neither confirmed nor denied them."

My word choice appears to be the wrong one by the way his eyes narrow. "You haven't *confirmed* nor denied them." He takes a long, slow agonizing lick of his lips. "Roger that."

Shit.

"Archer-"

"It's fine." The icy exterior I loathe slides into place as he begins to back up towards the living room. "I'm gonna go put out the fire and head to bed early. I know you like for us to hit the gym before therapy when the schedule allows."

"Arch-"

"Enjoy your sandwich. There's an extra thing of mustard in the pantry if you need it."

I'm not given the chance to say anything else to his face, and I have an inkling of my own that his glorious ass doesn't listen nearly that well.

I mean...I wanna take a moment to appreciate how round and firm it is in those jeans, but I know now is not the time. However, I wish it was. Fooling around on a Friday night sounds way better than fighting.

Following out of the room, I meekly suggest, "Can we please talk about this?"

"There's nothing to talk about."

"Except there is."

"There isn't."

"There is."

"There isn't."

"Damn it, Archer!" My body rushes around to block his ability to kill the fire. "Don't do this."

His stoic expression continues weighing down the butterflies in my stomach that I miss floating. "Do what?"

"Shutdown."

The lack of a rebuttal has me finding the backbone I need to get better about having.

"We *rarely* fight. I mean *actually* fight. And whenever we do, *you* do this shit. You get upset or mad or pissed off, stuff it all down, swallow your tongue, and then just fucking *bail*. Why?! Is it because you think I can't handle having an adult fucking argument or do you think I'm gonna kick you out for not being a 'yes man'? Or is it something totally off the wall I don't understand but want to?"

It's his turn to have culpability claim his stare.

"Which is it, Archer? What's the reason you're afraid to fight with me?"

"I…" One hand snakes around the back of his neck to squeeze. "I…" The shoulder shrug that follows is clumsy. "I'm not fucking *afraid* to fight with you, Jaye. I just don't like to do it. I don't like seeing that look on your face. I don't like feeling like an asshole. I don't like thinking that the woman I love now hates me because I said some stupid shit in an argument when I could've done the right shit which was walk away until we were both more level fucking headed."

Did he say…love? Did you hear that? Did I hallucinate that? Is this a lack of food hallucination again?

"But you wanna fucking fight, sweetheart? Fine. Let's fight."

Instantly regretting that choice of words.

"How the fuck could you not tell them about us?" He folds his arms protectively across his chest once more. "And *why* haven't you?"

Guilt settles back into my expression.

"Give me a bullshit excuse that I can poke holes in. Tell me it's because you don't see them very often when you never see them less than three times a week. Tell me it's because it hasn't come up in a conversation, when your mother clearly brought it up tonight, giving you an opportunity to tell her that you don't *need* to be fucking set up anymore! That you have a man in your life that gives you the shit you need! No, I don't have a fucking sportscar – or any car for that matter – and I can't give you diamonds for our fucking anniversaries and have to put up birdhouses in the Brandts fucking backyard to earn a few bucks just to buy you a salted caramel mocha on a Sunday, but I am fucking *here* for you! I am here for everything you fucking need!"

"You are!"

"Then why the fuck are you so ashamed of me?!"

"I'm not ashamed of you!"

"Then why the fuck am I this dirty little secret?!"

"Because you're mine!"

The shouted answer causes bewilderment to bulldoze his face.

"Because I know the *second* they fucking know, you're not just mine anymore, Archer. Our relationship isn't just *ours*. It's then up for discussion every…fucking…time…I see her. And she'll nitpick. And then scold but think that she's helping. And then she'll start in on the when are you proposing, when are we getting married, when will she *finally* have a grandchild of her own. Me not telling her has *nothing* to do with you and *everything* to do with not wanting to put myself through more of that bullshit."

"And your dad?"

"Background checks. We're talking more than just the basic running your name through a database. He'll look up phone records. Medical records. Tax information. Ex-girlfriends – or in that one case ex-wife. Insurance reports. And this is all before he quizzes *you* like you're in an interrogation room for the first-degree felony of dating his only daughter."

A hint of terror flashes in his green gaze.

"Yeah, I love my dad – like totally daddy's girl, you know this – but the man gets *a lot* overprotective when I'm serious with someone. The fact he hasn't done any of those things yet is a miracle. We're talking *real growth.*"

The corner of Archer's lip twitches like it wants to smile. "You're sure them not knowing about us has nothing to do with the facts that I'm homeless, jobless, and mentally unstable?"

"You are *not* homeless." My arms wind around his midsection. "You are *not* jobless." I let my fingers fold at the small of his back. "And no one in my family is mentally stable – self included – so you fit right in."

Laughter bounces his body, frame thankfully melting under my grasp.

"I love you, too, Archer. And if telling my parents is that important to you-"

"*It is.*"

"Then we can have them over for dinner on Sunday and tell them. You can cook – demonstrating to my mother what a keeper you are – and then show my dad around at all the shit you've fixed or installed. I'll make arrangements tomorrow while you're in with Dr. McMahan." He lets his hands run the length of my arms until I unwrap myself for our hands to connect. "I'm *proud* to have someone like you in my life, baby. *Never. Doubt. That.*"

Archer leans in closer and sweetly whispers, "And you never doubt that I love you."

Feeling the warmth in my stomach spread pushes to me challenge, "Then *make* love to me."

The unexpected declaration drops his jaw.

"Right here..." I gently tug him towards the couch. "*Right now.*"

Seeing an argument forming in his expression prompts me to pounce his parted lips. Roll my tongue around his. Detach one of my hands to caress the outside of his cock over his jeans.

All it takes is a harder grab to get him pulling away on a groan, "*Fuck, sweetheart.* It's been a *long* time. I'm don't know if I can give you the slow, gentle bullshit you're asking for."

"The only thing I'm asking for, Archer, is that you do everything possible to have me coming from this moment until first thing tomorrow, and I only say that because I know we gotta stop for you to make us coffee and you to go to therapy."

Having his own words tossed back at him works better than I hoped.

We go from standing to lying down only a smidge faster than we go from being clothed to naked. Torrid, teeth filled kisses are scattered across both sides of my elongated neck along with deep, guttural groans that mercilessly vibrate my entire body. Pleasure from the pain and pressure continuously curls my figure up to his. My hardened nipples repeatedly crash against his chest, needily moaning louder during each collision. Cries grow deafening for *more* contact. For the *right* contact. I wind my toned legs around his hips and use my ankles to encourage him to go where I want him rather than to keep prolonging the inevitable.

A light nip to my earlobe is delivered prior to Archer cockily teasing, "Can't wait any longer, can you, sweetheart?"

The pout he's presented quickly melts into a new round of moans as he languorously drags his tongue lower. Watching him taste every inch he crosses is delicious but the sensation that spreads through me like wildfire when he latches his teeth onto my nipple and tugs is infinitely more delectable. Within seconds, both of his hands join in on the intoxicating assault, caressing and cupping and

320

feeding him the dark points one right after another until they're eventually pushed into one soft, squished mess that allows his tongue to lick each one during its every thrash. Wetness wastes no time soaking my lower lips under the ceaseless teasing and being already brought to the edge before he's even touched me where I need it most leads me to making feral noises, I didn't even know I was capable of.

Finally satiated with his lecherous tormenting, Archer braces himself above me with one hand and uses the other to roughly part my wobbly legs. No warning or extra taunting is given. He simply thrusts himself inside and tries to keep a groan trapped behind gritted teeth. His sound restraint is met by my sopping wet muscles clenching in objection. Commanding he release the noise I want to hear, the one that will make them grow even more slippery.

My boyfriend's body bucks forward, his dropped low, stare planted on the area he's marking.

Carving.

Scribbling his signature on to make his.

"Fuuucckkkk, that feels amazing." A dark, sinful huff thoughtlessly slips past his lips on a growled announcement, "It's never felt this goddamn good before."

There's no stopping my figure from arching upward at the praise or my pussy from clamping down in agreement of the proclamation.

It hasn't.

Is that because we waited so long?

Or because we waited until we said I love you?

Archer promptly relocates the pad of his thumb to my slippery clit and gradually begins to roll it around. Hitches in my breath not only summon his hooded stare to mine but encourage him to push hard. Move it faster while increasing the speed of his thrusting to match. Over and over and over again, his long, thick cock, savagely tears through the tightness, sculpting the soaked territory into something that's his.

Belongs to him and only him.

Each time he dives deep, my hips hastily rush up to meet the action, wanting to welcome him to depths no one else has explored in ages. My heels rest on top of his firm ass, gently nudging in approval at first yet switch to a more aggressive nature when the whispers of an orgasm begin tickling my skin. Light taps transpose into unrestrained kicks that prompt him to pump faster.

More persistently.

He brutally pounds like the new missions are to break me and keep breaking me and never stop breaking me.

I allow my fingers to roam the defined biceps I've watched him build from our gym trips.

From building a life inside these walls for me.

Us.

I grant my nails permission to claw in ecstasy at his dark, thick locks, that recently got cut and steal the tiniest caresses of his stubble covered cheeks he keeps neatly shaped.

An orgasm ruthlessly rips through my system shaking my limbs, my voice, my damn soul, but the heaving from my other half never falters. He barbarically grunts and continues to thrust. Huffs and strokes his thumb quicker. Drops his forehead to rest against mine forcing me to feel each time he draws in a breath that's used to fuck me unrelentingly into our couch. Ceaseless cycles of pants and moans and screams cover us alongside sweat and stickiness. Our tongues randomly take swipes into one another's open mouths, both wanting to express our newly declared love as much as our insatiable hunger.

More body breaking shudders suddenly begin to splinter me; however, this time, Archer seems incapable of resisting them. The feeling of his balls tightening and dick swelling sends my grip to his shoulders, desperate for something to anchor onto as sweltering ropes of cum splash against the pulsating muscles. His groans overpower mine, convincing them to go airy, and push me into getting lost in the primitive symphony pouring past his bared teeth. I absorb his shakes. Greet them with my own. Embrace the way we're emotionally fusing as much as the ends of our orgasms are.

Unsteady breaths and feathery nuzzling are all we seem to be able to execute for the first few minutes. When I finally remember how to speak, my voice is a bit cracked and weak, "I think I'm broken."

"I'll fix you, sweetheart." Our noses lovingly brush together. "First, by feeding you." He presents a kiss to my left cheek. "Then by bathing you." Another loving press to the other side. "Last by reading to you." Archer shifts his gaze back to mine and showcases a wolfish grin. "And then I'll fucking break you. *All. Over. Again.*"

Why do I get the feeling this is about to be the longest, most incredible night of my life? Thank fuck tomorrow's Saturday. Because if it wasn't you better believe my ass would be calling in sick. Dflu aka dick flu. That's a thing. No? Well, it should be! What about insomnia? It would be okay to call in for that, right? Didn't get any sleep due to getting banged all night? Hm. Whatever. Thankfully, I don't have to come up with an excuse. At least…not yet.

Chapter 17

Archer

Greedy.

That's the word that sums me up perfectly now.

Rolling my sleepy girlfriend onto her stomach is as effortless as convincing her legs to widen for two fingers to slip inside from behind. She softly moans at the intrusion but doesn't resist. Doesn't demand more sleep, which we both need. Jaye simply lifts her knee a little higher and rocks with the motion, riding the two digits the same way, she loves to ride my dick. Feeling her grow wetter during every passing push causes my already hard shaft to swell to the point of pain. While it's not the easiest shit to ignore, I do it. I keep my focus on stretching her exhausted muscles, loosening them to a level where pleasure is all she'll feel. Letting my thumb tease her puckered hole she loves my tongue on instantly gets juices speedily and steadily spreading down to my wrist.

At that point, I replace my fingers with my cock, hands clutching her ass for support in the new position. Jaye's leg tumbles off the side of the couch, foot hitting the floor, and seeing her beautiful, curvy body splayed out for me like an offering fuels the ferociousness of my actions. Barbarously slamming deep, bounces her against the cushiony piece of furniture, but each hard hit leaves her toes with no choice but to claw the ground beneath them for leverage. My grip on her full cheeks harshens as her back bows on a breathy howl of my name. White-hot, wet heat swarms around my shaft, laving it from tip to base to balls, in thick creaminess that I hate myself for waiting so long to have.

The perpetual pumping of my dick is primitive.

Pitiless.

Pierces through the pulsations proclaiming she can't take much more to command that she does.

Demand that she takes my dick until I have no doubt she's completely satisfied.

Her orgasmic screams oscillate between being buried into the couch cushion and leaked into the room alongside each additional thrust that grinds her against the furniture. Knowing her clit is just out of my reach convinces me to slightly readjust so that every stroke I deliver causes the sensitive spot to brush against the sofa, assisting in the most boorish way possible. Jaye eagerly and needily throws her body into the hump movements, helping herself to another orgasm, proving she too is becoming greedy.

For me.

This.

One set of fingers abandons its post on her perfect ass to predatorily scrape up her spine and snatch a fist fill of her tangled curls. The snapping of her head backward frees a throaty moan and recalling that this position, this bestial claiming, is one she fantasized about for so long, a fantasy that only *I* will ever fulfill, prompts me to rapidly pound. And yank her into the hammering. Grunt and curse and hiss over the perfect fucking sound my balls make each time they slap her.

Her pussy screams match those escaping her lips severing any chance I have for lasting much longer. The overworked muscles swell around my shaft, trapping it deep, and unyieldingly milk from it every last drop of cum it can. Spurt upon spurt is swallowed and guzzled as though her body's still starving, desperate to be fed more of me despite the fact that's basically the only thing it's had all night.

Don't look at me like that. I did feed my woman! I'm a man of my word. I fed her, fucked her, bathed her, fucked her, read four pages of some smut novel, and fucked her again. My plan was executed...I just...had to rearrange it a bit.

Finally sated the two of us collapse not only back onto the couch but into each other's arms.

"Good morning, baby." Jaye sweetly hums, nestling herself against me. "Can we start every morning this way?"

Pride can't be prevented from plastering itself in my grin. "We *can*."

"Hot sex *and then* hot coffee."

I lightly chuckle over the statement. "It's a good plan, but you probably don't wanna go to work smelling like sex every morning, so how about hot sex, hot shower for you, and then hot coffee?"

She slowly nods during a loud nod. "Your plan is better."

My head tilts her direction, grateful to have her gaze meet mine shortly after. "How about we go another round in the shower, count *that* as our gym session, and then stop at Loca Mocha Casabloca on our way to therapy?"

Excitement bursts through Jaye's entire expression. "And *that* plan is better than the original." Love and mirth overwhelm it next. "How do you keep doing that? How are you even thinking right now?"

More arrogance coats my chortles. "Can you not? Have I *literally* fucked your brains out?"

"I think so."

This time we laugh together but unfortunately have it cut short by the doorbell.

"Wonder who that is," Jaye absentmindedly ponders while sitting up to get the pajamas she didn't spend much time in last night.

"Maybe Mrs. Tippet returning a cookie dish?"

My suggestion is met with another impressed hum. "That would make sense. She's usually up this early to go shopping for her bird."

"Mathew Macawnaughey."

We both grin at the terrible pun.

Yeah, alright. It's a little funny.

Once we're both properly dressed, we head for the door together, hands locked as if we're incapable of being parted for too long.

This is the first time I've ever been like this. Kind of worried I look too clingy. Kind of don't fucking care.

Jaye opens the door to reveal more than one surprise. The first is the sound of shouting coming from our least favorite neighbor and the second is her father.

Dressed completely in his lieutenant's uniform.

Hat included.

Fuck. Me. He looks like a hit man trying infiltrate a local precinct to take out a target. What? It doesn't matter that I read a book like that last week. It doesn't make the shit less true.

"Dad!" Jaye squeaks, body immediately flying away from mine to hug him.

"*Sugar.*" He uses his free hand to warmly embrace her, suspicious scowl shot my direction over her shoulder. When she pulls back, he playfully asks, "Gonna let me in? It's cold *and* loud out here."

The two of us step out of his way to allow him entry at the same time she asks, "Is that Gwenith?"

"The number one pain in the ass for the precinct *every* New Year's Eve?" Lieutenant Jenkins humorously nods. "That'd be her."

"Why's she yelling?"

"From the sounds of it, argument with her husband." He respectfully removes his hat from his head. "I heard what I believe to be glass shattering, so I went ahead and called it in. For *everyone's* safety."

She beams proudly up at him. "Of course, you did, Dad."

His stare cuts to me and rather than wait for his daughter to remember I'm present or that we haven't officially fucking met, I

330

push my shoulders back and extend an open palm his direction. "Lieutenant Jenkins, I'm Archer Cox."

"*Charles.*" He tucks the hat under his arm to shake my hand. "It's nice to *finally* meet you 'Pizza Dude', especially considering the fact you *live* with my little girl."

Our grips drop and so does my gaze to his cringing daughter. "I know I probably should've told you sooner, and I wanted to tell you sooner, but I didn't want you to do the thing where you start pulling his records-"

"And what? Discover that he spent a weekend in the drunk tank after a bar fight two years ago?"

"It was warmer than the street, sir."

His brown stare she obviously gets hers from lands on mine. "You were living on the street?"

"I was."

"Why not with family?"

"Orphaned and never adopted, sir."

"Friends?"

"Died in combat, sir."

"A shelter?"

"They were at capacity, sir."

"Can we maybe *stop* interrogating my boyfriend for a minute?" Jaye squeakily interjects. "You know the very thing I wanted to avoid, by *not* telling you sooner." His attention snaps back to his daughter prompting her to ask, "Not that I hate unannounced visits, but why the drop by? And in your uniform?" Her hands slam themselves on her hips in disapproval. "Did you wear this *just* to intimidate him?!"

Honestly not intimidated. Not by his outerwear anyway. The look of rage and murder lingering just on the other side of his gaze on the other hand, has me wishing we would've met in a public setting. With cameras. And witnesses.

"Lucky coincidence there." His grin is undeniably teasing. "I've got a charity event to attend this morning and wearing my uniform is required." Charles shifts his hat from one side to the other. "And I didn't drop by unannounced. I called. *Twice.* I also texted. Not receiving *any* sort of response from my daughter who is *always* up at this time, did have me nervous, but your mom insisted it was just the attire making me more suspicious." He casually extends the bundled objects in his hand towards her. "*This* is the reason I was stopping by. You forgot it after dinner, and I knew you needed it for work."

She winces again as she accepts the offering. "*Right...*The training manuals."

He slowly nods prior to sighing, "And I know dinner last night wasn't...*the best*...which is why you were in a rush to leave, which is also probably why you forgot them."

The books become cradled to her chest in a guilty fashion.

"What I wanna know is why didn't you tell us last night?" His set of questions hone in on her to both our surprises. "Why didn't you take the opportunity right then and there to come clean? To – at the very least – tell the two of us that you are involved with someone? I can understand not wanting to tell your mom right away that you were living together – which I want on record I *hate* you doing that without giving me the opportunity to properly meet-"

"You mean *grill*," Jaye sassily corrects.

"-*first* – but you should've said *something* to us. You're a grown ass woman, Jaye. You don't have to *hide* the individual you are involved with from us. That's disrespectful to *us* as well as him."

Holy. Fuck. I did not see this going that direction.

Suddenly, the heat of his glare is swung to me. "You have a shit ton to answer for too, grunt, but for now, I have a few things, I'd like to say to my daughter in *private*."

"Dad-"

"I understand, sir."

"Archer-"

"Sweetheart, you and your dad clearly need a minute." My eyes lock onto hers. "And I'm not about to let being with me *ruin* the relationship that's between the two of you anymore than it clearly already has."

"Arch-"

"It's fine. I'll make myself busy for a few, and when the two of you are ready for me be a part of the conversation, just holler." I do my best to offer her a small grin. "You know I'm not going anywhere. After all, this is my home too, remember?"

The words seem to be the right ones given the way her shoulders unglue themselves from her ears.

Rather than say anything else to Charles, I merely dismiss myself on a nod and retreat to the kitchen to start making coffee that we should probably have sooner rather than later.

Maybe he'll be impressed with my barista skills? Think that could win me some points? Oh. No. I did get an application from Loca Mocha Casabloca, but they wanted people with at least two years of experience in a professional capacity. Yeah. I haven't even been back to drinking the shit that long.

Their intense, increasingly loud conversation eventually migrates towards the living room encouraging me to take out the trash to continue to give them the space they need.

Outside – unluckily for me – isn't exactly less tense.

The cop car parked in front of Mrs. Prescott's house on its own is enough to fill me with dread; however, seeing the unpleasant side eye thrown my direction of the taller of the two officers immediately deepens it.

This isn't gonna be good.

My hand has barely touched the lid to our trash when Gwenith squawks, "Arrest him!"

I make the mistake of looking over again to catch her pointing a finger my direction.

"It's *his* trash! He's the one who's been trespassing!"

The dark-skinned officer that's closest to me asks, "Sir, have you been trespassing?"

Knowing better than to make any sudden movements, I simply remain frozen and state, "No, officer."

"Yes, he has!" Gwenith screeches, gym clothes covered body clomping closer. "He's been tossing *his* garbage into *our* trash to frame my husband!"

"Frame him?" Bewilderment can't be kept out of my tone. "Frame him for fucking what?"

"*Language, sir*," the taller, almond beige toned man instantly berates.

"My apologies, officer."

"Frame him into looking like *he's* the one who's been having an affair when it's really you!" She stabs an accusatory finger my direction. "*You're* the lying, piece of filth, that doesn't belong in this neighborhood." Her trembling frame continues to creep closer. "You may have everyone else fooled, but not me! Not me! No! *You're* the type of monster that would steal my husband's credit card! And use it to buy fancy hotel rooms for hookers! And take them for lobster dinners! And *cheat* on the innocent woman that you're holding hostage in that house!"

Maintaining my composure increases in difficulty. "I'm not holding anyone hostage."

"She's probably being raped and tortured!"

"I would never do anything to hurt her!"

"Don't yell at my wife!"

"Tell your wife not to yell at me!"

"Don't yell at my husband!"

"Tell your husband to be a man about his shit and tell you the fucking truth!"

"Everyone needs to lower their voices," the shorter officer firmly insists, hands conducting small calming motions.

"*Language, sir,*" the taller one reprimands again, this time fingers inching uncomfortably closer to his taser.

"*That thing* stole my husband's credit card bill to get the number."

"I did not."

"You did! I just know you did! I just know that's where all those charges came from! And why I found whorey lingerie tags in our trashcan! And a butt plug box! And empty condom wrappers in our trash!"

337

"We don't even use condoms!" I absentmindedly shout back.

Shit. The whole world didn't need to know that. God, what is it with this woman that makes it so hard to keep my shit together?

"Do you hear that?! He's just out there spreading diseases all around! Isn't that a crime, too?! Spreading herpes! I know he has herpes! I know that's the type of shit a pathetic, disgusting, dumpster diver like you has!"

My jaw drops in tandem with the bag in my possession.

"Arrest him!" She dramatically flails. "Arrest him for trespassing! And identify theft! Oh, and fraud! Oh! Oh! And lying about living there!"

"I do fucking live here!"

"What did I say about *language*?" the cop I know I've had a run in with prior hisses. "Do I need to-"

"*Officer Green*," Charles's voice unexpectedly interrupts from my side. "Officer Hurst."

Tone and demeanor instantly change for both at the same time they greet in tandem. "Lieutenant."

338

"Oh, thank goodness," Gwenith dramatically praises, hand thrown over her chest. "Back up has arrived."

She really is just bat shit delusional, isn't she?

"Mrs. Prescott," he politely acknowledges prior to tipping his head toward the man lingering closer to his SUV, "Mr. Prescott."

The weaselly fuck who has barely said a word nods in return.

Charles redirects his attention to the men in uniform. "I see the domestic dispute situation isn't *deescalating*." He folds his hands firmly in front of him. "How can I assist?"

"By arresting that *thing* next to you!" She shrieks, finger back to pointing at me. "He's a criminal!"

"He's not a thing!" my girlfriend's voice unexpectedly shouts back, joining the conversation. "And he's not a goddamn criminal!"

"Stop covering for that bum!" Gwenith bitterly commands. "We all know you're just using him because you're *so* lonely."

"No, *you're* lonely, that's why you're always making up bullshit about everyone in the neighborhood!"

"Jaye Jenkins," Charles calmly but firmly states at his daughter, "you are not to say another word. Am I clear?"

To no surprise, she presses her lips together, indicating she's obeying his command.

"Mrs. Prescott, it would be best for the situation at hand if you would refrain from making any further accusations without due cause. From my understanding, the original dispute began in the house between you and Mr. Prescott, is that correct, officers?"

Green takes the initiative to answer. "She is claiming that the cause of their fighting is because the man beside you-"

"Mr. Cox," Charles informs, not only showing me respect, but wordlessly demanding that they do the same.

That they acknowledge I have rights.

That I'm *human.*

Fuck, is this where Jaye gets her compassion from?

"Is because *Mr. Cox,"* Green immediately corrects, *"framed* her husband by trespassing into their yard to hide the affair he is having on what I now know is your daughter, Little Jaye Jenkins."

"I swear to God I would never-"

His hand lifts to silence me causing my mouth to clamp closed like my girlfriend's.

"She is also accusing him of trespassing on her property to steal credit card statements, which he then used to buy his supposed mistress a number of items," Hurst informs the rest of the allegations.

"I see," Charles quietly states prior to taking a moment of silence for thought. "Is there anything *you* would like to add, Mr. Prescott?" His eyebrows lift in an accusatory nature. "Or perhaps *dispute*? Is there anything you might like to say or explain to your wife in the presence of the law *outside* of a court? A court in which you will be put under oath. A court in which lawyers will dig further into the depths of your whereabouts in both business and personal aspects."

His eyes widen in fear.

Why do I get the feeling an affair is the least of the fucked up shit he's into?

"I told Gwenith I wanted a divorce, and sh-sh-she just fucking lost it."

"Edward!"

"She started throwing shit and screaming and honestly, I'm kinda afraid for my life."

"He tried to hit me!" Gwenith immediately squeaks, switching sides. "Right before you got here! He even tried to come after me with a knife!"

"I did not, Gwenith!"

"He did! He's a monster!"

"You're the fucking monster, you bitch!"

Seeing the situation back to where it belongs prompts Charles to kick his chin towards the front door for the two of us to make a stealthy exit.

The second we're settled back inside our house, I thoughtlessly grunt, "Your dad's a really good fucking detective."

"Yeah, it made shit like trying to hide the fact you ate the last double stuffed Oreo practically impossible." We share a small snicker together that's followed by her winding her arms tightly around me. "You okay?"

Instinct indicates to hug her back, yet the niggling brought on by Gwenith's bitterness has me quietly investigating, "Is that the real reason you invited me in?"

She shifts her gaze up to mine.

"Because you were lonely? Was all that shit about wanting a friend and someone to talk to just…I don't know…a lie?" Irritation builds in the pit of my stomach. "Just some shit you said so I'd stick around, and you wouldn't have to be in this big ass house all alone anymore?"

Horror hops onto her expression so fast it stumbles her backwards. "How fucking dare you."

"I-"

"How fucking dare you let that miserable old hussy get in your head like that!"

"I-"

"Get between *us* like that!"

"Ja-"

"I didn't just go toe to toe with one important man in my life to have the other suddenly forget that he matters too! That I have been fighting *for* this relationship every step of the way! From persuading you to take food from me to reminding you that I love you, that I've *been* in love with you basically from the first time I

343

saw you smile, in every way I can think of! You are my person, Archer Cox." She grabs a fist full of my white tee and yanks me closer to her. "You make me happy. You remind me it's okay to make myself happy. And most importantly, taught me to just be *me*. The *real me*, not the one I spent so many years turning myself into."

Shit...I almost fucked this up because of Mrs. Prescott, didn't I? Fuck, I swear that woman is like the herpes she claims I have. Which I don't. I'm completely clean in case you've forgotten.

Rather than say something sweet or sentimental like I probably should, I good naturedly taunt, "Did you really say hussy?"

Her infamous cringe crosses her face as it reddens. "I wanted to say harlot – you know, take it back like they do in some of the time traveling novels – but it just felt...wrong."

"But *hussy* felt right?"

She shoots me a glare and playfully swats at my chest.

"Careful, woman. Don't make me call the cops in here." The two of us can't hold in our laughs. "I mean they're right outside."

Like her father could hear the joke, he reenters the house, smug smirk wedged on his expression.

Fuck. Me. Should I be worried again?

344

"Perhaps being fingerprinted and behind bars for a few might do them *both* some good." His hands find their way into his pants pockets. "We take domestic abuse claims very seriously in this city for both men and women. And the fact they're both just so quick to make criminal accusations about one another as well as innocent bystanders isn't something I think should be taken so lightly. Green and Hurst are taking them down to the precinct now." Charles's stare swings specifically to me. "And Green will be reprimanded for his procedural misconduct, Cox. Bullshit behaviors like that are a *cancer* in his career. One that I'm not afraid to cut out."

"Thank you, sir."

"Now," seeing his expression harden has dread stirring in my system once more, "I've got a couple questions I want answered before I leave this morning."

"Can you make them quick?" Jaye sweetly interrupts. "We have therapy to get to in about an hour."

"You're in therapy again?" He cautiously investigates.

"I am, sir." The proclamation is far from my favorite, but I know how important it is to own it. To embrace my progress even if it's slower than I care to admit. "I suffer from anxiety and PTSD. Help wasn't always available; however, now that it is, I am...learning...*training myself* to accept it."

An impressed hum is presented. "And this help has come from my daughter?"

"Yes, sir."

"She's paying for it?"

"Until I can get a job, sir, at which point I will pay her back. *Every. Single. Penny.*"

"You will not," Jaye huffs from my side.

"I have kept a financial track record, sir. From groceries to medical costs."

"Archer!"

"Impressive," Charles compliments on a slow nod.

"No!" My girlfriend unhappily squeaks. "That's not impressive. That's ridiculous! And unnecessary! And I won't be accepting-"

"Why don't you have a job yet, Cox? Dragging your heels? Enjoy being a handyman too much? Hoping to knock her up and just be a stay-at-home father?"

"Dad!"

"No one will hire me, sir." Placing a hand on the small of Jaye's back is done to wordlessly help her calm down. "I have applied for everything I can think of and *continue to* apply for everything we come across. We pick up applications practically everywhere we go, but I have not been called in for a single interview. It's disheartening as fuck; however, I owe it to your daughter...*to myself*...to keep going. To keep trying. Jaye restored my faith in humanity, sir, and I will not let it go so easily." My head tips a little higher. "While I hope to have steady work soon, I would like to note that I do make myself useful throughout the neighborhood whenever possible. Dog walking. Weed pulling. Furniture assembling. Hell, I even watched Dane's kids for an hour, so he could run to the office to pick something up. Thankfully, they like books almost as much as Jaye does so it was easy."

She giggles and wiggles herself closer to me.

"I love your daughter, sir. And I respect her. And I would never do anything to use or abuse her. I'd rather eat a bullet."

"Do those things and you will."

"*Dad!*"

"I'll feed it to myself, sir."

Another impressed smile crosses his face. "I like you."

"Thank you, sir."

"You can relax, Cox." The grin grows friendlier. "You don't have to be so formal."

"Habit."

"Not a bad one." He offers me a small wink. "Now, I know you two have somewhere to be, but how about you show me that office Jaye's been texting me pictures of and tell me more about that pizzeria you tried to buy at twenty."

How the fuck does he know about that?

"You tried to buy a pizza place?!" Jaye loudly exclaims.

His expression transposes to a devious one at the same time he ushers a hand at the stairs. "I wanna know about that and a couple of other things before we have dinner with my wife tomorrow night."

I toss my girlfriend a small glance to see her proudly smiling.

Huh.

Love that she's a woman of her word, too.

"Jaye said you'd cook, but I know my wife." The two of us begin to ascend the steps side by side. "She'll process the situation better with familiar food and several glasses of expensive wine."

Unsure if it's okay to laugh, I simply smile.

Well, finally meeting him didn't go nearly as horrible as I was expecting. I'm sure meeting her mother won't be a Saturday walk through the bookstore, but it'll be fairly manageable...don't you think?

Chapter 18

Jaye

"You're nervous."

Archer's voice summons my stare away from where I was absentmindedly looking out my driver's side window and over to him. "What?"

"You only chew on your pinky nail like that when that big, beautiful brain of yours can't stop running in circles about time travel plot holes-"

"How did everyone not *guess* that he was clearly from the future?!"

"*Or* when you're nervous. Like before a budgeting meeting with your boss. Or a parent teacher conference to begin a reading program for a student that's struggling with comprehension. Or, hell, even when you're waiting to hear feedback from me about your illustrations."

"Do you really like the bunny?" My change in topic occurs between another bite of the nails. "Should it have bigger ears? A larger nose? Maybe a fluffier tail?"

"Maybe you should stop chewing on this," he lovingly pulls my hand away from my mouth, "and talk to me about why you're so nervous? I prefer you with nails." Archer's fingers fold with mine. "I like the way that shit feels when you scratch them down my arms."

The sexual thought has my teeth sinking into my bottom lip at the same time I accelerate through the light.

We've fucked so much in the last three days, I honestly don't know how I'm still able to sit up let alone drive to what I have no doubt is going to be the worst meet the boyfriend dinner in the history of meet the boyfriend dinners. And yeah, I'm including that Guess Who? remake they did with Bernie Mac and Ashton Kutcher.

"What's got you so stressed about this dinner, sweetheart?"

My eyes stay planted on the traffic in front of me.

"Is it about what I'm wearing to the restaurant? Because I put on a fucking sweater for this shit."

Hearing the mirth in his tone threatens to conjure a smile.

"It's even got a pointless button. That's how you know it's really fucking high class."

Not giggling is impossible. "You look incredible and smell even more amazing."

"And so do you," Archer promptly compliments. "I know how worried you were trying on a new dress, but you look fucking beautiful, sweetheart." My eyes cut him a small glance. "Almost *too* beautiful. I'd probably be more worried if your dad wasn't a Lieutenant."

I do my best not to blush under the compliment.

This dress is totally on the other side of my comfort zone. It's fitted and bold printed and the fact I'm wearing purple heels to go with it is absolutely the cherry on top of the take risks sundae, but I love what I see when I look in the mirror. I love even more that I feel fun and free in this versus stifled and stuffy. Hundred bucks says my mother hates it.

"You can relax, sweetheart. Just because we don't go eat at fancy places all the time doesn't mean you have to worry about me. I know how to fucking behave in public."

"You're not the one I'm worried about," my under the breath mumbling is heard yet acknowledged by the smallest sympathetic grin.

Perhaps I'm just stuffing pages with nothing. Overreacting. Making Mom out to be a monster when she's really just…a little overbearing. I'm sure she'll be happy for me. And of course grateful, she's one step closer to getting grandkids in her head. You know Archer and I have actually touched on the topic. Kind of hard not to when you work with kids fulltime. He likes the idea of being a dad even though it makes him nervous given how awful his own was. He'd also like to have a job and more stability before we dive any deeper into the discussion. Can't blame him there.

352

Our arrival at Silver Steakhouse – the upscale restaurant known for being a favorite of my parents – is followed first by a valet taking my car keys and next by my boyfriend distractedly wandering off the wrong direction.

Is he running away?! Could he have not clued me in on the plan! I so would've gotten my Wendy Darling on with him!

"Baby…?" I cautiously call from where I'm creeping behind him. When there's no response, I try again, *"Archer?"*

He holds up a single digit, rounds the corner, and comes to an abrupt halt that causes my body to slam into his. Before I have the chance to ask questions, he states, "I know him."

"Who?"

My boyfriend casually points to the man in tattered clothing that's a few feet over searching for change on the ground. "His name is Danny. Danny Reyes." A painful pause is wedged between sentences. "He uh…he lost most of his money in a Ponzi scheme. Lost his job first. House next. Wife walked out with his two kids. Moved them to Montana." Archer's body leans against the edge of the brick building. "One minute he had all the money in the world he could dream of and the next…" The shoulder shrug that's presented looks so dejected. "He was um…He was one of the nicer guys out here. Taught me how to time it right to pick through the fresher tossed out meals at the upscale restaurants. Most of these places have their bus boys take shit straight to the dumpster, so it doesn't leave a bad smell lingering around." His gaze drops to mine. "Learned early on, eat the protein while its fresh. Bread has a longer backpack life."

353

Unsure of what's appropriate to say in this situation, I merely give his arm a loving, reassuring squeeze.

"Give me a sec?" Archer quietly questions.

After receiving a nod, he pushes himself off the wall and struts over through the cold night air to the man desperate for a win. I silently watch a small exchange begin. Danny looks taken back. Confused. Yet rather than use that as a viable reason to walk away Archer persists. Does his best to remind the male of who he is. How they know each other. Whether or not it works is unknown to me; however, whatever the case may be it doesn't affect my boyfriend's decision to fish cash out of his pocket to give him. Danny resists the offer only once but appears to thank Archer repeatedly for the kindness.

His arrival back in front of me precedes an unexpected heartwarming statement. "I know not everyone gets a Jaye Jenkins in their life," the grin he flashes is sweet, soft, "but everyone could definitely use a little more of her compassion."

Swooning struggles not to be heard.

"Gave him the cash Ms. Donovan gave me this morning for putting her trashcans away while she was out of town at her father's funeral. I tried to tell her she didn't need to pay. I was just…being neighborly, but she insisted. Praised me for saving her HOA fees. I figured I could just use it to tip the valet tonight." He smiles a little wider. "*This* seemed like a better call, though."

"Oh, absolutely, baby." My arms fly around him as I lift myself up to plant a chaste kiss on his lips. "You're amazing, you know that?"

"I know you like saying it." He gives me a small hug in return. "And I selfishly like *hearing* it." We exchange a round of snickers. "I just hope you know that's not why I did that. That's not why I do any of the things I do for others."

"Trust me…I know."

Linking hands, we make our way inside and over to the open booth table my parents are already occupying.

The instant Dad's gaze falls on me he happily exclaims, "Good evening, sugar!"

"Hey, Dad!" I greet in return, leaning down to hug him.

My father warmly speaks to my boyfriend next. "Cox."

Archer extends his hand out for the shaking. "Charles."

Keeping my voice even as I sit across from the woman who gave birth to me is almost fucking impossible. "Hey, Mom."

"Evening." She uses her not wine holding hand to point at my attire. "New dress?"

355

"It is."

"It's nice. Bit loud for dinner, but still lovely."

Backhanded compliments. Aren't they everyone's favorite?

"The colors remind me of those on the cover of *One Fish, Two Fish, Red Fish, Blue Fish*, which is probably what drew Jaye to the dress in the first place since she's such a big Dr. Seuss fan." Archer settles into the seat beside me at the same time he adds. "And I agree, Mrs. Jenkins. The dress is lovely for dinner."

Impressed by his statement as much as his stance renders me momentarily speechless leaving him to introduce himself.

"Margret Jenkins," she extends her free hand across the white tablecloth covered table, "you can call me Maggie."

"Archer Cox."

"My husband says you prefer to be called Cox." Her hand falls into her lap. "Is that correct?"

"It is. Jaye's really the only one who's ever called me Archer." He places a hand lovingly on my thigh. "I prefer to keep it that way if possible, ma'am."

"Like I'm the only one who can call you Mags," Dad warmly reminds on a gentle nudge to her side.

She giggles at his flirting and blushes the tiniest bit.

I don't how he does it. I don't know how he can just calm and charm any situation he's in. My uncle Teddy can too. Come to think of it...so could Grandpa. I wonder why that gene just skipped me?!

"So, I've taken the liberty of ordering a couple appetizers," Mom nonchalantly announces. "Their stuffed mushrooms are superb, plus they're great for protecting brain health and promoting healthy cholesterol levels, which I think is safe to conclude that that's something that *everyone* at the table can benefit from." Her stare lingers a little too long at me revealing who that statement was truly intended for. "I assume you're not allergic to them. Given that Chris, Jaye's fiancé-"

"*Deceased fiancé,*" I quietly correct.

"-wasn't allergic to them, I can't imagine that whoever she replaces him with would be."

Yup. So far...about on par for what I expected.

"I have not replaced Chris, nor would I ever *try* to replace Chris, Mom." My hand slides on top of Archer's for support. "I've simply moved forward."

357

"I know, sugar." She swiftly states with an untrusting smile prior to meeting Archer's stare. "Forgive my…poor word choice."

My boyfriend flashes a polite grin on a small nod.

"You two feel free to order whatever your heart desires. It's on us." Mom doesn't pause long enough for a rebuttal. "We're just so excited to meet you and get to know you better."

"Agreed," Dad lovingly echoes and grabs his glass of wine.

"Obviously, we're having red – it'll pair better with the steak – and I *know* my daughter will probably order a glass of Moscato even though it's riddled with sugar she *shouldn't* be having." Her head tilts in a lecturing nature. "Chris was always great about keeping an eye on how many glasses she had to keep the extra weight off-"

"*Mom.*"

"*Mags.*"

"What?" my mother scoffs as if she doesn't understand what's just left her mouth. "I'm simply explaining to the new person at the table our family's patterns and routines."

"With all due respect, ma'am, you're informing me of things I already know about your daughter – her preference for Moscato – and trying to assign me a task that is not yours to assign."

Her jaw cracks a little lower and so does my own.

"Jaye is more than just her body type or how she looks or does not look in certain things. She's her own person. With her own food preferences – something I don't always agree with-"

"Skittles are better than M&Ms."

"No, they're not," Dad and Archer state in unison.

Who do you agree with?

"*Nonetheless,*" he resumes speaking in a calm tone, "I don't *make* choices for her. She makes them for herself. And I *support* them because that's what a real friend, a real *partner* does, ma'am. Not criticize or control."

I'm not entirely sure *who* looks the most surprised among us. Me, Dad, or the woman who I'm still learning to stand up to the way he effortlessly is.

Thankfully, the waiter arrives to welcome us to the restaurant, explain the unique setup of their open kitchen which allows the consumer to see directly into how their food is being handled, and grab our drink orders. I opt for having water rather than ordering something that could be used to start World War Boyfriend while Archer does the same simply announcing he's just not in the mood for alcohol.

Between you and me? I kind of think he wants to be sober so he doesn't accidentally say some rude shit my mother probably needs to hear.

Almost the second he leaves, the mushrooms arrive.

My parents help themselves first yet when I go to reach for one Mom snips, "So, your new boyfriend doesn't like mushrooms."

"*Or*," Dad interjects before I can, "he's doing the well trained thing where he allows everyone else at the table to go ahead of him."

"Chris never-"

"I am not Chris, ma'am."

The statement startles her and damn near causes me to drop the mushroom off the side of my plate.

And here I thought I was going to have to be the one to say it.

"You're right," she quickly caves on an innocent surrender of the hands. "You're absolutely right. I have got to let that go. I need to get to know *you*."

This feels like a setup.

A setup that's going to end with us not eating steak and having to stop for dinner a Gloria's Grande Burger on the way home.

"Why don't you tell us all about yourself? Where'd you grow up?" What do you do for a living? The rushing of words comes to an abrupt halt. "Oh! Oh! Better yet, why don't you start with how you two met? I know all about the one involving Chris wooing Jaye with concert tickets to Fall Out Boy and Green Day and Flu Fighters-"

"*Foo Fighters*," I correct again at a muted level.

"They're a band, Mags, not a CDC team."

Dad's comment gets a small smirk out of me that he acknowledges with a wink.

"How did *you* meet her?" She loudly pushes at the same time she scoots to the edge of her seat. "How did you *win* her over?"

Archer opts for staying still versus attempting to gather food. "We met when she offered me dinner one night."

361

"Aw," my mother unexpectedly coos prompting me to look up. "Had you forgotten your wallet or brought the wrong credit card?"

"No. I was," the adjustment in his seat shifts my attention to him, "living on the street and starving and digging in her trashcan for scraps."

Watching him maintain the stoic stature on his face is remarkable.

Inspiring.

His ability to keep his chin up, to face the ugliest truths that would disgust the masses, is just one of the many strengths he has that I'm learning to have to. I'm not ashamed of how we met or our love story. And I'm not embarrassed by the life he was surviving before me. In fact, I've come to use it like a reminder that there's a possibility for greatness to be found at every moment.

All of a sudden, my mother starts to snicker uncontrollably. I immediately dart my attention her direction just in time to see her playfully bump into Dad. "He's kidding!"

My father's brow crinkles in confusion.

"He's telling some sort of joke, we don't get, but that he'll explain!"

"Yeah, I uh…I don't think so, Mags."

"*Of course*, he's joking," she insists, still awkwardly laughing. "That's probably how he got our daughter to fall for him. He's probably a total hoot!"

This is where I get my out-of-date language from, isn't it?

"Probably made her laugh and laugh and laugh until she almost cried." Her amused gaze falls back to Archer. "You a prankster, too? Maybe one of those people who love to pop out from around corners to get people scared and laughing?"

"That just makes him sound like a killer clown," Dad grumbles between bites.

"Um…," my boyfriend uncomfortably shifts in his seat a second time, "no ma'am. I'm not a prankster. And what I described regarding how we met was not a joke."

She snaps her glare to me. "Tell me he's joking."

I don't.

"*Jaye Jenkins*," her voice undeniably seethes, "you tell me this young man is joking *right now* or-"

"It's not a joke, Mom."

"What?!"

"Archer was a homeless vet when we first met. And while there was no wooing with concert tickets or expensive meals or romantic trips to Iceland-"

"You went to Iceland?" Archer mumbles in question to me.

"There was lots of reading. And talks about books. And cooking. And exploring places I had always wanted to try but couldn't seem to find the guts to. He didn't whisk me away to be this...trophy...wife...I never actually...wanted to be," the confession stumbles out surprising both of my parents. "He simply...encouraged me to...find my own happy. And everyone is entitled to their own happy."

Fury and outrage pumps so noticeably in her expression that the waiter decides to walk the other direction as opposed to approaching our table. "You said he *was* a homeless vet." She glares at him again, yet he still doesn't cower. "Where do you live now? *What* do you do now?"

"He lives with me."

"In Chris's house?!" my mother shrieks much too loudly.

"In *our* house!" I firmly snap back.

"Voices," Dad promptly reminds on a stern finger point.

"Chris *bought* that house," she needlessly reminds.

"And he *hated* it."

The gasp out of her doesn't demolish the courage pouring out of me.

"He bought that house *for me*. He bought it because *I* wanted it. Because I didn't want my kids living in a downtown high rise. He hated that place so much that some nights he made up excuses just to stay where he really wanted. That house has *never* been more than a museum for the prestigious shit he felt like showing off and an expensive workshop for a hobby that he loved *more* than he ever loved me."

"Don't say that."

"I *can* say that, Mom. You…didn't…*know him*." Straightening my spine is done on a breath of confidence. "And had you? Had you really known more than just the fact he was your best friend's son, that he had more money than he knew how to spend, that he had some of the snobbiest habits, then you'd be fucking *appalled*. He was selfish. He was careless. Sometimes he was downright heartless. And worst of all…worst fucking of all…*I* wasn't treated like a blessing in his life but a *burden*." The pounding in my chest harshly continues. "And no mother, no mother who loves her daughter, like I *know* you love me, would *ever* want her to be in that type of relationship let alone marriage."

"Maggie-"

"*Mrs. Jenkins*," she hisses at my boyfriend.

"Mrs. Jenkins," Archer politely begins again, "I don't have a job. I apply. No one responds. I apply again. And I'll keep applying until someone takes a chance on me the way your daughter did. And in the meantime, I will continue to renovate our house."

"You've done a great job, Cox."

"Thank you, sir." He nods at Dad and looks back at Mom. "I will continue to cook. Clean. Help out neighbors when they need it. Take notes at the stupid HOA meetings."

"You take notes at those things?" Dad thoughtlessly gags. "You deserve a medal."

His smile is pushed away to proceed with his speech. "While I don't bring anything financially to this relationship yet, I can guarantee you that no one – and I mean *fucking no one* – has loved or will love your daughter as deeply as I do."

"You didn't know him! You don't know how he loved her!"

"I can tell you that he didn't."

The bluntness to the statement causes my father to wince.

"No man who truly loves the woman he's with would force her to hide away her favorite books because they clashed with his shit. No man who truly loves the woman he's with would reject a thoughtful gift like pajamas. No man who truly loves the woman he's with would spend so much time critiquing her choices instead of appreciating her uniqueness."

Both of my parents glance my direction in bewilderment, yet it's Dad who ponders, "Did he really do that type of shit to you? I mean I never really liked the guy but-"

"Don't say that, Charles!"

"Why?" my father casually brushes off. "It's the truth. Chris was a pretentious shit. Even his own parents thought so. And more importantly, if he treated our daughter like garbage, Mags, then fuck him. He didn't deserve the tolerance I had to exude because I made the mistake of believing our daughter was happy."

"She was happy!"

"She just said she wasn't!"

"She's clearly lying!"

"Why would she lie?!"

"He-he-he *brain* washed her!"

"*Voices*," gingerly leaves my lips.

"I've seen this type of shit before." Mom hastily nods to herself. "There are at least ten Netflix documentaries about men like him. *Cult* leaders. Preying on poor, innocent, defenseless, naïve women."

"I am *not* naïve." I viciously bite on a small pound to the table. "And I damn sure am not defenseless. I knew exactly what I was doing. I *know* exactly what I'm doing, and I know who I'm doing it with."

"You shouldn't be-" is the start of the sentence that gets cut off due to Archer's sudden slight twitches.

Seeing the start of an episode has me instantly looking around for the trigger only to realize the flash fire in the kitchen must've caught him poorly.

Mom huffs her outrage. "What in the hell-"

"*Sweetheart is now*," he quietly whispers to himself while slightly rocking. "*Steak is now.*" More rocking. More reminders. "*Lieutenant... Lieutenant...Where's our-*"

"*Charles* is now," I remind and inhale deeply, to indicate he should do the same.

Archer sucks in a gulp of air prior to whispering, "*Sweetheart is now.*"

"*I am now,*" the cooed response assists in settling his shoulders. "*You are safe now.*" His grasp on my leg loosens. "*You are loved now.*"

He slowly nods and lets his hazy green gaze find my brown. "*I am loved now.*"

My hand gently lands on his cheek at the same time I question, "Are you with me?"

A faint hit of red hits his cheeks as he nods. "I'm here."

"Where?"

"Silver's Steakhouse."

"With?"

"*You.*" His fingers give mine a small tap to release him, so I do. "And your dad." Another long breath is expelled. "And your mother."

"Who does *not* want her daughter dating a junkie!" Mom shrieks just about above a whisper. "I know your type." Her eyes narrow the hardest they possibly can. "You're not *really* a veteran. You're a disgraceful junkie who developed a coke habit or a *meth* habit that got his ass thrown out on the streets! I see your kind all the time in the hospital. Pretending they have every illness on God's green earth just to get another hit!"

"Ma'am, I am *not* a junkie."

"Then how do you explain all this?" her hand waves around at the same time I shake my head at the waiter to not come over.

"I suffer from PTSD." While making the announcement is more frequent for him, it's no less difficult. "I…occasionally…have moments where…I'm triggered by something in my environment."

"Do you *know* your triggers?" Dad cautiously inquires. "Is my daughter at risk?"

"Of course she's at fucking risk, Charles!"

"No, sir, she is not," he promptly reassures. "And I *do* know my trigger. And I am getting help in the form of therapy as well as medication. The episodes have always been sporadic; however, they are becoming shorter in length and on the occasion, I can catch them before they even start. This is thanks to the medication and techniques taught to myself and supported by Jaye."

"Do you think you're capable of holding a steady job with it?"

"Absolutely, sir."

"*Charles.*"

"Charles." Archer kindly tips his head. "I don't think they'll be an issue, but *if* I am ever hired for a job again, I will disclose that information."

Dad offers him an almost proud grin that his wife swiftly swipes away. "He's lying."

My father's sigh is so heavy it knocks me back in my seat. "He's not lying, Mags."

"He has to be."

"Why? Because you don't like that our daughter isn't shacked up with another guy that was on the cover of *Forbes*?"

Archer snaps his head over at me. "Chris was on the cover of *Forbes*?"

"Just...once..."

"He's making all this shit up," Mom grumbles and reaches for her wine. "All of it to manipulate her. And *you*, which is clearly working. And me, which it *isn't*." She chugs down a gulp. "You should be better about spotting a con man, Charles. Where are all those skills that made you a damn good detective?!"

"They were used to verify that the man sitting next to our little girl is who the fuck he says he is. You *know* I ran all of his information long before she gave it to me."

See.

"I've known who he was, where he's lived, where he's been stationed, how many times he paid his car payment late, and so much more, practically since they met."

"*Dad.*"

He tosses me a sarcastic stare. "I *asked* you for the information first. Just because you didn't give it, didn't mean I wasn't going to get it. We both know that."

Ugh. We do...but still!

"Archer Cox was an orphan who was raised in foster care and served in the United States Army. He was severely wounded. Honorably discharged. The trail from what should've been recovery to the moment he landed on our daughter's doorstep is a fucked-up mix of missed paperwork, laziness, and proof that people often stop giving a shit about you when you stop being able to provide

372

something for them. His list of couple priors correlate to some of our harsher weather days – his stints used to escape the cold and bitterness – and his medical record indicates no signs of current or heavy past substance abuse." Dad picks up his fork. "The young man's only crime is agreeing to come to dinner tonight." He stabs at the mushroom. "No one deserves the shit you're putting him through for no reason."

"It's not for no reason! I'm worried about our daughter! You've seen how outrageous she's been behaving lately."

"You mean how she's stopped just doing everything that makes *you* happy and started making *herself* happy. Like she said?"

New waves of fury boil out of Mom in a flustered, incoherent tizzy.

"Mom," pushing the appetizer plate away is done in tandem with proceeding, "I thought it was important for the people I love to finally meet, which is why we wanted to have dinner together tonight; however, it is clear that while *I'm* ready for this moment, *you* are not."

Her jaw tumbles unexpectedly to the table.

"I refuse to subject Archer to this bullshit any longer." Gently pushing to encourage him to get out of the booth begins. "And you know what? You may hate that he's nothing like Chris, that he'll never be anything like him, but to me? That's one of the best parts."

More rage rips through her wide-eyed gaze.

"Enjoy your dinner, Mom." I offer my father the best smile I can find. "*Dad.*"

"Enjoy your Gloria's, sugar."

"How did you-"

He presents me a wink alongside a chuckle.

The man really is too good at his job.

"We'll try this again when *she's* ready." One more glance is given my mother's direction. "When *she's* ready to accept that the man I once loved is *gone.* When *she's* ready to accept that I have actually moved on like she hasn't." Meeting Dad's stare occurs again. "Text me when you get home to let me know you made it safe?"

"Isn't that my line?" Dad playfully jeers.

He's given a good-natured eye roll, a goodbye kiss on the cheek, and a cordial handshake from Archer.

Our ride home consists of the aforementioned stopped for Gloria's Grande Burgers, although instead of getting it to go, we opt to eat there. We don't discuss the disaster we left behind but use the chance to talk about the book club book he's a little further in than he was on Friday. Gushing about books calms me down like he knows it will while it also lifts his mood to feel like he truly has the active role in my life we spent the evening claiming he has.

Upon entering our house, Archer immediately ditches the sweater alongside our shoes, giving me a reason to snicker enroute to the couch. "The sweater was not *that* uncomfortable."

"It felt like Dune, Dane's toddler, had me in a hug he refused to let me out of."

"It wasn't that tight."

"You could practically see my tattoos etched through the damn thing."

I flop onto the sofa on a girlish giggle. "I fucking wish."

He pauses instead of sitting down. "You know if you want me to take my shirt off, all you gotta do is ask, sweetheart."

We walked around naked all afternoon yesterday and most of this morning. It made it very easy to fuck literally all over the house.

The memories of yesterday prompt me to declare, "I think you should move in with me."

Archer drops down onto the couch beside me at the same time he lightly chuckles. "I uh…already did that, sweetheart. Almost five months ago. This is the address on my driver's license."

Realizing that didn't come out the way I wanted causes me to roll my eyes. "I mean, I want you to move all of your shit out of the garage and into the house. Into the master bedroom. I want us to…repaint it. And get rid of the photos I hate so much. And change out the furniture. And get a real bed. A bed that's *our* bed instead of this couch, which we *made* into our bed."

His hands fold together as he leans slightly forward to rest his arms on his knees. "You sure you're ready for that?"

"I am," I declare without hesitation. "I *really* am."

"Are you? Or is this about what happened at dinner with your mother?"

"This has nothing to do with her."

He tosses me a sarcastic eyebrow lift.

"Okay. It has a little to do with her."

"*Jaye-*"

"But not in the way you think!"

Archer kicks his chin towards me to continue.

"I meant what I said. This is *our* home. Which means you keeping your shit in the garage and me hiding away from a bedroom I never felt comfortable living in to begin with is fucking ridiculous. If this is really *our* house, *our* home, *our* sanctuary, then we should be living in *our* bedroom. One that has colors and books and style we both like. Who gives a shit if it ends up looking like a coloring page done by a first grader?" A small, happy laugh slips loose. "What matters is that it reflects *us*. Who *we* arc. The relationship *we* have."

Archer takes a slow, long lick of his lips.

Nods.

Drops his stare to the ground for a moment in thought.

Shit. Am I wrong? Should we wait a bit longer?

When his green gaze drifts up, I see familiar hunger that has me pushing my thighs together. "We should probably fuck one last night on our *old bed*, huh?"

Giving him a saucy, teasing nod is instant. "Of course. Out of respect."

Chuckles leave us both yet fade shortly before he's pulling me into his lap to smash his lips against mine. Our mouths refuse to wait any longer to part and going from clothed to naked is a set of actions that's completed in record timing.

All it takes is one push inside to erase all the horrors of the evening.

To remember that this is right.

That we're *right* together.

For each other.

Wet waves whirl around his swollen shaft, primitively washing away any worries that might be lingering from the ugly untruths he was forced to hear and re-instilling the loving ones. Rather than let him take me, I take him. I plant my palms firmly on his bare shoulders. Begin to work his cock by lifting myself to the tip of his dick and dropping down as low as I can possibly go, pumping his full length on every stroke.

Groans of approval or appreciation or both are attached to every nip and lick and suck being delivered to my collarbone.

And the top of my tits.

His calloused hands roughly cup both, thumbs lightly rolling around my nipples, teasing them incessantly, leaving me with no choice but to throw my chest out into every bounce. Buck like a drunk girl at a karaoke bar trying not to get knocked off a mechanical bull. My brazenness and audaciousness – two big things to be accredited to our relationship – is openly welcomed by the man using his hard hold to harshly pull me down into his frenzied thrusting.

Animalistic grunts steadily flood the room alongside my increasingly loud chants of his name.

Each time it leaves my lips his cock noticeably swells.

And every time it noticeably swells my pussy pulsates.

Pleads in a primordial code to fill me to the brim in a way I've never been, let alone by anyone else.

Not even Chris. Our sex sessions – when they happened – always included a condom and pulling out. The idea of kids was fine for him but the reality – in retrospect – wasn't.

"*Fuck, take whatever you need from me, sweetheart,*" Archer lasciviously grumbles face becoming buried between my tits. "*I'm fucking yours.*"

The proclamation combined with the vibrations threatens to pre-maturely yank me over the cliff of climaxing. Digging my nails in deeper to his muscular shoulder is done in tandem with him winding his arms around my torso. Trapping me to him. Imprisoning him in my sweat soaked cleavage. Naturally, my head drops backwards during the frantic bouncing while my knees continually crash into the couch cushions struggling to support our tempestuous behaviors. All of a sudden, thick, creamy juices begin coating his cock in a more consistent pacing, proclaiming to us both that the orgasm I've been holding at bay is tired of being there. Feeling the soaking change causes my boyfriend to groan louder.

Growl like a crazed beast determined to brand me on the inside and out.

In love with the idea, in love with someday that branding growing into a baby, expanding our family, leads to me completely letting go. "*Archer!*"

Howling his name to the same tempo my muscles are constricting is mindlessly done. My wild withering is shamelessly met by muffled pants and unsteady jerking. His typically precise and unfaltering piercing progresses into a carnal mess of clumsy carving that doesn't stop until searing spurts are reigniting my fading orgasm. Unexpectedly coming a second time from what feels like endless rushes prompts additional clenching and shuddering and rapturous hollering. Our equally twitching frames instinctively fuse together transposing us into one drenched, trembling, ball of airy sighs.

Guess orgasms really do make everything better. I read it in a book once. And I know not everything you read in a book is true, but I can honestly say…from firsthand experience…that one is.

Chapter 19

Archer

"Could we not have this fucking discussion while I'm carrying this heavy ass shit?" I gripe on my way past Jaye for Dane's truck that we've been loading furniture into.

"No," she loudly rejects, folding her long jean jacket covered arms across her chest. "I wanna have it now. *With witnesses.*"

Pushing the nightstand further across the space occurs at the same time I counter. "You mean with potential allies."

"Careful, Cox," Charles warns as he arrives at the bed of the truck to put in the drawer pieces he carried. "You're gonna make her pout."

Without missing a beat, that's exactly what she does.

He turns around to see the sight and teasingly taunts. "*See.*"

It's impossible not to shake my head in amusement.

Charles is a fucking great man. From the way he treats his daughter, to the way he's welcomed me into his family with open arms is phenomenal. He even pulled a few favors to help me get an interview for the loading dock at Harry's Hardware about a week after we met. He then spent two afternoons post work coaching me through the process. Practicing. Eating cookies and critiquing the things he knows those hiring look for. Jaye was so fucking giddy about us bonding that she could barely wait until he was out of the driveway to jump my bones. The rehearsal shit panned out for me. I aced the interview. Passed the second. And was hired a couple days later. My background check just finished processing on Friday, so now I get to start tomorrow – Monday. Does it pay really well? Fuck no. Are the hours unfucking godly? Unfortunately, yes. Which is why my curly haired beauty is losing her shit in our driveway instead of helping us move out the furniture to make room for the new bedroom pieces we finally agreed upon.

Dane and Charles both laugh at the situation yet seeing Jaye's face sterner than ever prevents me from doing the same. Tossing my hands up in the air out of irritation precedes grumping, "Fuck, Jaye, what do you want me to do? Not take the job?"

She scrunches her nose like she's preventing herself from saying yes.

"That is not a fucking option, and you know it."

"Then let me-"

"I'm not letting you buy me a goddamn car!"

"You can buy me a car," Dane playfully pokes during his stroll over. "I'm not nearly as selfish as that ground pounder there." He tosses her an overly cheesy smirk. "I'm much more of a giver."

383

"You're gonna make me *give* you a foot to the ass if you keep that shit up," I good naturedly jab back.

"Jaye, you know why he doesn't want you to buy him a car," Charles reminds in a firmer tone. "And I don't blame him."

"But I don't want him walking home from work!"

"I don't mind walking, sweetheart."

"*I* mind you walking! It's not safe. You could get hit by a car or a bus or a train-"

"There aren't any trains anywhere near that location. And you know that. Because if there were *this* wouldn't be an issue still."

"What about when it's raining? Or a million degrees outside? Or snowing?"

"We could buy me a bike?"

She presents me with a sarcastic scowl.

"Wow. Look. At. That. Face," Charles chuckles, heading back to the house to gather more items. "That's the one that wiped out the dinosaurs."

Dane joins him on the laughing and jogs away to join his side.

"Take this shit seriously," she snips at a lower volume.

"*I. Am.*" My arms fold across my thrift store Guns N' Roses t-shirt. "You just don't like the alternatives I'm suggesting and me *not* taking this job is – *I repeat – not* an option."

"Archer-"

"Sweetheart, I *need* this."

Her entire body seems to melt from the weight of the statement.

"Do I wanna get up at three in the morning to go in at four? Fuck no. Do I wanna have to wait around to be picked up by you or your dad or that jarhead I can't believe I call my friend? Absolutely fucking not. But the situation is what it is, Jaye. This is the first real job I've been offered since I was discharged. We've searched for this for *months*. Don't force me into abandoning the first…semi-independent win I've had in years." My head tilts slightly to one side on a whispered begging. "*Please, sweetheart.* Don't make me choose you over it."

The woman I love to see smiling rather than frowning defeatedly tosses her arms in the air, stomps over, and wraps them

385

around me. "Fine. But I hate this. Not the you having a job thing. I like that. I think *you'll* like that. And I can't wait to hear all about your work gossip-"

"I don't gossip."

"You will," she casually brushes off. "I just…hate that there's a huge new elephant in our relationship to eat right after it feels like we just finished one."

Her reference to our late spring cleaning summons a soft grin to my face.

Originally, we were just focused on the bedroom yet during the process of looking at furniture and deciding what to change, something even more life-altering was decided. Jaye was ready to remove all of Chris's old things, including the model cities. Those went to his parents – who seemed to not only be happy she's moved on but like that I'm a hands-on type of man – while everything else has gone and is going to various charities around the city. Some things have been given to homeless shelters, some have been given to charities that assist in the rebuilding of lives – from domestic cases to disaster relief – and some local programs that go out and give directly to those in need. The whole thing has taken longer than we expected but honestly? I think it was good for Jaye. She picked the speed. She picked what went where. She chose how to finally close that chapter of her life before we move onto our next one. I'm proud of her.

"We'll eat this new one, the same way we've eaten all the others." It's my turn to wrap my arms around her, hands folding at the small of her back. "One bite at a time." Our mouths briefly brush for a soft kiss. "Now, how about you put those cookie making hands to a different use and help load up the boxes we need to take down to the shelter that's at Chester and 7th?"

Jaye joyfully nods and delivers one more peck prior to bouncing off to complete her task.

In an almost conveyer belt like fashion, old pieces come out of the house while pieces that arrive from the delivery teams go in. I do everything I can to make the transition as smooth as possible. While Jaye handles boxes – using the now almost completely vacant garage – I conduct traffic through the front door. Move the California king mattress with Dane just in time for it's smaller king replacement. Keep pathways clear and the man I know one day I'll call my father-in-law properly hydrated.

The four of us work all morning into the early evening cleaning and building and relocating items elsewhere. As a thank you for their time and energy, Jaye declares she's taking us all out to dinner, an invitation Dane nor her father passes on.

Just as my friend pulls away from the curb in his truck, wanting to drive himself over to the Pitter Patter Pizza Pub – just in case his favorite bartender is working – another car enters the cul-de-sac, this one freezing both Jaye and Charles's frames as it arrives in front of our house.

Don't worry. It's not either of the Prescott's or their divorce attorneys who I feel bad for. That split is gonna be a shit storm.

Seeing Mrs. Jenkins exit the vehicle is a surprise that manages to stumble me slightly backward.

Haven't seen her since Steakageddon. Her and Jaye haven't spoken in almost a month. I know it bothers my girlfriend – she's literally said the shit – however she refuses to stay in cycles that don't work for her or who she's growing into. She loves her mother – again she literally said it – but needs her to respect the changes she's made. And that she's making. Especially in regard to me.

Mrs. Jenkins slowly approaches where the three of us are standing. "Good evening, everyone."

"Hey, Mags."

"Hi…Mom…"

"Hello, Mrs. Jenkins."

She stops at the edge of the driveway, keeping her distance. "I knew today was moving day and I…I just wanted to stop by and…and…"

The lost end of her sentence prompts her daughter to finish it, "See how it went?"

Mrs. Jenkins coyly nods.

"Good!" Jaye joyously shrugs. "The shelters all seemed really appreciative of the donations and Dad and Dane only managed to chip one doorframe during the furniture removal process."

"That was all him," Charles casually brushes off.

I rest my hand on the small of her back at the same time I say, "It's an easy fix, sweetheart."

"It is for someone as handy as you must be," Mrs. Jenkins states to me in what almost sounds like a friendly way. "Given that you've done some spectacular renovations." She nervously folds her hands in front of her. "At least um…at least from the pictures I've seen."

"Thank you, Mrs. Jenkins."

"*Maggie.*"

Rather than repeat the preferred nickname, I simply seal my lips together.

"I would love to…see them in person." Her chin tips a little higher despite her jaw's trembling. "Perhaps we could go to dinner to celebrate the changes and your new job?" She does her best to smile. "Congrats on the new career, Mr. Cox. Charles told me all about it."

"And that I taught you everything I know which is *how* you got it."

He's delivered an eyeroll prior to me politely correcting the woman I thought despised me. "It's just *Cox*, Maggie. No need for the mister."

She slowly nods her comprehension.

"We're actually meeting Dane – our neighbor and Archer's best friend-"

"I wouldn't call him my *best* friend."

"*Only friend*," Jaye sasses from beside me, "down the road at Pitter Patter Pizza Pub. I'm gonna treat everyone to pizza for pitching in today." Leaning into my hold for a wordless request of support, she offers, "You're welcome to join us if you think you can treat my boyfriend with the respect he deserves."

Fuck. Me. I didn't wanna have a My Big Fat Greek Wedding moment before dinner. What? Yeah. We watched the shit last night. It was playing at the drive-in which is on the outskirts of the city. I'll admit. Movie was pretty fucking chick flicky but getting head in the middle of it made me forget all about that.

"I'm sorry for the way I treated him," Maggie begins, stare shifting over to me, "*you.*"

Silence seems to be the wisest move for me to make for the moment.

"You didn't deserve the shit I said. I was…upset and angry and sad and scared-" her voice abruptly stops on a headshake. "Nonetheless, you didn't deserve the behavior you received. I would like another opportunity to truly get to know you."

"Why the sudden change of her heart?" Jaye inquires without hesitation.

"A pair of old friends reminded me how short life is. And how you never know when it could be *your* last moment with someone you love. They reminded me to *treasure* those that are still with us."

Chris's parents.

"And my *partner* who has…*always* told me the ugly things I need to hear yet don't necessarily want to, also highlighted my poor behavior. He forced to me face the truth."

"Which is?" my girlfriend cautiously continues to investigate.

"Chris is gone. He has *been* gone. And me trying to replace him *for you*, to *fill his Birkenstocks* with another man that was just like him was wrong. That's not what *you* needed. That's what *I* needed. It was my way of coping with losing someone so close to us."

391

Her confession catches Jaye by surprise but not me.

Everything she said and did that night clued me in on that.

It was almost a Hardy Boys mystery level of easy.

What? Oh. One of the elementary school kids in the afterschool program has been reading them as part of his custom literary program, which means Jaye's reading them too, and in turn me. Don't worry. I'll keep up the reading habits even with a job. Isn't that what lunch breaks are for?

"I'm sorry for my mistake, sugar." Tears do their best to stay out of her voice. "I really do just wanna see you happy, and you honestly seem the happiest I've ever seen you with Cox."

"I am."

She energetically nods at her daughter. "And I wanna see more of that person. And this person you're becoming. And get to know you as well as the man in your life the same way your dad has."

"This is all just a ploy to get me to share my cookies again," Charles playfully scolds on a finger wag.

"Not everything is about cookies, Dad," Jaye giggles.

392

"I reject your preliminary assessment."

More laughter circles around the group only stopping when Maggie asks, "Is it alright if I tag along to dinner?"

"I'm okay with it as long as Archer is."

Great.

No fucking pressure on my shoulders.

"And if he isn't, Mom," Jaye's shoulders push back lengthening of her spine, "then no. You can't come. His feelings – whatever they may be – are valid, and I will support them just like he has always supported me."

All eyes land on me leaving me in my least favorite position.

The spotlight.

"You're welcomed to join us for dinner, Maggie. I think a second chance and a little *compassion* can go quite a long way if we let it."

My girlfriend happily hums while her father releases an impressed grunt.

"Wanna ride or drive yourself, Mags?"

"Why don't I ride with all of you?" She sashays over to her husband. "Hear more about today's events and tomorrow's big day."

The four of us begin the process of piling into Charles's SUV instilling in me a foreign feeling of peace I'm thankful for.

My gut tells me that that emotion won't always be so unfamiliar. And you know what? I honestly think with a little more time and a little more effort from everyone that it'll be one elephant we'll all finish eating together.

Did you enjoy reading Compassion: The Extended Edition? I would appreciate you leaving a review if you did!

https://amzn.to/3zI6GdI

Want more of this couple? Make sure you check out Silent Knight: A Compassion Christmas Novella to see how their future unfolds!

https://amzn.to/3FGIqfT

OTHER WORKS

Here are links to other stories/places/people that were mentioned/referenced in the book!

Clover Rose University (The Bro Series) – https://amzn.to/3fwH2lr

Presley Morrison (The Love Duet) – https://amzn.to/3U3DtSQ

South Haven (Already Designed) – https://amzn.to/3U8gVjN

The Frost Luxury Hotel (Freeform) – https://amzn.to/3t1NV13

Dornan Law Firm (Walking Away) – https://amzn.to/3UkKRJ5

Bennett Enterprise (The Bennett Duet) – https://amzn.to/3UjJRFa

Merrick McCoy (The Adrenaline Series) – https://amzn.to/3OeHeSH

Sloan Mathers (Aleatory) – https://amzn.to/39zUkdu

Georgian ArKtecture (Waiting) – https://amzn.to/3UjJRFa

Haworth Enterprises (Bulletproof) – https://amzn.to/3FHbALN

Unbreakable (The Senses Series) – https://amzn.to/3DC38L8

GRATITUDE:

The list of people who assist in this entire process is truly too many to name. So rather than run the risk of forgetting anyone, I want to just say thank you to EVERYONE. Readers, bloggers (new and old), friends, family, reviewers, and street teamers…you have all shown me amazing compassion and love over our time together. Thank you for supporting me and making every step of the journey filled with more kindness than anything else.

Until next time…

FOLLOW ME!!!

Website (Signed Paperback Purchases Available)

https://www.xavierneal.com/

Facebook

https://www.facebook.com/XavierNealAuthorPage

Facebook Group

https://www.facebook.com/groups/1471618443081356

Twitter

@XavierNeal87

Instagram

@authorxavierneal

Pinterest

https://www.pinterest.com/xavierneal/

Bookbub

https://www.bookbub.com/authors/xavier-neal

Goodreads

https://www.goodreads.com/author/show/4990135.Xavier_Neal

New Release Alerts

https://www.xavierneal.com/newsletter

Tik Tok

https://www.tiktok.com/@authorxavierneal

Spotify

http://bit.ly/XNSpotifyProfile

Store Front

http://tee.pub/lic/authorxavierneal

FULL List of My Works

Standalones

Cinderfella (YA Contemporary) - https://amzn.to/2pBHZff

The Gamble (Romantic Comedy) - https://amzn.to/2uf4ZFw

Freeform (Romantic Comedy) - https://amzn.to/2IPna7W

Part of The List (Contemporary Romance) -
https://amzn.to/2udYwuz

Walking Away (Contemporary Ménage Romance) -
https://amzn.to/2pAOEGf

Can't Match This (Romantic Comedy) - https://amzn.to/2XapsVw

Hike, Hike Baby (Romantic Comedy) - https://amzn.to/2PNj456
(Available in Audio)

Baewatch (Romantic Comedy) – https://amzn.to/3izNvaG

Sleigh Bride (Holiday Romantic Comedy) -
https://amzn.to/2J0Qk8D

Aleatory (Contemporary Age-Gap Romance) -
https://amzn.to/3xKJQ2L (Coming to Audio)

Picnic Perfect (Romantic Comedy) - https://amzn.to/2UZdgeN

Eden (Dark, Taboo Romance) - https://amzn.to/3mumx98

Baby Got Pack (Romantic Comedy) - https://amzn.to/3rsQpoO

Waiting (Contemporary Age-Gap Romance) –
https://amzn.to/3QwTXBa (Coming to Audio)

Senses Series

(Sports Romance/ Romantic Comedy) (Complete Series)

Vital (Prequel Novella)- FREE ON ALL PLATFORMS
https://amzn.to/2ueL5KJ

Blind- https://amzn.to/2GmEMcO

Deaf- https://amzn.to/2IK71Rf

Numb- https://amzn.to/2pAOYVt

Hush- https://amzn.to/2pzV2gS

Savor- https://amzn.to/2HZsVP1

Callous- https://amzn.to/2pAPmTV

Agonize- https://amzn.to/2ILLaZw

Suffocate - https://amzn.to/2GjLU9T

Mollify- https://amzn.to/2GgRJoJ

Blur- https://amzn.to/2pD1rrK

Blear - https://amzn.to/2DQGb6a

Blare- https://amzn.to/33nnqV8

Senses Box Set (Books 1-5) – https://amzn.to/2Gkxruw

Adrenaline Series

(Romance/ Romantic Suspense)

Classic (FREE ON MOST PLATFORMS) -
https://amzn.to/2I0wd4D

Vintage- https://amzn.to/2HXksMw

Masterpiece- https://amzn.to/2G0tWKj

Unmask- https://amzn.to/2Gn2tBK

Error- https://amzn.to/2pBakC6

Iconic- https://amzn.to/2G1Q8Ua

Box Set (Books 1-3) - https://amzn.to/2IP7GRe

Prince of Tease Series

(Romance/ Romantic Comedy)

Prince Arik- https://amzn.to/2pAuhbF

Prince Hunter- https://amzn.to/2IKzuGu

Prince Brock- https://amzn.to/2ufmghN

Prince Chance- https://amzn.to/2LuclMw

Prince Zane- TBA

Hollywood Exchange Series

(Romance/ Romantic Comedy)

Already Written - https://amzn.to/2G0F2ix

Already Secure- TBA

Already Designed (The South Haven Crew #1) -
https://amzn.to/2G8A0fP

Already Scripted (The South Haven Crew #2) - TBA

Already Legal (The South Haven Crew #3) - TBA

Already Driven (The South Haven Crew #4) - TBA

Already Cast (The South Haven Crew #5) - TBA

Havoc Series

(Military Romance/ Romantic Suspense) (Complete Series)

Havoc- FREE ON ALL MAJOR PLATFORMS - https://amzn.to/2HYWOyZ

Chaos - https://amzn.to/2ug1Ox5

Insanity- https://amzn.to/2I3eABs

Collapse - https://amzn.to/2G3cAww

Devastate- https://amzn.to/2IO9GcL

Havoc Box Set (Books 1-3) - https://amzn.to/2G17519

The Just Series

(Second Chance Romance)

Just Out of Reach- https://amzn.to/2ubzfBe

Just So Far Away- https://amzn.to/2DR57KM

Private Series

(Romantic Suspense) (Complete Series)

Private - https://amzn.to/2IN7P7R

Public- https://amzn.to/2pAF7it

Personal- https://amzn.to/2vejdHt

Popular (A Private Series Standalone) – TBA *(This novel will be about how J.T. and his wife, Janae got together.)

Duched Series

(Romantic Comedy) (Complete Series)

Duched- https://amzn.to/2G4Xlim

Royally Duched- https://amzn.to/2pAnvDh

Royally Duched Up- https://amzn.to/2G089SP

Duched Deleted (FREE Novella ON ALL PLATOFRMS)- https://amzn.to/2GlOQTy

The Bros Series

(Erotic Romance) (Complete)

The Substitute- https://amzn.to/2ub9CAc

The Hacker- https://amzn.to/2FZFxJr

The Suit- https://amzn.to/2poTcyX

The Chef- https://amzn.to/2Dgi7MR

Must Love Series

(Sweet, Romantic Comedy)

Must Love Hogs- https://amzn.to/2IMmmkg

Must Love Jogs- https://amzn.to/2pBIiqp

Must Love Pogs- https://amzn.to/2ueUUIu

Must Love Logs- https://amzn.to/2IFGrL7

Must Love Flogs- TBA

The Culture Blind Series

(Contemporary Romance)

Redneck Romeo- https://amzn.to/2vYuPhM

Cowboy Casanova- https://amzn.to/2sxwqGT

Horseback Hero- https://amzn.to/2BhT91r

Blue Jean Bachelor- TBA

Camelot Misfits MC Series

(MC Romance/ Romantic Suspense)

King's Return - https://amzn.to/2TTnNCI (Available in Audio)

King's Conquest - https://amzn.to/2IaYZo8 (Available in Audio)

King's Legacy – https://amzn.to/2YfvY1i (Available in Audio)

Wiz's Remedy – https://amzn.to/2PMmJDK (Available in Audio)

Locke's (Currently Untitled) Novel - TBA

Trick's (Currently Untitled) Novel – TBA

Synful Syndicate Series

(Dark Romance)

Unleashed- https://amzn.to/2VVhcfT

Unchained- TBA

The Bennett Duet
(Dark, Mafia/Mob Romance) (Complete)

Dark Ruler – https://amzn.to/3z5oEWl (Available in Audio)

Dark Reign - https://amzn.to/3H9v3SO (Available in Audio)

Haworth Enterprises Series
(Romantic Suspense)

Bulletproof - https://amzn.to/3FHw8nr (Available in Audio)

The Hockey Gods Series

(Sports Romance/Romantic Comedy)

Can't Block My Love – https://amzn.to/38HYH0z

My Fair Puck Bunny – https://amzn.to/33t2nSw

The Forward Must Cry – https://amzn.to/3ijTfpm

Defenseman No. 9 – https://amzn.to/3sqAgiJ

Taming of The Crew - https://amzn.to/3jo5gwR

The Draak Legacy

(PNR Romance)

Saving Silver – https://amzn.to/3J5jG06 (Available in Audio)

Getting Gold - https://amzn.to/3ejkdNW (Coming to Audio)

Pleasing Platinum – https://amzn.to/3rsCQ9g (Coming to Audio)

The Love Duet

(Contemporary/Second Chance Romance)

First Love – https://amzn.to/3xrUnlt

Last Love – https://amzn.to/36hyjit

Complete Boxset (w/bonus material) – https://amzn.to/37RNpeK

The Debt Tales

(Dark Fairy Tale Retellings)

Twisted Debt – https://amzn.to/3c2eyhM
Savage Debt - https://amzn.to/3E08QrX

Compassion Series

(Slow Burn Contemporary Romance)

Compassion: The Extended Edition: https://amzn.to/3zI6GdI

Silent Knight: https://amzn.to/3FGIqfT

Made in the USA
Middletown, DE
13 June 2023

32551617R00229